Notorious

Also by Carey Baldwin

Fallen
Judgment
Confession

Notorious

A Cassidy & Spenser Thriller

CAREY BALDWIN

WITNESS
IMPULSE
An Imprint of HarperCollins*Publishers*

Excerpt from *Fallen* copyright © 2015 by Carey Baldwin.

EPub Edition FEBRUARY 2016 ISBN: 9780062387080

Print Edition ISBN: 9780062387097

10 9 8 7 6 5 4 3 2 1

For Sarah and Chloe
Best friends who met by bobby pins

Notorious

Chapter One

Sunday, October 13
10:00 P.M.
Dallas, Texas

WHEN HEADING FOR a secret rendezvous with her lover, it simply wouldn't do to appear to be sneaking off. So it was with a proud, unflinching spine, that Cynthia Beasley Langhorne ascended the grand staircase at the Worthington Mansion—one of Dallas's most celebrated historic landmarks.

Golden light from opulent chandeliers flooded the plush, red carpet runner on the steps, giving her the eerie feeling she was wading into a river of blood. To keep from tripping, she lifted her Stella McCartney gown above her ankles. Its blue silk-chiffon swooshed, whispering secrets against her skin and tickling her bare legs. The mingled scents of money, power, and perfume floated up from the ballroom, along with the strains of Mozart and crashing cymbals. To those looking on with interest, and there were plenty of gawking eyes fixed on her, she supposed she appeared to be gliding with ease. But in truth, the crushing weight of her charmed life made each demure step as tortuous as a death march.

Bracing herself with a deep breath, she cast a glance over her shoulder at her handsome, unreachable husband, who was posted in the middle of the marble foyer below. She kept her head turned long enough to catch Dutch's eye, allowing a few paparazzi to capture her impenetrable smile. Mona Lisa had nothing on her. No one would ever guess her thoughts or her true purpose—at least so far, no one ever had. And that was her curse in life. Blessed with wealth and notoriety, her heart would remain forever unseen, her diary her only confidante.

In spite of her determination, her steps slowed involuntarily, giving Dutch every chance to stop her. If he had so much as raised an eyebrow at her, she might've turned back and run straight for his arms. But, of course, he didn't, and his indifference bolstered her faltering courage. She tossed her head, knowing the effect of her silky, auburn hair swinging across her bare shoulders would be dazzling. The music lulled, as if paying its respects like a gentleman rising to his feet when a lady exits the room. A flurry of flashing lights was accompanied by the electric sound of cameras clicking.

When her husband had asked her where she was going, she'd answered truthfully, "I'm meeting Matthew Cambridge, darling. I promise I won't be long."

Dutch's eyes had glinted dangerously—but only for a moment. Then he sent her an insouciant smile. "Tell Matt that I'm the one who brought you to this god-awful-boring fund-raiser, and I'd like to dance with my wife at some point, let's say before midnight."

"Before midnight it is," she'd promised.

Then he'd taken her hand, and she'd willed him not to let it go—not to let *her* go. But let her go he did.

Now a resigned sigh escaped her lips because it was too late for regrets. Her husband was married to his work. His passion was reserved for the FBI, and there was nothing to be done about that. Though she would give her own life to protect the damnable fool, the separate paths she and Dutch had chosen were paved with the cold stone of one irrefutable truth.

He doesn't love me.

As her brown eyes locked with his frosty blue ones, she raised her chin and blinked away the moisture that blurred her vision. When her chest tightened, she commanded her body to relax, then raised her hand to her lips and blew him a kiss. She turned her back fully, then continued her march—not because she didn't love her husband but because she did.

And because if she didn't go through with this, the only thing that mattered would be destroyed.

Up the stairs, down the hall, and behind a closed bedroom door, she shed her clothing. She folded her silks, laying them neatly on a side chair, then hung her delicate gown in the closet. A chill seeped down to her bones, and a shiver swept over her. Without her garments, she felt as vulnerable as a soldier going into battle without armor.

But she had no choice.

The cost of defeat would be unbearably high.

Naked now, she arranged herself seductively on the bed,

pressing her hand on her stomach to suppress the wave of anticipatory nausea. Pretending she was somewhere else, she closed her eyes. A creak of floorboards signaled her paramour's approach. The door whooshed open. She steeled her resolve and forced her eyelids up.

But what she saw, there, in the doorway, turned her blood to ice and froze a scream, forever, in her throat.

Chapter Two

MOST DAYS SPECIAL Agent Atticus Spenser loved his job—but today sure as hell wasn't one of them. At the moment, he and his partner, forensic psychiatrist, Dr. Caity Cassidy, were "off the books," working a special assignment: protect the interests of the tall, red-haired, pain in the ass striding beside them.

Fellow agent Alex "Dutch" Langhorne had always seemed more like a cactus needle swimming beneath Spense's skin than a colleague, and as far as he could tell, the feeling was mutual. But during a recent fund-raiser for Texas governor and presidential hopeful, Matthew Cambridge, Agent Langhorne had found his wife, Cindy, brutally murdered; her nude body posed in an upstairs bedroom of the Worthington Mansion. And like any family, dysfunctional or no, when one of their own was in trouble, the FBI rallied.

So now, accompanied by Dallas police detective, Monroe Sheridan, they approached the newly cleared crime scene on foot in order to get the lay of the land. To Spense's trained eye, the expansive grounds revealed no obvious escape routes or hiding places or even a decent place for a kid to build a fort—only yards of manicured green lawn, redbrick paving stones, and widely spaced trees. Spense's family had lived a short stint here in Dallas, and the pungent scent of honeysuckle reminded him of that time.

"What are those?" he asked, spying some climbing bushes covered with familiar-looking orange berries.

"Pyracantha." Caity's knowledge of all things botanical sometimes got him wondering if her doctorate were really in horticulture. The smile she sent him made him glad he'd expressed an interest in the local flora.

If he were being honest, he'd have to admit his current foul mood was as much due to the fact his vacation had been canceled, yet again, as it was to his contentious relationship with Dutch. Spense had hoped to get Caity alone on a nice secluded beach somewhere far away from murder and mayhem. She needed to learn how to unwind, and he'd prepared the perfect tension-release plan: sand, sangria, and a whole lot of Spense.

Instead, here they were, sweating it out in the damn Dallas heat. He'd almost forgotten the way the humidity could turn a polyester shirt into a wet suit. Pressing a handkerchief to his forehead, he glanced over at his fellow agent, who didn't appear inclined to break a sweat. Was it ice in Dutch's veins keeping him cool or simply his European heritage? If anything ever happened to Caity, Spense knew he'd never be able to hide his distress. He applied the handkerchief to the back of his neck. He and Langhorne were cut from very different cloth.

"Dammit to hell." Detective Monroe Sheridan's expletive broke into Spense's thoughts, and he looked up to find the source of the man's consternation: A few yards ahead, in the mansion's drive, a kid circled on a beat-up yellow bike. Steering with one hand, the boy appeared to be snapping pics on his phone with the other.

"Stop! Police!" Hand on a holstered Taser, Detective Sheridan charged straight at him.

Jackass. Spense's temperature rose several points above Sheridan's IQ—or at least above the man's commonsense quotient. "Take it easy," he called out to Sheridan.

Too late. The kid raised his hands, shouting, "Don't shoot!" His front wheel lifted in the air, then the bike tilted, first dumping the boy on the ground and finally clattering on top of him.

Caity sped after Sheridan. It took Spense and Dutch only a few long strides to catch up to where she now knelt beside the fallen boy.

"What's your name?" she asked softly as she began checking out his cuts and scrapes and examining his twisted limbs.

"My friends call me Artard, but my name is Aaron." The kid's voice came out high and shaky. Not surprising, considering he probably thought Sheridan had been ready to shoot him. Even if he knew the difference between a Taser and a pistol, from a distance, he couldn't have told them apart.

"Well, which do you prefer?" Caity asked matter-of-factly, not hinting at the offensiveness of the nickname. Spense's chest expanded. Caity was like that. She knew feeling sorry for the kid would cause him even more embarrassment. She understood a lot of things most people didn't.

"Aaron."

"All right, Aaron. I think you'll live. You feel okay? Like you can stand up?"

Aaron's gaze darted to Sheridan, and his eyes widened.

Caity threw an arm around him.

"Nothing to be scared of," Dutch said. "You're not in trouble or anything."

"Oh hell yes, he's in trouble. He's interfering with my crime scene." Sheridan folded his arms, glaring down at the boy.

"Not your crime scene anymore. It's been cleared," Spense reminded the detective.

"It's still private property. I ought to arrest his little *Artard* ass for trespassing." Sheridan bent and scooped a cell phone off the ground.

"Hey, you can't take my phone!"

The kid was right. The detective needed a search warrant to look at the contents of the phone.

A mean glint came into Sheridan's eyes. "I might still drag you down to the station. Haven't made up my mind yet." He made a show of scrolling through the pics. "Delete. Delete. Delete," he said, tapping the phone. Then Sheridan grabbed the kid's collar, as if to yank him to his feet.

Spense inserted himself between Sheridan and Aaron and knocked the detective's hand away.

"Watch yourself, Agent Spenser, or else . . ."

"Or else what?" Spense spun around. He was a good half foot taller and had at least fifty pounds of muscle on the detective.

"Just watch yourself, that's all."

Spense took the boy by one arm, and Caity took him by the other, then they gently helped him to a stand. Blood oozed down from a scraped knee, and his shorts were dirty and torn, but other than that, he seemed to be none the worse for the tumble.

"Be sure to wash those abrasions with soap and water when you get home. A little Neosporin wouldn't hurt either. But you don't need stitches." Caity was still scrutinizing Aaron's injuries.

"He said *agent*? Are y'all with the CIA?" The kid had a Texas drawl, and again, Spense was reminded of his childhood. His family had moved out of Dallas, rather abruptly, when he was six. He didn't recall much, but some distant part of him went nostalgic in a really weird way. Aaron's nickname reminded him of what some had called him back in the day. Only then, nobody sugarcoated a thing. *Retard*, plain and simple was the name that had been hurled at him on the playground.

Caity brushed debris from Aaron's shorts. "Not CIA. I'm a psychiatrist."

Spense thumped the kid conspiratorially on the back. "I'm with the FBI. Special Agent Spenser." He tilted his head at Caity. "Dr. Cassidy isn't an agent, but she works along with us, helping to solve crimes. She's what we call a civilian consultant."

"Is she your girlfriend?"

The kid had a pair. Spense liked him even more than when he'd first spotted him playing junior detective, checking out a major crime scene on a decrepit old bike that had probably been handed down from an older sister—most boys weren't into yellow with flower decals. "I'm working on that, Aaron. Maybe you could put in a good word for me."

"I don't think she cares what a kid like me thinks."

"Sure she does. See how her mouth is twitching over there?

Every time she looks at you, she has to work real hard not to smile. That means she likes you. She likes you a lot."

Aaron's muted brown eyes brightened. "She does that with you, too. I'd say you've got a good chance with her."

"You're very observant, kid. I think you'd make a good profiler someday. In fact, you remind me of myself when I was younger."

"You're a *profiler*? Like on *Criminal Minds*?"

"Yep."

"He's a good one, too," Dutch said, surprising Spense with a rare compliment and more conversation than they'd had during the entire forty-five-minute ride in traffic after Dutch had picked them up at the airport.

"I bet he could profile you down to a T," Caity added.

"Would you profile me? Please?" Suddenly Aaron couldn't take his eyes off Spense, and that made Spense feel an unexpected rush of responsibility toward him.

Sheridan dragged a hand across his face. "Look, I get it. I might've been a little hard on Artard here. But do you two have to keep making it up to him up all day long? We came here for a reason."

"We have plenty of time," Dutch said.

Spense wondered if he had a human side after all. Then again, maybe his colleague just wanted to avoid the crime-scene walkthrough and Sheridan's questions as long as possible.

Spense widened his stance, studying Aaron. "If I *were* to profile you, I'd start by noting that you're a lover of Flaming Hot Cheetos."

"How'd you know that?"

"Easy, there are red powder stains on the tips of your fingers," Caity chimed in.

Aaron stuck his hands behind his back, hiding the evidence.

The kid's giant grin alone was enough to keep Spense going, but the happy glow on Caity's cheeks gave him an added incentive. Plus, he never minded showing off a little.

"You're extremely loyal to your friends, even though you hate it when they call you Artard." He lowered his voice. "By the way, if you don't like that nickname, I think you should say so."

"That's horseshit. You got no way to know if he's a loyal friend or not," Sheridan protested.

"Sure I do. After all, he didn't try to save himself by ratting out his buddy—the one who's hiding just around the corner." Spense jerked his head, and they all followed his gaze to a narrow trail of flattened grass in the yard—it looked to have been made by a bicycle tire and led straight to the side of the mansion. "And what else, let's see . . . you hated girls until about six months ago, when you discovered that the most beautiful girl in the world goes to your school."

"How did you know *that*?"

"Because you're fourteen."

"But how—"

"Easy. You're obviously older than thirteen."

"*Obviously.*"

"And if you were *fifteen*, you'd have your learner's permit already. If you had your learner's permit, you wouldn't be checking out a crime scene on your bike. You'd have cruised by in the car, with your older sister as your driving supervisor." Spense whipped his Rubik's cube out, scrambled and unscrambled it, then handed it to Aaron with a flourish. "This is for you—I've got plenty more. Practice up, and you'll find out what your brain can really do if only you'll let it."

"You're some kind of a genius or something, aren't you?"

"Don't be too impressed, kid. The older sister was a lucky guess . . . sort of—that bike used to be hers, right?"

Aaron nodded.

"Want me to take a picture of you holding up my FBI creds?"

Caity held out her hand to Sheridan, wiggling her fingers insistently. He let out a long sigh before handing over the illegally confiscated phone.

"Say cheese," Caity prompted.

After posing for a couple of shots, Spense scrawled his personal number on the back of his card and gave it to Aaron. "Call me next week, and if I'm still around, I'll take you and your buddy down to the FBI building. We can have lunch in the cafeteria."

At last, the buddy poked his head out from around the side of the mansion and began walking his bike toward them, slowly at first, then picking up speed. "Will you show us the *X-files*?"

Another true believer. If he had a nickel . . . Spense laughed and clapped Aaron on the back. "I think you guys are going to have to settle for a tour of the cafeteria . . . but maybe I can throw in the FBI gift shop, too. Now leave your information with Agent Langhorne in case we need to contact you." He nodded at Dutch. "And then hit the road before Detective Hard-ass over there hauls us all downtown."

As the boys walked their bikes off to the side and huddled around Dutch, Caity tiptoed up to whisper in his ear, "You're going to make a great father someday."

"If I remember my high-school biology correctly," he replied, in a low tone, "I've gotta get past second base with you, first."

A soft, seemingly involuntary sound came from her throat, and a pretty flush colored her cheeks.

He grinned. All signs pointed to his hitting a home run in the near future.

"Sorry to interrupt this little episode of *Undateable*," Sheridan groused, "but we've got work to do."

Now that Aaron was out of harm's way, Spense nodded his agreement. There was a mystery to be solved, and he was itching to get to it.

Wednesday, October 16
4:00 P.M.
Plano, Texas

A SIMPLE HIT had been all that was ordered; however, the woman had earned a slow death, if not a magnificent one. Fortunately, Malachi's reputation as *the Thresher* was spotless, and his various employers generally left the manner of homicide to his discretion. He touched the target's forehead with his fingers, anointing her husk with the ointment—a blessing of sorts—then rose to his feet. He tilted his head and surveyed his work.

She looked quite at peace, lying there on her dingy kitchen linoleum, in spite of the messy way her insides were pushing and shoving their way out of her body cavity, as if trying to escape a cruel world.

Malachi did not hold a romantic view of the afterlife—rather he believed in ashes to ashes, dust to dust, for all but a chosen few. Certain lives were more important than others, and thus the accomplishment of taking them was that much greater: a truth that small minds could not comprehend.

The traditional view, as handed down from the pulpit of his mother's church, was that all lives held equal worth. Thus, by logical extension, all men deserved the same death. But anyone with the courage to open their eyes and take a good look at the pinhead lolling beside them on the bus, the train, or in the next office cubicle would see that merely having the property of life does not in and of itself make a creature worthwhile. Amoebas live, but they do not matter. Perhaps a number of others might agree with him on that particular point, but then their puny minds would go on to delude them into believing that they were better than said amoeba.

Wrong!

Possessing the quality of a beating heart, the ability to think and emote, was simply not enough. Being human doesn't mean you matter. Some men matter, but most do not. Malachi mattered precisely because he had the ability to discern the difference.

That was his gift: He could hear the hum of a human's soul.

If said human had one, that was, because, of course, not everyone did.

He'd not heard the hum on his target today, but still, the woman had displayed a rudimentary spirit, trying to outwit him with lies and false promises in a futile attempt to get away. Such behavior was admirable, and even though she did not possess a soul, he knew he would take pleasure in her pain. Her courage marked her as more than an amoeba. Smiling at her shell, he slipped on his noise-canceling headphones, then vacuumed the room, wiped all surfaces clean of prints, and exited out the back door.

After stowing his vacuum in his trunk, he climbed into his new SUV. His phone vibrated in his pocket. He checked the number, and as he'd feared, the call came from a certain employer—his one and only dissatisfied customer. Malachi could not allow his previously unblemished record to be spoiled by one little mishap. Especially a mishap that wasn't even his fault. One way or another, he was going to have to clean up the mess in Dallas.

Chapter Three

Wednesday, October 16
4:15 P.M.
Dallas, Texas

AFTER SPEAKING ON the phone with Aaron's mother and securing a promise from him and his buddy that the two would walk their bikes straight home, Caitlin joined Spense, Dutch, and Sheridan inside Worthington mansion—a historic old home that had been converted first into a hotel and later into an event venue. Looking around, she stifled a groan. The décor was over-the-top, with dozens of chandeliers, gold-leaf wallpaper, and enough nude statues scattered about to make Liberace blush.

"How'd it go with the mother?" Sheridan asked.

"All taken care of," she replied, making her smile twice as friendly in order to hide the fact her blood was still blistering hot from the way Sheridan had ridden roughshod over a fourteen-year-old kid.

Once the detective had taken time to think about things, it, apparently, had dawned on him that deleting those photos from Aaron's phone was illegal, and that if the family filed a complaint, he'd created a potential nightmare for his department. So Sheridan had asked her, since she was "a headshrinker and what-have-you," to smooth things over with the boy's parents. She'd readily agreed.

Helping the detective out of a jam now would increase the chances he'd share information with Spense and her later. They weren't an official part of the investigation, and Sheridan had included them in today's crime-scene walk-through only as a courtesy to the Special Agent in Charge of the Dallas field office, Jim Edison . . . and because Dutch had refused to do one without them. They had a meeting set up with Edison tomorrow night, when he returned from Washington, D.C. Meanwhile, the plan today was for Dutch to guide Sheridan through the events of Sunday night even though he'd already been questioned at length.

The detective's wide shoulders hunched, like a predator ready to spring his trap. Perspiration beaded around his hairline, darkening the edges of his short brown hair, and accentuating the moonlike shape of his face. Bringing Dutch back to the scene of his wife's murder was undoubtedly designed to trip him up on his previous story, or possibly get him so worked up and guilty, he'd break down and confess. As far as she could tell, this kind of tactic only worked on television crime shows, but on the plus side, it was a good opportunity for Spense and her to get up to speed.

"Dutch." Caitlin paused and worked to delete the eagerness from her voice. Like Spense, she loved a good puzzle, but this wasn't a crossword. A woman had lost her life in this house, and they owed her respect. "We're ready when you are."

Directing his gaze to the floor, Dutch stuffed his hands in his pockets. Not likely Sheridan would be on the receiving end of that wished-for confession. It didn't appear Dutch would be getting worked up anytime this century.

Spense shot her a troubled glance. She knew Dutch's flat affect bothered him. But to her, Agent Langhorne seemed to be the type of individual who shut down in the face of strong emotion. The more intense his feelings, the less he allowed them to show. At least that was her current operating theory. The alternative would be to acknowledge that Dutch was cold-blooded, and that was a road she wasn't willing to travel without compelling evidence.

"Let's get going. I've got a date with October baseball," Sheridan said, his impatience turning each syllable into a quick staccato beat.

In a pointed show of support, Spense clapped Dutch on the back. That must've cost Spense a bit, she thought. She'd been reading the doubt in his eyes ever since their plane had touched down in Dallas. Spense knew something about Dutch that she didn't. She'd overheard Spense whispering on the phone with Edison, remarking that with Langhorne's history, it wouldn't take long before the press would be kicking down the closet doors and dragging his skeletons back into the limelight.

Could he have done it? One of law enforcement's most-sought-after hostage negotiators, a man who risked his own life on a regular basis to save others? The question made her head—and her heart—ache.

At any rate, Dutch still wasn't talking, and their "walk-through" was going nowhere fast. They were still loitering in the foyer, staring up at the grand staircase. Was Dutch stalling, or re-living? She noted the faraway expression in his eyes and decided it was the latter.

Sheridan drummed his fingers on his chest. "We can do this here, Agent Langhorne, with your buddies present, or we can go down to the station and take the gloves off."

Spense sent Sheridan an I-eat-your-kind-for-breakfast look. "I'm watching you, Detective, so don't step out of bounds."

The detective scowled at the ceiling, then grunted. "No worries. I'm a by-the-book kind of a guy."

"Except when it comes to minors, apparently," Spense said. "Keep on the straight and narrow from here on out." If Spense had his suspicions about Dutch, Sheridan would be the last to know. Spense's loyalty to the FBI ran deep. Still, if it turned out Langhorne did have a hand in his wife's death, she had little doubt Spense would turn him over to the authorities as unhesitatingly as he'd agreed to come to his aid in the first place.

Sheridan muttered something Caitlin didn't quite catch, then powered on a handheld recorder: "Present today are Special Agent Atticus Spenser, Dr. Caitlin Cassidy, and Special Agent Alex Langhorne." He paused. "Agent Langhorne, you understand that you are not under arrest. You're free to go at any time?"

She detected just enough movement in Dutch's chin to be interpreted as a nod.

"For the record please." Sheridan waved his recorder in the air.

Finally, the man spoke. "I'm not under arrest. I can leave anytime I want."

Everyone present understood the reason for Sheridan's request for an on-the-record statement. If Dutch knew that he wasn't under arrest, and there was no involuntary detention, Sheridan didn't have to Mirandize him. Anything he said could be used against him despite the lack of counsel present.

Though Sheridan wasn't exactly small—he had a muscular

build and big bones—he was shorter than both special agents. Running one hand over his hair, he stretched his neck and back, working to gain perhaps a half inch of height before continuing. "Agent Langhorne, please describe the time and circumstances under which you last saw your wife alive."

Taking a page from Sheridan's book, Dutch stared at the high ceilings. Caitlin was half-worried they might crash down on them from the weight of all those gigantic chandeliers, and what with all the neck craning going on today she might not be the only one. Next, Dutch focused on the gilded wallpaper.

"Do you need me to repeat the question?" Sheridan asked.

"Please," Dutch said.

The flush climbing up Sheridan's face called attention to a group of very faint acne scars on his chiseled cheeks. His full lips stretched tightly, revealing his teeth, even and white, except for one stray on the bottom that had pushed its way forward and was slightly yellowed. On balance, he was not an unattractive man . . . until you got to know him a little. "Your wife is dead. You were the last one to see her alive."

"Me and one hundred other people."

"Technically, but you were definitely the first to see her after she died."

"You mean except for her killer."

"Sorry, I meant to say you discovered the body."

"Sure you did."

"How about you quit jerking me off and tell me everything about the last time you saw her alive." Sheridan sighed. "Then maybe we can get out of here in time to see the Rangers beat the Yankees."

All three men nodded, and for a moment, Caitlin thought they just might bond over a common desire to see the Texas Rangers make it into the World Series. But then a couple of beats passed, and the hard looks returned to their faces.

"Like I told you before, I was standing right here, and . . ." Dutch's gaze went to an impressive marble staircase, covered with a red runner. "Cindy was standing there." He pointed. "About halfway to the top." As he spoke, his eyes moved up and to the right.

Caitlin tipped her head at Spense, wondering if he'd noticed Dutch's eye movements. Looking up and right generally meant a person was recalling rather than fabricating an event. Relying solely on neurolinguistic clues wasn't something she'd recommend, but so far, Dutch's nonverbals led her to believe he was telling the truth: The last time he'd seen Cindy alive, she'd been headed upstairs . . . but the guests, the dancing, all the action at the party was happening on the first floor of the mansion. She closed her eyes, picturing Cindy on the stairs—the *Dallas Morning Gazette* had been running her "last photograph" all week. Caitlin's breath hitched as she visualized Cindy's stunning blue gown, her sad, golden brown eyes, and the resolute set to her coral lips.

Where were you going? Why so determined?

"Did she speak to you?" Sheridan asked, startling Caitlin. Opening her eyes, she refocused her attention on the men and realized he'd been talking to Dutch, not reading her thoughts. Her breathing returned to normal.

"She was too far away for us to hold a conversation. But we did make eye contact." At last, dropping an octave, Dutch's voice carried some semblance of grief.

"Clearly, I meant did she speak to you before she went upstairs," Sheridan retorted sharply.

"That's not what you asked me. I'm not a mind reader."

"And I'm not a fool."

"That's debatable."

"Let's move on," Spense tried, in a neutral tone.

"I'm *attempting* to get his side of the story so we can catch the SOB who did this." Sheridan threw his hands up.

"It's not a story. And you're not interested in finding my wife's murderer."

"Then what am I interested in?"

"Closing the case. You want to arrest the husband and collect your merit badge." He held out his hands, placing them together at the wrists. "Go ahead. Cuff me. Take me down to the station like you threatened to do with that boy earlier even though you have no evidence."

"Oh, we got evidence." Then Sheridan clamped his jaw abruptly, as if he'd slipped up.

"*If* you've got anything on me, it has to be circumstantial, because I did *not* kill my wife."

"Circumstantial evidence's the best kind, buddy, and we got that in spades. Maybe we got more though—who's to say? Now if you don't want to cooperate . . ."

"I'll cooperate. I'm just not kissing your hairy ass."

"You've gotta admit that's fair." Spense spread his arms magnanimously. "We'll cooperate, but no hairy-ass kissing. Everyone's in agreement on that point, right?"

"Right." Dutch smiled—well, almost—at Spense, and Caitlin felt her chest loosen as some of the troubling tension between Dutch and Spense dissipated. At least momentarily, they seemed united against a common enemy.

But the detective wasn't amused. His shoulders shot up. His

pink face turned red, and he threw a daggered glare at Dutch. This was no game, and Dutch needed to choose his words carefully. For now, he appeared to be the prime suspect, and if he wasn't forthcoming with Sheridan, it might remain that way indefinitely. The sooner the police eliminated him, the sooner they could turn their attention to tracking the real killer. As glad as she was to see Spense and Dutch on the same page, they couldn't afford to alienate Sheridan.

"Dutch, please, in your own words, just tell us what happened. Detective Sheridan can't do his job without your help. None of us can." He knew his freedom was at stake. Maybe even his life, yet he remained taciturn, and that troubled her. As much as she empathized with him, she needed him to fight.

Dutch shifted his stance, looked away, and stayed silent for a few moments. When he finally met Catlin's eyes, she noticed his had grown moist.

So he wasn't made of stone after all.

"Cindy pulled me aside and told me she had to go meet Matt."

"For the record, you mean Matt Cambridge . . . *Governor* Matthew Cambridge?" Sheridan was waving his recorder around again.

"We've been through all of this before, Detective."

"How is that a problem? You having trouble keeping your story straight?"

"It's the truth. I'm simply getting tired of going over and over the same ground."

"Sorry you're bored. But I'd like to hear *again* what reason your wife gave you for sneaking off to meet the governor of Texas, alone, in an upstairs bedroom, in the middle of a fund-raising ball."

"She didn't offer any explanation. And she didn't say she was meeting him in a bedroom, or that they would be alone. She was hardly sneaking off, as any of a dozen reporters who photographed her, will tell you. She even paused on the stairs to give them a photo op. I don't appreciate your tone or your implications. This is my wife we're talking about."

"But you saw her go upstairs." Sheridan took a step toward the grand staircase and stabbed his finger in the air. "Where the bedrooms are. It must've seemed strange she'd go off on her own to meet Governor Cambridge."

"It really didn't. Cindy's been very involved with Matt's campaign. She's the one who organized the fund-raiser, and along with Heather, she handpicked the guests."

"For the record, you're referring to Heather Cambridge, the governor's wife, the first lady of Texas?" Sheridan stumbled on her name, and Caitlin got the impression he was a bit starstruck. Unlike the Hollywood detectives from their last case, he wasn't accustomed to hobnobbing with celebrities. Heather Cambridge, like Cindy Langhorne, was a renowned beauty, and well-known throughout Texas. Matt Cambridge was one of the most talked about men in politics and considered a frontrunner for the upcoming Democratic presidential nomination. Because of the Cambridge connection, this case had made national headlines. It was understandable Sheridan might be feeling the pressure—but to Caitlin, that seemed all the more reason for him to take extreme care with the investigation. Instead, he seemed to be rushing to judgment.

"Yes, I'm referring to Heather Cambridge. She's been Cindy's best friend, her only real friend, I'd say, since grade school. The four of us have spent many evenings together socially. So it didn't strike me as strange that my wife would meet Matt upstairs. I assumed she planned to advise him on whom and how to schmooze. There were a lot of high rollers here, and she knew most of them quite well."

"Your wife was giving schmoozing advice to the *governor*." Sheridan dosed his tone heavily with sarcasm.

"She's quite the expert. On schmoozing, I mean."

"*Was* quite the expert."

"Quite." One corner of Dutch's mouth lifted in a nervous twitch.

Sheridan gaped at him. "Is this funny to you?"

"Not in the least." Dutch stepped close to Sheridan, and the detective backed down, crouching away from Langhorne.

"What happened next?"

"What do you think? She went upstairs."

"And what did you do?"

"I ducked out of the party for a while. I hate these types of things—if not for Cindy, I wouldn't be caught dead at a fund-raiser."

Spense squeezed his eyes shut and pinched the bridge of his nose. Caitlin saw a muscle twitch in his jaw. That *caught dead* remark was painfully insensitive, but Dutch acted as though he didn't notice. Yet, he was far too clever not to realize the implications of his words. It was almost as if he were eager to take the blame for his wife's death. The muscles in her throat contracted as memories of how bravely her father had fought for his freedom, yet still failed in that endeavor, came flooding back.

"We'd agreed to meet back up by midnight," Dutch forged on as though he were speaking of any ordinary occurrence. "So I went for a walk to clear my head. I was suffocating in here—what with all the power-hungry assholes sucking up the oxygen in the room. Once I thought I could stomach the crowd again, I came back in and looked around for Cindy."

"Did you find her?" Sheridan's expression implied that Dutch had indeed.

"You know I didn't."

"Whatever you say."

Please don't take the bait. Caitlin sent Dutch a warning look, and he nodded at her. Hoping he could feel her support, she smiled at him, suddenly realizing that she might be the only person in the room who genuinely believed in his innocence. She'd liked Dutch from the start though she wasn't quite sure why. When she'd met him for the first time, back in Hollywood, during the Fallen Angel Killer case, she'd felt as though she already knew him . . . from somewhere. She couldn't put her finger on what it was about him that drew her to him, but her gut told her that despite his undeniably off-putting manners, he was a good man—and an innocent one. Still, he was playing a dangerous game with the detective.

"Like I said, I did *not* find my wife anywhere. So, I asked Matt—Governor Cambridge—if he knew where she was." Running a finger inside his collar, Dutch hesitated. "Anyway, he said he hadn't seen Cindy all evening except when they said hello at the door. He was surprised she thought they had some sort of meeting set up—claimed it was news to him."

"You must've been alarmed at that point," Sheridan's voice seemed matter-of-fact, where it could easily have taken an accusatory tone. Maybe he'd realized he didn't have to bait the suspect. The suspect was doing a perfectly good job of making himself look guilty with no help from anyone in the room.

"No. I wasn't alarmed."

"It didn't bother you that your wife lied to you?"

"We're married. Married people lie." And with that deadpan delivery, his cynical view of relationships came across loud and clear. She pictured Cindy again, looking back over her shoulder. There was so much longing, so much heartbreak in her eyes.

At least that's how it seemed to Caitlin from the photographs.

What did you have to do that was so very important? Who was waiting for you?

There was a long, empty silence before Sheridan asked, "What time did you speak to Cambridge?"

"Maybe you should confirm with him, but I think it was around 11 P.M. I mingled a bit, then went back outside—to the parking lot. I was tired, and I took a nap in my car."

"Did you try to call your wife?"

"She doesn't carry her phone when we're out socially. She considers that gauche, and believe me, she spends a lot of time making sure her manners are perfect. She doesn't want anyone pointing out that she didn't go to finishing school." His eyes moved up and right again. "Cindy's a hell of a woman. Did you know she didn't even graduate high school? And yet here she is, advising a man who could very well become our next president."

Caitlin touched her heart. The way Dutch spoke about Cindy in the present tense made it seem he was having a hard time letting go, in stark contrast to his practiced cynicism.

"So other than a brief conversation with Cambridge, between 10 P.M. and 12 A.M., during the time we know Cindy was murdered, you can't account for your whereabouts," Sheridan said.

"I just did."

Good Lord, Dutch was either obtuse, which she knew to be false, or he really didn't care if Sheridan clapped him in irons.

She fanned her face. Despite the air-conditioning, she felt hot and queasy.

"But you have no alibi witnesses."

"If I'd murdered my wife, I assure you I would've had an alibi prepared."

"Would you?" Caitlin asked.

Dutch looked up in seeming surprise. She was surprised, too. She hadn't meant to blurt that out.

Spense arched a questioning brow at Caitlin. "Dutch is sharp as any criminal weasel I've ever known."

"Thanks for your support," Dutch muttered but didn't look displeased.

Spense ignored him and continued addressing Caitlin and Sheridan. "He's a member of the upper echelon of law enforcement. No way would he hang himself out to dry for his wife's murder by skipping the alibi."

"Not if he *planned* to kill her. A crime of passion, on the other hand, could've left him holding his dick without one."

Apparently, Sheridan had never made it to finishing school either.

"Or else he's innocent, like he explained, and that's why he didn't take time to create an alibi," Caitlin said. "But what I'm wondering, Dutch . . ." It was hard to get her breath, but she had something she wanted, no, she *needed* to say to Langhorne. "I'm wondering why you don't even try to supply a reasonable answer. Someone could've seen you on the grounds, or as you came and went from the mansion. Maybe a valet saw you sleeping in your car. But you haven't offered anyone up. It's like you don't care one way or another if Detective Sheridan arrests you." Her palms were moist, and she wiped them on her slacks. "But as it turns out, I care very much what happens to you." Aware her voice had risen above a polite decibel level, she lowered it. "And I'm getting fed up with being the only one. Never mind everyone else—the Bureau, the police, the public—*you* should at least be on your own side. How do you think Cindy would feel if she saw you just giving up like this?"

He was looking at her as if he could see all the way through her. "Cindy would be mad as hell."

While Spense and Sheridan exchanged a confused glance, Caitlin shook out her tingling hands. She was as baffled as anyone by her outburst. She hardly knew what had come over her, but ever since she'd walked into this house, she'd felt Cindy's pain like it was her own. No matter what ugly accusations the press made about Cynthia Langhorne, she deserved justice. And Catlin did not intend to stand by and watch her husband literally dare Monroe Sheridan to arrest him.

"Okay," Dutch whispered.

"Okay what?" she asked.

He reached out and put a hand on her shoulder. "Okay, I'll stand up for myself." Dipping his head, he gave her another penetrating look. "I know what you went through with your father, Caitlin. I know you did everything in your power to help him, and believe me, I appreciate what you're doing for me, now. I'm sorry if I seem ungrateful because I'm not. You're absolutely right about what Cindy would want, and I'll be damned if I'll let whoever did this to her get away with it. So, I promise you"—he squeezed her shoulder—"that from here on out, I'm going to answer any questions you . . . or the police might have."

"Caity . . ." Spense had a worried look on his face as if he thought her past was clouding her judgment.

"This has nothing to do with my father," she snapped. But even as she said the words, she knew they weren't true. This had everything to do with Thomas Cassidy. Her father had been executed for a murder he didn't commit, and she'd been helpless to stop it. Well, not this time. She wasn't going to sit around and nod and smile while Dutch played Russian roulette with Sheridan. "I will not stand by and watch you throw away your life. And I don't want the bastard who did this to your wife to go free, but that's exactly what's going to happen if you don't tell us everything."

"Ask me anything. I promise, I'll tell you the truth," he said.

"Why didn't you go upstairs to look for her?" Caitlin wanted to move off the topic of her father as quickly as possible.

Dutch fixed his gaze on Sheridan. "See, here's the difference between her question and yours, Detective. Dr. Cassidy actually wants to hear my answer whereas you already have the answer in mind. Not the most efficient way to get to the truth." Dutch's face and posture opened as he turned back to her.

"To answer your question: I should have gone upstairs to look for my wife. I wish to hell I had, because maybe then I could have saved her life. But instead, I behaved like a coward. I left the party. I simply withdrew from her, which was my habit, because I didn't want to discover her with another man. I assumed, at that point, since she'd lied to me about meeting Matt, she was meeting someone she didn't want me to know about. I—I didn't think I could stand to find her in a compromising situation. I know she's had affairs, but I didn't want her rubbing it in. I could have stood it, though. I realize that now. It would've been far better than what I found when I did go up."

Caitlin hated to ask, but it seemed important. "You say she had affairs. You knew that for a fact, or heard rumors? Did you and your wife have an understanding?"

"We didn't have an open marriage if that's what you're asking. These past few years, Cindy swore she was faithful, but I know I didn't make her happy. And there were so *many* rumors. But as long as I didn't see it with my own eyes, I still had hope for us."

"You were angry with her over those rumored affairs. I don't have to ask that. But what I do have to ask is were you angry enough to kill her?" Sheridan leaned in, waiting.

Dutch kept his eyes on Caitlin. "There he goes again. Asking a question when he's already decided on the answer. But I promised you I would, so I'll respond. I loved my wife, Detective, and I did not kill her."

Without knowing all the facts of the case, it was impossible to say with certainty he was telling the truth, yet she believed him. Every instinct she had told her Dutch Langhorne was an innocent man. She cast a sideways glance at Spense, but she couldn't read his reaction. He was wearing his poker face, and there was no decoding it. He slipped one hand in his pocket and her heart turned over. That was so Spense. She knew he was searching out his Rubik's cube. He must've forgotten he'd given it to Aaron. With Spense, it was always the little things that made her melt at the most unexpected moments.

And that was something she needed to get under control if they were going to both work together and *fraternize* when they were off duty. A crime scene was no place to go schoolgirl.

She pressed her lips together and focused on someone who didn't make her the least bit weak in the knees: Monroe Sheridan. Just like Dutch said, the detective had made up his mind from the get-go that the husband did it. Now he draped an arm over the banister and shook his head at Dutch. "Of course you admit to having heard the rumors. They're all over the Internet."

His voice was mean and taunting. He was deliberately trying to get a rise out of Dutch by bringing up Cindy's reputation. Caitlin didn't like where Sheridan was headed. He was supposed to look out for the woman, not grin while dragging her through the mud.

"All the Dallas ladies love to post about—"

She'd had enough. "Your job, Detective, is to get justice for Cindy Langhorne. Maybe you should keep that in mind the next time you speak."

He turned on her. "I'll say whatever I damn well please, Dr. Cassidy. I don't mind looking at you one little bit, which is the main reason I'm allowing you to be here, but when it comes to my investigation—"

She stretched herself up to her tallest stance, and for Dutch's sake, resisted the urge to spit in Sheridan's eye. Spense, on the other hand, didn't exercise as much self-control. Before she could stop him, he got hold of Sheridan's lapels and yanked him around to face him. "You want to disrespect me, or Agent Langhorne, Detective, go ahead. Knock yourself out. We don't give a rat's ass what you think of us, do we Agent Langhorne?"

"Not even a hair on a rat's ass." Dutch came over and stood shoulder to shoulder with Spense—the two men forming a barrier between her and Sheridan. She had to duck left to see around the high wall of muscle.

"But disrespect Dr. Cassidy one more time . . ." Spense said, in a deadly-calm voice " . . . and you're gonna need replacement parts for that frat-boy smile of yours."

MALACHI CLICKED HIS seat belt in place, removed his noise-canceling headphones, and hit the ANSWER button on his cell, "Thresher speaking."

"It's me, Hawk." The voice on the other end of the line was scrambled into an unpleasant, low-pitched frequency that sounded a lot like Chewie from *Star Wars*.

Most employers didn't take such care to conceal their identities. The majority were dolts who carelessly revealed their names, phone numbers, and more. But the Hawk not only used an alias, it made sure Malachi could not even identify its gender. In a way, he admired its cleverness. He wished he'd thought to conceal his own voice with a scrambler when he'd first started out, but he hadn't, and it seemed late in the game to do so now.

"Do you have the diary?" The voice undulated painfully into his ear.

Malachi switched to speaker.

He'd been born with a hypersensitivity to sound. His mother used to say he had dog ears because he could hear frequencies canines did and certain others that even man's best friend could not. This hypersensitivity of his acoustic nerve was real, and not imagined—though he'd been treated by a number of psychiatrists who'd tried to convince him it was. A *fixed delusion*, they'd called it.

Narrow-minded quacks.

But he knew the truth. The more ethereal noises flooding his airwaves existed—even if the audiologists couldn't document them, and the shrinks refused to believe in them. Souls *hummed*, and only he could hear their music. If he approached a man, and there was no humming, then there was no soul dwelling within. "I don't have the diary yet, but I promise you'll have it soon."

There was a long pause that gave his ears a bit of much-needed relief.

Then the Hawk said, "I thought I made myself clear. I need the diary, and I need it now. We had an agreement, but you haven't held up your end. And believe this: If I have to take matters into my own hands, the consequences for you will be severe."

"I'm a man of my word. I keep my promises—which is why I can't simply drop one assignment when another becomes urgent. I have to finish what I start."

"You've already failed me."

"I don't see it like that." What happened in Dallas wasn't his fault. And he was willing to adjust course and do whatever was needed to retrieve the diary as promised. This situation represented exactly the kind of problem that arose when employers didn't leave the details to him. "I've finished my other job, and I'm at your disposal."

"You'd better be."

He lightly ran a fingertip over the newly sharpened blade of the hunting knife that lay on the front passenger seat. The Hawk should be careful how it treated him. Malachi tuned his ears, straining to hear a possible hum beneath the distorted voice. Of course, there wasn't one. He'd yet to find an employer in possession of a soul. Most of his targets didn't have souls either, but he got paid well for his work. And every now and then, he got to take a meaningful life.

It had been far too long since he'd encountered a humming target, and he was growing impatient with the measly fare put before him.

Every soul he took added value to his own, and when his time came, his death would surely be a magnificent one. This was his due because he was more than fair, affording a good death to those who deserved it—and even to some who didn't. And when he heard the humming, he made the death as special as circumstances permitted. He could be quite creative when given the opportunity.

If a life held any value at all, even a soulless one, he considered taking it a privilege. Afterward, he liked to purify his own body. His ritual varied. Sometimes he bathed himself in bleach. Other times, he'd light candles and lie by the corpse. Or more often, when he was short of time, like he'd been today, he'd simply rub his body with mint ointment, allowing the vapors to cleanse his spirit as he set about his work.

"Hello?" The Hawk sounded impatient, even with its modulated voice.

"Still here. Still at your disposal." He pressed his fingertip against the tip of the knife, then smiled at the drop of blood that bubbled forth from beneath the skin.

"How long will it take you to get to Dallas?" Hawk asked.

"I can be there in under an hour, depending on traffic." He laid the phone in his lap, covered his ears with his hands, and started the engine. Once the engine noise died down, he grabbed the wheel and pulled away from the curb, heading for the highway.

"I'll call you back," the Hawk said abruptly. This was the third conversation he'd had with it when it had suddenly had to hang up. That, and the circumstances of the mission he'd been given, left him the impression the Hawk held a position of some importance in the world. But he was neither foolish enough nor curious enough to speculate further on who his employer might be. He preferred to focus on the task in front of him, and on his own special talent.

Malachi had always had the underpinnings of his gift, but at first, it wasn't finely tuned. Though by now, he'd built up quite a bit of tolerance, as a child, he couldn't bear certain sounds: the low rumble of the washing machine, for example, would make him clap his hands over his ears and scream. Then the screaming would cause the neighbors to knock on the door, and soon it was all too much, and he'd faint. When his mother vacuumed, he'd hide under the bed and cry until she'd finished. Once, at church, the bells rang out, and their resonance made him thrash around on the floor with his eyes rolling back in his head. That led the pastor to advise his mother to get him a medical diagnosis.

So she took him to a neurologist. The EEG and CT scan came back normal. But then, at the pastor's urging, the doctor ordered a PET scan, and voila, it lit up like a rainbow, with greens, yellows, and reds—he'd seen a picture of it that his mother saved, and it reminded him of a sun flare he'd seen in his science book. The specialist explained that certain colors represented increased neural activity in his limbic system—the part of the brain that controls emotion.

He was then placed on antiepileptics, but the medicines did nothing to quell his fits. In the end, his mother stopped all the drugs. Instead, she sent the laundry out and ceased vacuuming when he was at home. They stopped attending church. Which, truly, was no great loss and saddened him only because his mother missed the false comfort it had given her.

He changed lanes, then turned on his Escalade's navigation system. He knew how to get to Dallas, of course, but he wasn't sure of directions to the particular Preston Hollow address. A map came up on the screen. He shifted into cruise control.

Life hadn't been all bad. There were benefits to his keen hearing, even though it caused him discomfort. Just as animals sense fear in others, he could hear fear rolling off a person's skin. Unlike the soul, which has a nice, soothing hum, fear squeals like a pig.

In grade school, he'd put that knowledge to good use. He knew which boy would make an easy target, and he would rob his lunch or humiliate him on the playground. These were only innocent pranks, but they helped hone his gift. With time, his skill grew so great he could not only detect emotions, such as fear, elation, and arousal; he finally recognized the one thing that set him apart from all the other children—his ability to hear the soul.

His was a true gift and not meant to be wasted. To put it to good use, he decided to end his mother, since hers was a rather lonely existence. His father had died of a heroin overdose before he was born, and she'd never found another companion. Instead, she focused all her time on Malachi, smothering him with affection. This affection was unrequited, as loving someone was not his talent.

He could not *feel*.

Or perhaps he did care a little for the woman because even though she did not hum, and therefore he knew she had no soul, he honored her with a death that mattered. His very first meaningful death. Not as spectacular as he would've liked. But then again, he was only eleven, so chopping off her ears prior to strangling her seemed rather extraordinary at the time. The police never so much as suspected him. They placed him in a foster home without a second thought.

And so it began.

There was a rickety auditory vibration, not a soothing hum, of course, that the lowly exuded. They sounded quite a bit like broken washing machines, and whenever he came across such individuals, he knew they could be swiftly disposed of. With others, he had to spend more time, studying them, tuning in. But that was back in the early days.

Eventually, he became so skilled that merely walking into a person's habitat was enough to determine that individual's mortal worth from the echoes bouncing off the walls and shimmying out from beneath their beds.

Encouraged by his growing discernment, he practiced killing the lowly—who required no special consideration—until at last, he considered himself ready to seek out gainful employment in the form of contract work. There was plenty of that to go around. He got his first jobs by hanging out with local thugs, but it didn't take long for him to branch out and develop his own connections. It was hard to get good help, and in the hit-man business, if you were adept at what you did, the demand far exceeded the supply.

He hired himself out as *the Thresher*—he was good at separating the wheat from the chaff—taking great care never to come face-to-face with his employers. All monies were left at prearranged drops. Since no one knew his real name, or what he looked like, he was not only safe from the police, but his reputation grew far beyond that of an ordinary man. Once, he heard a rumor that the Thresher was seven feet tall and could crush a man's windpipe one-handed.

The pay was excellent, and the work remarkably easy to find. There was always someone who wanted to off a spouse or a co-worker. But when that type of thing—which seemed to be somewhat seasonal, picking up around the holidays and slowing down during the summers—dried up, he supplemented his income with small jobs. Breaking in and stealing the cat from an ex-wife, or "repossessing" a philandering husband's favorite set of golf clubs, for example. Malachi rarely needed to travel outside of his native Texas to find employment though he had ventured to bordering states on some occasions.

His phone rang again. "Thresher speaking."

This time the Hawk didn't bother with a greeting. "How far away are you?"

"Twenty minutes. You'll have the diary soon, but I'm going to need more money."

"Not after the way you screwed up."

"It wasn't me who screwed up. It was just a set of unfortunate circumstances that I was unable to predict because you failed to give me a full set of information. All you told me was to get the diary and eliminate the target. I needed more information about the target's personal life. Now the situation is even riskier. The area is crawling with police."

"I decide what information you do and don't need—but just to give you fair warning, the FBI brought in a couple of hot shots to run interference for Langhorne—Atticus Spenser and Caitlin Cassidy. You can Google anything you want to know about them."

"That doubles my risk."

A scratching sound that might've been a scrambled sigh came out of the phone's speaker. "Deliver the goods, and you'll get an extra ten grand."

"Twenty-five."

"Ten."

"Am I authorized to do things my way? Use any means necessary to carry out my mission? Because I will not be micromanaged."

"Just get the fucking diary. And remember what I said about consequences if you value those big balls of yours." It hung up.

As he pressed his foot on the accelerator, he noticed his heart picking up speed along with the Escalade. His mission just got a lot more complicated, and his reputation was riding on it.

Chapter Four

Wednesday, October 16
4:30 P.M.
Dallas, Texas

DUTCH LED THEM up the massive staircase, down several corridors, and into a far wing of the Worthington Mansion. When he pushed open a door marked *Presidential Suite*, an unexpected gust of hot air and a rancid odor hit Caitlin in the face.

Sheridan crossed to the window and closed it. "Been airing the place out. Stank something awful in here."

Death's putrid smell laced itself through her stomach and cinched tight.

"Mrs. Langhorne expelled her bowels when she was killed." Then, as if Caitlin wasn't aware, he added, "That's not unusual."

She nodded, only half-listening. Her gaze had been immediately drawn to a wooden, four-poster bed frame—the mattress was missing. In spite of the heat, she shivered, as though a ghost had just walked across her grave.

"The body was posed. When I arrived on scene, Mrs. Langhorne was spread-eagle naked in a pool of her own blood and feces. And this one"—he jabbed a finger at Dutch—"was hanging out in that recliner over there, gawking at his wife's body. Didn't bother to cover her up."

"It was a crime scene," Spense offered.

A glazed look came over Dutch's eyes. "That's right. I didn't want to disturb the crime scene."

"Uh-huh. And what the hell were you doing in here if not murdering your unfaithful wife?" Sheridan asked.

"By midnight, I suspected something was wrong. So I came upstairs and checked every room on the second floor. They were all locked, except this one."

"Your wife's gone missing from a party for two hours, and you finally get around to checking on her," Sheridan said.

"We'd agreed to meet before midnight. I had no idea she was in danger."

"I'd think most men would want to keep a better eye on the little woman."

Sheridan's body language and tone set Caitlin's teeth on edge. Assumptions might be necessary from time to time to move forward with a case, but made prematurely, they became a dangerous enemy of the truth.

"Sorry to disappoint you, but I don't live my life by most men's rules. And definitely not by yours."

"Don't care if you do or you don't, not even a hair on a rat's ass—as you put it before. But a jury . . . now they just might. So you weren't in any hurry to check up on Cindy, and once you found the body, you claim you took yourself a seat and did nothing. For a solid hour. What took you so long to call for help?"

Dutch shrugged.

Caitlin could see him slipping backward into shutdown mode. "I can't imagine what that must've been like for you, Dutch, but this is important. What were you doing from the time you found your wife's body, around midnight, until the time you called 911?"

"At one o'clock in the morning." Sheridan held out the recorder.

"I guess I was in shock."

"I guess so. I mean your wife is laid out naked on the bed with a bullet in her chest and her legs wide open." Sheridan stroked an imaginary goatee. "Or *maybe*, you spent that time staging the scene to make it look like some whack job did it, then got rid of the gun."

"You took a BlueView of my hands. Swabbed me yourself. You know there was no gunshot residue on them. I wasn't destroying evidence. I was in shock."

That's it, Dutch. Fight back.

"Thanks for reminding me about the lack of gunpowder on your hands. Of course, a member of law enforcement, a special agent such as yourself, would've washed off the residue and gotten rid of the murder weapon before calling for help. Don't you agree?"

"If I were guilty, yes, I would've done those things—and a hell of a lot more. I would've created an alibi, for example."

"Crime of impulse. You didn't plan it ahead, so you couldn't manage the alibi. But after the fact, your training kicked in. You posed the body. Wrote the word *SLUT* in all caps—that was a nice touch, I gotta say—on your wife's forehead with her lipstick, got rid of the gun . . . somehow . . . and then washed your hands."

"How did he get a gun inside if the murder wasn't premediated?" Caitlin challenged.

"Security must've been tight since Cambridge was the guest

of honor. That would mean the gun would've had to have been planted beforehand. Ergo, the crime was premeditated, and Agent Langhorne would've created an alibi for himself."

"He's a federal agent and a family friend of the Cambridges. You think the governor's boys checked him for heat? He just swaggered in the door with his off-duty carry. Doesn't mean it was or was not premeditated."

"Did you bring your off-duty with you?" Spense asked.

It would be easy enough to verify if he'd passed through security, Caitlin thought.

"No. At a function like this, no reason to complicate things by bringing a gun," Dutch answered. "There was a metal detector at the front entrance, but neither Cindy nor I walked through it. We came early to help Heather, and it wasn't set up at the time."

"Seems strange to me you weren't carrying, considering the nature of the function. What if there had been trouble?"

"I didn't bring my pistol because Cindy asked me not to. She hates guns, and I try not to carry them when she's with me unless it's really necessary."

"Which is it? You didn't bring a weapon because you didn't want to complicate things, or because your wife didn't want you to? Or are you lying? Here's what I think: You brought it. You used it, then you got rid of it."

Spense sat down in the recliner that was positioned a few feet from the bedframe. He rocked his head back and stretched out his legs. "Anyone move this recliner?"

All eyes turned to Spense.

"No," Sheridan said, after appearing to think on it a minute.

"It's facing the door, not the bed."

"So what?"

Something clicked into place in her head. She saw the look on Spense's face and knew they were on the same page. Spense bolted to his feet. "So Agent Langhorne couldn't have been *gawking at his wife's body* if the chair was facing the door."

"Make your point."

"He was lying in wait in case the killer returned to the scene of the crime. That's why he didn't call the police. Once he realized Cindy was dead, and there was no bringing her back, he wanted to take care of the killer on his own."

Dutch's face colored. Spense had hit it right.

"Who's to say your boy didn't shoot her, then lie in wait for the lover?" Sheridan asked. "He's a cold-blooded killer, any way you slice it."

"Wouldn't you have waited for the murderer—if it had been someone you loved?" Spense asked Sheridan.

A chill ran down Caitlin's spine—because she understood exactly what Spense was saying: that *he* would have been lying in wait, ready to take his revenge with his bare hands. Her head went light, and she grabbed the bedpost to steady herself. The long plane ride, the lingering smell of death, the heat—it was all getting to her.

And she couldn't stop picturing Cindy. Images flashed in her head, alternating between Cindy headed up the stairs in her beautiful gown and Cindy lying naked and bloodied on the bed. She peeled her hand off the post. The crime scene was talking to her, and she had to listen, whether she wanted to or not, for Cindy's sake. The answers, at least some of them, were right here in this room.

"No one heard the shot?" she asked. "If the killer used a silencer, we're back to premeditation."

"No silencer. At least we don't think so. The presidential suite is far away from the ballroom, and several guests claim they heard a car backfire shortly after ten o'clock. Our theory is that given the remote location of the room, the band music—possibly even crashing cymbals—the sound of the single gunshot was covered well enough for it to be passed off as incidental. But I like the way you're thinking." Sheridan handed her a set of crime-scene photos. "Captain asked me to share these with you two—no harm to the case since your boy was present when they were taken anyway."

He'd had them all along and was just now handing them over despite his captain's instructions. She could tell by his reluctance and his tone he thought Dutch was getting special consideration because of his law-enforcement status—and in truth, he was right. Otherwise, Sheridan wouldn't be discussing the case with them at all. She took a seat in the recliner Spense had vacated to view the photos. "Blood spatter on the headboard and the spread. Looks like she was shot on the bed itself. Not placed there after."

Sheridan nodded. "We believe the victim went upstairs to meet her lover, not the governor. We think she got undressed and lay on the bed, waiting for this mystery man. But her husband followed her upstairs. He waited a few minutes, then burst in and found her naked. He shot her, then, in a fit of rage, he grabbed the scissors from the desk, and shredded the dress that she'd hung in the closet." Sheridan walked to Caitlin's side and indicated a photo of Cindy's designer gown, the shoulders still attached to a hanger, the delicate chiffon skirt shredded to bits.

Dutch's face turned a color that made Caitlin think of the sky just before an impending storm. It was hard to say if his sudden emotion was because the sight of the dress reminded him of his loss or because Sheridan's blatant accusation infuriated him the way it did her.

Spense pulled out a notebook. Caitlin was glad of it, because that meant he'd handle the notes, and she could concentrate on the scene and the behavioral clues the killer, and the victim, had left behind.

Talk to me. I'm listening.

"I assume you've verified the governor's whereabouts at the time of the shooting with his protective detail? How many men did he bring with him? What kind of advance scouting was done for the mansion?" Spense had his pen poised and ready.

"We did verify his whereabouts. Unlike Langhorne, Cambridge has an alibi, and an airtight one. The security detail stated he never left the first floor during the entire fund-raiser."

"And Mrs. Cambridge?"

"Her guard states she was occupied downstairs with guests all evening."

"You think the security detail's word is ironclad, even though, I'm sure, some have been with the governor for years and might be extremely loyal."

"Actually, that's not an issue, unlikely though it would've been in the first place if you're suggesting that the governor's men would cover for him. Cambridge left his usual protective detail in Austin. He requested Dallas DPS officers, specially trained to assist with visiting VIPs, for security. They did a sweep of the mansion beforehand and were posted at the front and rear exits. Cambridge did bring a personal guard—who shadowed his wife the entire evening—but left the rest of the detail behind at the capital in favor of utilizing local resources."

"Why the hell would he do that?" Spense asked.

"No idea," Sheridan said. "Not my place to ask."

Caitlin had a thought. "Matt Cambridge is running for president. I'm guessing he didn't want the press to accuse him of gouging public funds for his protective detail while he was in Dallas for campaign purposes. It costs more to travel with a detail than to assemble one locally. That way, you avoid hotel and airfare expenses."

"See your point, but let's get back on track." Sheridan waved his hand dismissively.

"Okay, under your theory, why did Agent Langhorne follow his wife upstairs? It seems outrageous for him to suspect she'd meet her lover at a fund-raising ball. Too public." She stuck her finger in the air and turned to Spense. "And remind me, I want to come back to something very important we haven't yet touched on."

Sheridan hesitated, looking from Dutch to Spense and back again. "At the risk of getting my teeth rearranged, Dr. Cassidy, I'll take a stab at that one. Cindy Langhorne thrived on notoriety. We've interviewed her best friend, Mrs. Cambridge, at length, and we have reason to believe Cindy wouldn't have minded getting caught with her pants down. She wanted her husband to notice her.

"So maybe she let him overhear her making plans on the phone. Or perhaps he had her under surveillance. I'm not convinced by Langhorne's *no alibi is my alibi* gambit. I think this thing could have been meticulously planned out—a murder in the middle of a society event—by someone cold and calculating and intelligent, someone who knew the venue, knew the plans, and had the skill set to pull off something like this." He cracked his knuckles with finality. "Someone like Agent Langhorne."

"If Cindy was fleeing the room, trying to escape an enraged husband, she would've been shot in the back, not straight through the heart," Caitlin rushed in before Spense or Dutch could go off on Sheridan. There was something about being at a crime scene that made it easy to put herself in the victim's place. And she simply couldn't picture the scenario described by the detective.

"We believe he shot her from across the room, just as he walked in the door, before she even had a chance to sit up. Of course, you'd need to be quite a marksman to shoot a woman straight in the heart with one bullet from the doorway, but I understand Langhorne is champ out on the FBI shooting range."

"Sure, the person would need to be experienced handling firearms, but come on, Detective, it's hardly a military-grade skill to shoot an unarmed woman who's lying on the bed, possibly with her eyes closed, from a distance of, what, twelve feet. If I'm not mistaken, plenty of Texans know their way around a firearm."

"Not wrong about that," Sheridan admitted.

What about my dress? The lipsticked 'SLUT' on my forehead? Caitlin could practically hear Cindy whispering questions in her ear.

"He shredded my dress." Caitlin covered her mouth.

All three men shot her a questioning look. She shook her head. She was losing it. Overidentifying with Cindy in her efforts to tune in to the scene. "I meant to say the killer shredded *Mrs. Langhorne's* dress. That means this was a deeply personal act. He wanted to punish her. Instead of stabbing her again and again and again, he took the scissors to her dress, over and over and over. Whoever killed Mrs. Langhorne intended to shame her, that's why he posed her like that for the world to see."

Spense nodded. "More evidence of crime-scene precautions. This might or might not have been premeditated, but it was certainly cunning. Had the killer taken out his anger on the body, he would've been covered in blood and unable to escape detection for the duration of the party. By stabbing the dress, he gets to vent his rage but keeps his hands, and his clothes, clean."

Her throat closed at the idea of a crime so calculated and cold. This was no ordinary killer. This was someone capable of exerting extreme control to avoid detection. Her eyes fell on Dutch. He certainly had both the intelligence and the discipline to pull something like this off. But . . . all she could think about was protecting him. She had to believe in him . . . for Cindy.

Closing her eyes, she imagined herself lying on the bed, half-conscious, with the lifeblood seeping from her. Hatred shrouded the room as the attacker ripped up her dress.

Woosh woosh woosh.

She heard the sound of fabric tearing.

"Now everyone will know what you really are," the killer whispered in her ear.

Something oily traced her forehead. She couldn't open her eyes, couldn't see her assailant. So she concentrated on the letters being slicked onto her skin.

SLUT.

Caitlin's eyes popped open. "Did you check the forehead for DNA? Lipstick can be a great transfer medium."

"She's right," Spense and Dutch said in unison.

"That may be, but shit, it's Cindy's lipstick, so if there is DNA, transfer it'd be from her own mouth."

"It's not her lipstick," Caitlin said, her heart kicking up a gear. "In the crime-scene photo, the lipstick is red, but Cindy's lipstick that night was coral."

"What color's coral?" Sheridan looked around the room for help.

"Orange," Spense said.

"Peach?" Dutch suggested.

"Then no, it wasn't coral. Cindy Langhorne was wearing red lipstick. Check the photo of her body," Sheridan insisted.

Sure enough, in the crime-scene photos, Cindy's lips were scarlet—like the letters on her forehead. Even under different lighting, the pastel coral wouldn't appear dark red. Her lipstick had been changed. "I suppose she could've applied different lipstick right after she went upstairs . . ."

"Cindy never wore red," Dutch said. "She thought it made her look cheap, and as I've said before, she was very interested in keeping up a refined appearance. She didn't want anyone recalling that she came from the wrong side of the tracks. I can't help thinking that whoever did this to her must've known how much she'd despise being remembered this way."

"Then the killer probably brought the lipstick with him and wiped hers off, replacing it with red," Caitlin said.

"Like one of those serial killers who plays dress-up with his victims—paints their nails and shit. I see what you're saying, but we got plenty of suspects"—Sheridan looked askew at Dutch—"without bringing a serial killer into this. Even if it wasn't Langhorne, it could've been a jilted lover or a pissed-off wife. I just don't buy what you're trying to sell."

"I'm not selling anything, Detective. I'm telling you to be sure the lipsticked forehead gets checked for DNA because it's not Cindy's. Take a look at the photos in the *Dallas Morning Gazette*, and you'll see I'm right. Cindy Langhorne wore coral to the ball."

As the detective pulled out his phone and searched, likely to verify that Caitlin's memory was correct about the lipstick in the photograph from the *Gazette*, Spense tapped her shoulder.

"What?" she asked, still trying to shake off the creepy feeling of imaginary lipstick on her forehead.

"You said to remind you to come back to something."

She took in a sharp breath. "Something important." They'd talked around so many things since they'd entered the mansion, and yet somehow the subject of who Cindy's mystery lover might be hadn't yet been broached. "We're all agreed Mrs. Langhorne did not meet Matthew Cambridge in this room. So, Detective, whom do you think she was expecting? You're laying out your case that this was an illicit rendezvous, but you haven't told us who you think her lover was."

Sheridan's jaw worked, and he went for the nonexistent goatee one more time. "I got no idea."

"Did Heather Cambridge have any thoughts on the matter?" Spense asked.

"No. According to her, there was nobody at the moment. At least not that Cindy had confided to her. And Agent Langhorne maintains he doesn't know." He turned to Dutch. "That is still your statement, right?"

Dutch said nothing.

Caitlin searched Dutch's eyes. "If we had that name, we'd certainly have another direction to look in this case."

"Not your case." Sheridan wagged his finger.

"I was using the *we* figuratively. Agent Spenser and I are well aware of the fact we haven't been invited in on this thing." She turned back to Dutch, and as she watched his face, she had the sense that he might be holding something back. Did he still want to take care of the killer on his own? She tried to meet his gaze again, but this time he looked away quickly—too quickly. What was he hiding? "Dutch, I believe you if you say you don't know about an affair. But looking at this from a woman's point of view, if I did have a secret lover, and I couldn't confide in my best friend about him, I'd have to get my thoughts out somehow or other."

Spense turned to her, his expression intrigued. "So if you couldn't confide in your best friend, who would you talk to? A priest . . . a doctor maybe?"

"Well, I don't know about Mrs. Langhorne, but if it were me, I'd journal it." She smiled. She really might be onto something. "You know, like *Dear Diary* . . ."

Chapter Five

Wednesday, October 16
5:15 P.M.
Preston Hollow, Texas

"THE BUREAU MUST be paying you fellas a hell of a lot more than the Dallas PD pays me," Detective Sheridan spread his arms indicating Dutch's luxurious Preston Hollow home, then slammed the door to his unmarked cop car and caught up to them as they approached the house from the motor court.

Sometimes people improve on longer acquaintance, but Spense didn't hold out much hope that Sheridan would turn out to be one of them. The detective had followed him, Dutch, and Caity from the Worthington Mansion. No denying the Langhornes lived in one of the most exclusive suburbs of Dallas—or the whole of Texas for that matter. The two-story country French residence sat nestled among mature trees on an acre lot. The motor court had four bays, one of which housed Mrs. Langhorne's red Maserati.

"Looks like I went into the wrong branch of law enforcement." Sheridan didn't give it a rest.

"It's my wife who has the money," Dutch said.

Sheridan undoubtedly knew that already, but for whatever reason, he seemed to want to make Dutch say it. From Spense's point of view, it was just one more of the digs he'd been subjecting Dutch to all day. No doubt a thinly veiled accusation would follow.

"Your wife *had* the money, don't you mean? It's all yours now that she's gone. You really married up, man. No wonder you don't care who she screws."

Spense was just about to issue Sheridan his second warning of the day when a dog began barking like he'd cornered a squirrel. Sounded like it came from the south neighbor's yard. Spense held up one hand in a stop sign. "Everyone stay put."

"Just a dog, Spenser. Heard our cars drive up." But Sheridan halted along with the rest of them, casting a wary glance around. "You always this jumpy?"

Spense pushed back his jacket but didn't draw his Glock. "Anything look off to you?" he asked Dutch.

"Not so far." Dutch took a few steps closer to the house.

"A place like this? He's got a security system. If there was a break-in, we'd know it. I don't suppose you called ahead, and now you're just stalling to give the staff time to hide that diary."

"I thought you had a date with October baseball, Detective," Caity said.

Her patience with Sheridan seemed to be growing thin. It was obvious she'd been trying to keep the peace all day, but this last accusation, leveled at Dutch, must've been the straw that broke her back.

"I'm the one who suggested there might be a diary to begin

with. We offered to look for the journal, and bring it to you if one happens to turn up. But you insisted on following us and poking around yourself. And even though you have no warrant, Agent Langhorne agreed. Now you're accusing us of obstructing your investigation." Spense heard Caity's breath hiss out from between her teeth. "As far as I'm concerned, you can go suck an egg."

Sheridan put both hands in the air feigning surrender. "Damn the lady's got a mouth on her. She sure put me in my place."

"Dr. Cassidy is plenty capable of putting you anywhere she wants you." Spense knew Sheridan could never take Caity in a verbal sparring match—he didn't have the vocabulary or the wit. But *go suck an egg* was the most she'd toss at him because she thought they needed to *establish a rapport with the locals*. Spense, on the other hand, would take the guy down without a second thought. But at the moment, he couldn't afford to let Sheridan distract him. "He's got a point about the security system." Still something didn't seem right. That was one, unhappy canine out there.

"Didn't set the alarm. And I gave the staff a month's paid leave. They're torn up about losing Cindy, and I got nothing for them to do anyway." Dutch paced back and forth in front of his house. "Looks okay from out here, but Gizmo's not usually a barker."

"Why didn't you set the alarm?" Sheridan eyed Dutch suspiciously.

"The security system is there to protect my wife—not our possessions. And if her killer wants to come gunning for me next, I can handle myself fine. In fact, I hope he does because I'll be ready and waiting."

Spense held out his hand for the house key. "I'm going in first. Everyone stay here until I give you the all clear."

"I'll cover. You clear." Dutch fished out the keys.

Spense kept his palm open, waiting. "No. You stay here. It's probably nothing. This is just a precaution, but in case it does turn out to be real, I need you to stick on Caity."

"Consider me Super Glue." Dutch tossed him the keys. "It's the one with the Rangers logo."

"I can cover you." Sheridan's offer came late and halfhearted. Spense ran an assessing gaze over him and decided he looked nervous. He just might be one of those cops who'd never fired his service weapon outside of the range, in which case, Sheridan would be more liability than help if there was an intruder on the premises. "Like I said, just a precaution. If you wanna help, you can wait here and keep an eye out for a rabbit."

Sheridan's shoulders dropped, and his face relaxed. "If you're sure."

"I'm sure." Sure he could handle it better without having to worry about the detective's doing something stupid, like he'd proven himself capable of doing with Aaron earlier in the day.

As Spense headed for the door, he tried to tune out Sheridan and Dutch in the background. Their arguing made it hard for him to focus.

"*This is a setup, isn't it?*"

"*No idea what you mean.*"

"*You probably tossed the place to make it look like a break-in.*"

"*How'd I get the dog to bark?*"

"*I'm just saying it's convenient. You suggesting I stop by the house, and now something's up. I'm just theorizing of course.*"

"*You insisted on coming over.*"

"*You lured me here with that story about a diary.*"

Spense turned the key and breached the doorway uneventfully, leaving the two men behind, still bickering. He exhaled a long, relieved breath, as their voices faded. His brain sharpened itself on the quiet. One slice at a time, he cleared the downstairs. *Cut the pie,* his instructor at Quantico used to say.

Room after room, he made his way methodically through the home. Finally, the downstairs was clear. But this was one mother of a house. Luckily, the upstairs would have less square footage. It should go quick. Especially now he had his rhythm. He heard the whirr of the air conditioner cycling on and ignored it. That was a right sound. He only cared about the wrong ones.

He started upstairs, keeping his weight on the balls of his feet, moving as noiselessly as possible. On alternating steps, he checked back over his shoulder. Yeah. He'd cleared below, but nothing is ever one hundred percent. He kept moving forward. Stairs were tricky. Couldn't slice them like a pie—couldn't always see ahead. At some point, you just had to go.

He was there now.

Pistol out front, he dashed up the rest of the steps. Made it safely to the landing. Now for more pie. Leading with his gun and his eyes, he made his way down the hall and into the master bedroom.

Shit.

The room had been tossed. A painting lay shattered on the ground, its backing ripped away. He dodged bits of broken glass, the emptied drawers, and overturned chairs. The door to a walk-in closet stood slightly ajar. He kicked it open the rest of the way, and leapt aside.

Silence.

He cleared the closet—also tossed, before moving on. Upstairs, everywhere he went, the intruder had left his mark. This must've taken time. Whoever did this knew Dutch would be gone a good while. Spense stowed that away for future reference. No time to process clues now, but then another salient thought occurred. The intruder started upstairs. The downstairs was clean—they'd interrupted him before he made it there. Either he'd just left or was still in the house . . . somewhere.

A river of cold air rushed over Spense's skin, but he no longer heard the mechanical sound of the central air. He was in his zone. That place where the adrenaline pushed out all the distractions that lived in his head. That place where all sounds disappeared—except the ones that mattered. Even the dog's barking was a shadow of its former self . . . and then he heard the creak. That wrong sound he'd been waiting for.

Footfalls.

Other room.

Then scraping. Behind that next closed door, someone waited. Spense felt another's presence, and he knew whoever it was could feel him, too. They were too close not to be aware of each other. He stuck his gun out the door and followed it into the hallway, keeping his back off the wall where a ricochet might hit him. He arrived at the closed door. Kept to the side. The wood wouldn't protect him from a bullet if the intruder decided to shoot through it blind. Spinning, he kicked the door open and burst through. "Police! Freeze!"

He looked left, then right. *Clear.* The window stood open, curtains knocked to the ground. He flashed across the room and scanned the area outside the window. A giant weeping willow guarded the back of the house, its branches strong enough to hold a man's weight—long, thick, and perfect for climbing to the ground. He heard a soft thud, and looked down. A figure, tall and muscular, rolled down an incline, jumped up, and took off running.

Spense shoved his pistol in its holster, freeing both hands. As he crawled out, his head cracked against the windowsill, sending dull vibrations ringing through his skull. With his body half-out the window, his knees hooked over the sill, anchoring him, he stretched out his arms. But he couldn't grab hold of that supporting branch. No time to doubt himself, he scrambled back, threw his legs in front and got himself into an upright sit in the window. He concentrated on the branch.

See the branch.

Get the branch.

Jump!

His chin hit something hard, slamming his teeth into his tongue. Blood trickled down his face. He wrapped his arms around the tree's fat trunk, monkeyed his way from branch to branch. The rough bark tore his flesh as he slid down, down, down. He scrambled just far enough to know the fall probably wouldn't break his legs. Braced his feet together.

Jump!

He landed feetfirst, and his knees absorbed the first brunt of the impact, then his shoulder slammed into the ground. Something burned, but he didn't care. Adrenaline propelled him onward. Back on his feet, his pistol drawn, he gave chase. "Stop! Police!"

A male figure dressed in jeans and a dark shirt scrambled over a tall masonry fence into the neighbor's yard. The intruder had a good head start, but Spense wasn't far behind. His senses went on highest alert—for innocent civilians and kids. And for new threats—like that barking dog.

How dangerous could a Gizmo be?

His mind raced as he hurtled over the fence, a few beats behind his rabbit. He dropped into the next yard, where a blue pool glistened in the evening light. Shadows fell across the neighbor's back lawn, heavily edged with bushes. The intruder could be anywhere . . . then a man darted out from behind a fountain, spotted Spense, and froze. He'd have to run right past him to make it to the gate.

Advantage: good guys.

Spense held his pistol steady and aimed, while, at light speed, his hyperaware brain catalogued details of the man's appearance. Dirty blond hair. Scar on right cheek. About six feet. Gym rat. Late twenties. Their gazes connected—and Spense knew if he ever saw the guy again, he could easily recognize him by the bizarre emptiness behind his blue eyes—painted orbs, jerking around with no human purpose.

"FBI! Hands behind your head. Get on your knees."

Crazy eyes raised his hands slowly. Took a step backward.

"On your knees! Now!"

Bam!

From nowhere something knocked Spense's feet out from under him, and his pistol to the ground. He flew backward into the pool—the water like concrete when it met his back. His head hit the side of the pool. Then darkness enveloped him, filling his eyes, his nose, his mouth. As consciousness receded, weird images passed across his mind: eyeballs on springs, bulging from their sockets, a canine missile launching into outer space, a bathtub filled with black blood.

Fight it or die.

Battling the instinct to inhale, he made a fist and thumped his chest, forcing himself to exhale the contents of his burning lungs. Bubbles floated up around him. He kicked hard, shot to the surface, and gasped a breath that stung like hell. That first gulp of air went down like a shot of straight bourbon. His brain jolted into awareness, and he swam toward the edge of the pool. Then his foot hit the plaster bottom. He'd made it to shallow water. He stood up. If his head weren't throbbing like the devil, if he didn't know that his rabbit was long gone, he might've laughed. He'd been knocked into a pool by a dog named . . . wait . . . could that be *Gizmo*?

Shaking his head, he blinked water from his eyes. Dutch should've warned him that his neighbor's dog, Gizmo, was a Doberman. He braced his arms on the side of the pool and was just about to hoist himself out of the water when someone called out. "Stop or I'll shoot."

The trembling voice came out of a bald guy wearing nothing but a pair of lime green boxers. The Glock shaking in his hands looked a lot like Spense's.

Spense lifted his hands. "FBI. You think you could put down the gun, sir? I can explain everything."

A gentleman in a dark suit appeared behind boxer guy. Boxer guy passed him Spense's Glock.

"You in the pool. Hands behind your head, then turn around. Ease on over to the steps and get out of the pool nice and easy. Keep your back turned."

Spense did as he was told, then, anticipating the next command, he knelt on the ground. "FBI. Creds in my pocket."

Boxer guy stuck his hand in Spense's pocket, fumbled around then pulled out his wallet.

Seconds later the suit said, "You can get up, Agent Spenser. Sorry about that."

Spense got up and turned around. He knew a government agent when he saw one. What the hell? "You Secret Service?"

Suit didn't answer, but boxer guy pointed to his right and squinted. "See that gate down yonder?"

Spense nodded.

"Behind it, that's George and Laura's place."

As if that explained everything. Gizmo nudged Spense's wet crotch with his cold nose.

"Sorry, again." The owner motioned the Doberman to heel. "I'm talking about Dubb ya."

"Dubb ya?"

"You still got water in your ears, son. I say George. Dubb Ya. *Bush*. Lives right down yonder. So we got a hell of a neighborhood watch around here."

Chapter Six

Thursday, October 17
2:15 A.M.
Preston Hollow, Texas

CAITLIN TIPTOED DOWN the hallway and eased the door to the library open, cringing when the hinges squeaked. Spense and Dutch were both asleep, and she didn't want to disturb them. They'd all been forced into guest rooms on the first floor because the upstairs remained in total disarray. Though the crime-scene techs had come and gone, the cleanup would have to wait until morning.

After his submersion in the neighbor's pool, Spense had submitted to her brief mental-status exam and a quick listen to his heart and lungs—acting randy and cracking wise the entire time. To hear him tell it, it had all been a big adventure—jumping out of trees, chasing bad guys, confabbing with the neighbor. He'd been especially animated when describing that neighbor and his colorful choice in underwear. More than once, he imitated the man's Texas drawl and pantomimed the part where the Secret Service showed up. He razzed Dutch repeatedly for not warning him about Gizmo. She suspected Spense would've been damn well pleased with the whole evening if only he hadn't lost track of his *rabbit*. She also suspected he hadn't given a second thought to the fact that he'd lost consciousness in a swimming pool and very nearly drowned.

Satisfied, after observing him sleep for several hours, that he was breathing easily and hadn't aspirated enough water to cause him any harm, she'd kissed Spense on the forehead and gone back to her designated guest room. Dutifully, she put on her pajamas and climbed into bed, but she couldn't sleep. The realization that without a single bullet being fired, Spense could've been taken from her, drove her to prowl the house. She found the kitchen and made herself a cup of warm milk, but it didn't seem to help. After sipping it, she wasn't the least bit drowsy.

And that's how she wound up here, at the first-floor library. A good book would be just the thing. A good book would make her forget, for a few minutes at least, that Spense was a certain kind of man.

The kind who answered when trouble knocked.

The kind who ran *into* the blaze, in case there might be others trapped inside.

The kind who would never play it safe, and therefore was sure to find himself in harm's way on a regular basis.

And the terrible truth was that even if she could, she wouldn't change a thing about him. Because then he wouldn't be *Spense*. Falling for him was dangerous business—but she didn't know how not to. Swiping her eyes, she whispered a little prayer to keep him safe and stepped into the library.

She closed the door behind her, but not all the way, to prevent the noise of the latch. She considered searching by the ambient light coming in through the windows and the flashlight app on her cell, but it would certainly be difficult to locate a book that way. Patting her hand around for a light switch, she found nothing, but her eyes began accommodating to the low light, allowing her to see a little better. Then a shadow at the desk revealed itself to be no shadow at all. For what seemed like an eternity, but couldn't have been longer than a heartbeat, she stood paralyzed. Panic clutched at her throat, but then, her psychiatric training kicked in. This was one scenario she was better equipped to handle than Spense.

She infused her voice with authority, but spoke quietly so as not to startle. "Put down the gun."

Dutch, keeping the pistol pressed to his temple, swiveled his chair around to face her. In the moonlight-varnished room, his face, hair, and clothes held little color. She might've been looking at a black-and-white photograph of the man. Without the vibrant red of his hair, without the startling blue of his eyes, he became a stripped-down version of himself. Only the essential definition in his face remained—the shape of his eyes, his strong jaw, that hauntingly familiar mouth and chin . . . his expression. It was as though she were seeing him, really seeing him, for the very first time.

And what she saw shocked her.

Like a song with the bass turned up, her heartbeat thudded in her ears. A thousand concerns battled for precedence in her mind, but instantly, she focused on the most important one. "Put down the gun, Dutch. I'm going to walk over to you now."

"Okay." He didn't lower the pistol. "You can come closer."

She stepped forward and stumbled, her bare foot catching the edge of a rug.

With his free hand, he switched on the desk lamp. "Careful."

Her feet had turned to lead, but she managed to make her way across the room. He sat at a massive desk made of some kind of dark wood. Cherry maybe. Up close, she could see his cheeks were wet, his eyes swollen and red-rimmed. A half-empty bottle of whiskey stood open on the desk next to an empty tumbler.

She reached her hand out, palm up, and looked him directly in the eye, "Give me the gun."

The room went silent.

Too silent.

Neither one of them was breathing.

With their gazes locked, his finger tapped the trigger.

She knew he expected her to look away. "No way," she said. "If you're going to pull that trigger, you'll have to look me in the eye when you do."

His Adam's apple bobbed up and down. A few tense moments passed, then he dropped his gaze . . . and lowered the gun.

She exhaled a long breath.

He released the magazine, showing her it was empty. "I wasn't going to shoot myself. It's not even loaded."

Oh, he wasn't getting off that easy. As if this was all so innocent. "Maybe you've got a bullet in the chamber."

He shoved the magazine back into place, raised the gun to his head and pulled the trigger.

Click.

Her knees gave way, and she had to grab the desk for support. Her heart pounded hard and fast against her ribs.

He had the balls to smile at her. "I told you it wasn't loaded." He arched one brow at her. "You should've taken my word for it."

Leaning in, she reached out and slapped his face, leaving a red mark in the shape of her hand.

He rubbed his cheek. "Sorry."

"Not good enough. That was cruel, and you know it."

"It was for your own good."

"Gee thanks." Her hands balled into fists, and she stuck them behind her back. Her body trembled as her stomach twisted into a hard knot.

"I just thought you should know who you're dealing with. I've been watching you watching me, and I know what you're thinking."

"Is that so?" She clamped her teeth together and willed her breathing to normalize. He didn't get to make her feel this bad for more than a few seconds.

"You're thinking, poor Dutch. He's holding all his grief inside. He's acting tough, trying to make us believe he's bad, but deep down inside, he's really good."

"Wow. That's exactly what I was thinking." She pulled her hands from behind her back and braced her palms on the desk. Leaned in close enough to smell the booze on his breath. "Right up until you pulled that trigger. That was quite a stunt. How dare you put me through that, then tell me it was for my own good?"

"Because I'm not a nice guy, Caitlin. You're wasting your time trying to help me. But if I'd simply said so, you wouldn't have believed me. I had to find a way to make you understand what an asshole I really am. You didn't believe me when I told you the gun wasn't loaded, so I thought I'd prove both points with one trigger pull."

"Well it worked." She sat down hard.

He poured two fingers of whiskey in his glass and held it out to her. She took a slug and passed the glass back to him. "Okay, asshole. If you're really so terrible, why are you protecting Spense and me?"

His turn to drink. He polished off the whiskey and set the glass on the desk.

"I'm waiting," she said.

"Don't know what you mean."

"When Edison offered you an advocate from the Bureau, you specifically asked for Spense and me. Now you're doing all you can to piss us off or scare us off. You're trying to get rid of us. I'm sure of it. I think that you think we're better off not getting involved." She leaned back. "I just don't understand why. If you didn't want us here, why ask for our help in the first place?"

His answer: stretching his legs and giving her the one-shoulder shrug.

"You don't want to talk things out, fine. We should get you to the hospital now anyway. We can finish our discussion later." Maybe the gun wasn't loaded, but he hadn't been holding it to his temple for grins. He hadn't expected her to walk through that door, so it wasn't for show either. He'd been rehearsing. Next time it might be loaded.

"No hospital."

"You can go voluntarily, or—"

"Or what. You'll call the police? Have me admitted on a three-day hold? You can try, but you won't succeed."

"I'd rather not have to commit you. But you're a danger to yourself, so if you won't go in on your own, I'll be forced to do whatever it takes to keep you safe."

"I'm safe now."

"Most suicides are impulsive. You've just lost your wife. You've been singled out as a likely suspect in her murder. This is probably the lowest point in your life. Right now. This minute."

His chest heaved. He turned away from her, refusing to meet her eyes.

"If we can just get you past the next few days . . ."

"You can't force me to go. Even if you convince the cops to drag me down to the emergency room, I know the questions I'll be asked. And I know just how to answer them to get out pronto:

"*Yes, I have thought about dying since I lost my wife, but I know this too shall pass. Occasional thoughts of suicide cross my mind. I won't deny it—but a plan? Why no. I haven't given the slightest thought to how I would do it. The gun? I never held a gun to my head at all. The room was dark, and Dr. Cassidy misinterpreted. I'd be happy to hand over all my bullets, to her, if she's concerned. And I'll make an appointment with a grief counselor in the morning. Scout's honor.*"

He turned his palms up, as Spense often did. "I'll be released within the hour, and there won't be a damn thing you can do about it."

She knew it was true. If she were on her home turf, maybe she could persuade the attending in the ER. But here, she wouldn't have the clout to override a patient who knew the drill and gave all the right answers. Even if Dutch was a danger to himself, he could make it seem to the doctors that he wasn't. He was simply too sophisticated, and he knew the system too well. There was no way to force him to get help.

But she still had hope she could convince him to go in on his own. "I'm not buying it. You can turn over your bullets, your pistol, whatever. I know you can get your hands on more anytime you want. So how about being honest—with yourself, if no one else. I *know* that when you put that empty gun to your head it was a dress rehearsal. You were working up your nerve."

"No disrespect to your shrink skills, but I wasn't. I've got the nerve. I'm a stone-cold SOB, sweetheart. You want the truth?"

"Of course."

"I put that gun to my head because I want to die, and I needed to feel the cold barrel of that pistol on my skin. But first, I emptied the magazine to be sure I wouldn't do it. It's not a matter of working up the nerve. It's a matter of *needing* to live more than I *want* to die. I've got a reason to stick around."

Her throat went dry. He'd admitted he wanted to die. His voice, his mannerisms were convincing. He just might be telling the truth about having a reason to live. "Better make it a good one if you're going to convince me. I'm not going to be fooled by bullshit."

"Okay, how's this? I'm not checking out until I find the fucker who killed my wife."

He had to be telling the truth. The hard look of determination in his eyes. The rage in his voice when he spit out the word *fucker*. Hate was a terrible way to overcome despair. But if hatred for his wife's murderer kept him alive, she'd take it. At least he had a purpose in life. And she knew from experience, if he could only get through this moment in time, his heart could begin to heal. It would be a long process, but he'd be past the most dangerous part. This wasn't depression—it was grief, and he had every reason to be despondent.

A half smile crept across his face. "I can see the phone in the pocket of your robe, but you haven't called 911 yet. I think you might believe me—when I say I love my wife, and that I intend to bring down her killer. Or do you think I killed her, too?"

"Too?"

"Spense isn't convinced of my innocence."

There was simply no point in lying. Dutch could see through her falsehoods as easily as she could see through his. "Maybe he's not sure. But he *wants* to believe you're innocent, and he'll do anything he can to help find the killer."

Dutch turned his head aside, staring out the window. "Spense doesn't much like me."

"You haven't given him a reason to. Most of the time, you act standoffish with him, and the rest of the time you're downright rude." She took in Dutch's profile, letting her gaze flow from his face, to his shoulders, down his body. His pajama leg was pushed above his ankle. A shiver ran down her spine, and she sat up straighter. Like Spense, Dutch had a distinctively shaped birthmark on his right ankle, centered directly above the lateral malleolus.

There was no question in her mind at all. Not since she'd first entered the library and seen Dutch sitting in the dark like a black-and-white photo. Why he'd always seemed so familiar—it had all come to her in that moment. She just hadn't had time to deal with it, what with him holding a gun to his head. She didn't know how she'd missed it before, back in Hollywood, but once she'd noticed the resemblance, there was no unnoticing it. It was like one of those optical illusions where you can't see the picture hidden among the dots . . . until you do.

"Since we're being honest, since you're asking me to trust you, I'd like you to answer a question. You told me earlier, back at the mansion that you'd tell me anything I wanted to know."

"Are we done with the hospital nonsense?"

"It's not nonsense, but for now, yes. You've convinced me you're not going to kill yourself the minute I turn my back."

"Okay then, ask me anything."

"How are you related to Spense?"

He poured himself another shot of whiskey, swirled it in the glass. She wondered if he would keep his word or pretend not to understand her meaning.

He tossed back the whiskey, wiped his sleeve across his mouth, and looked her dead in the eyes. "By three months, I'm his older brother."

Chapter Seven

Thursday, October 17
2:20 A.M.
Denton, Texas

NOTHING LIKE A narrow escape to work up an appetite. Malachi hadn't eaten in nearly twenty-four hours, so he stopped at a Denny's off the 35. Besides, he wasn't eager to report back to his employer that he'd not only failed to get the diary, he'd very nearly been caught by that FBI hotshot. But there was really no reason to check in with the Hawk until he had the goods. He'd been given the green light to handle things his own way, and that's just what he planned to do.

He liked the server who'd taken his order, a tired-looking thing with wiry gray hairs sprouting out of her bun. She reminded him of his mother, who used to work at Denny's, too. When he looked up to find a new waitress, standing pink and sweaty-faced with a steaming plate in her hands, he stuck out his lower lip. "Where's Coleen?"

"I swapped tables with her. Here's your Moons over My Hammy and tomato juice." She set the food in front of him and leaned one hip against the table. "That's nice you took notice of her name." She covered the name tag on her uniform with one hand. *Sugar.* "Did you catch mine?"

"No," he lied. Sugar seemed more interested in flirting than going about her duties. That was okay, but he was starved and wanted to dive into his breakfast.

"They call me Sugar on account of I'm a sweet one." She popped her hand off the tag and leaned forward, pushing her cleavage in his face. "See there. For real."

Something stirred down below, and he decided he could eat and hold court at the same time. "Cute."

"Thanks."

He took a big bite of his sandwich and burned the roof of his mouth. To soothe the pain, he grabbed his juice and swished a bit before swallowing.

"You from around here?" Sugar asked.

"Argyle," he answered between bites.

"My brother's got a pig farm there. Maybe you know him?"

"No. I don't."

Sugar swatted his arm with her apron. "I haven't even told you his name."

"I'm not acquainted with any pig farmers." He rubbed himself beneath his napkin until he turned hard. "You got a coffee break or something, soon?"

"I believe I do."

He leaned in, straining to hear, and disappointment set in. He should've known. Broken washing machine—that's all she was.

Hardly worth the trouble. His erection deflated fast. "I'll take the check."

"You scarfed that down." She leaned in again, and he could smell a sweet perfume, mixed in with the grease.

But his interest had waned. And he had work to do before he slept. He had to map out his next moves. He still didn't have the diary. And there was a bigger problem: Nobody was allowed to see his face and live. The good news was he was looking forward to eliminating that problem—one Atticus Spenser.

"I can take my break now if you want."

"No thanks. Gotta run."

Sugar wasn't special, but earlier tonight, inside that big house, he'd heard a sound he'd been craving for a long time.

Humming.

He'd stumbled upon a soul, and judging from the echoes ringing through that house, there might be more than one. His knees knocked furiously against the tabletop. He could hardly wait for the harvest.

Chapter Eight

Thursday, October 17
2:25 A.M.
Preston Hollow, Texas

CAITLIN'S CHIN SNAPPED back like Dutch had dealt her a physical blow. It wasn't that it was such a surprise. It was more that she'd been desperately hoping, for Spense's sake, that Dutch would say *cousin*. In her heart, though, she'd already known. Spense and Dutch were too much alike to be semidistant relations. She'd never seen cousins with matching birthmarks—that was rare enough in siblings, or parent and child. And their height, their builds, their iron wills . . . even their facial features, minus the coloring, were practically identical.

Dutch wheeled his chair back from the desk. "I'll get you your own glass. I'm sure you could use another drink, and forgive me, but I'm tired of sharing."

Since she didn't have to drive him to the ER at this point . . . "Why the hell not?" She forced a smile, and he left the room.

She didn't want to think about the impact this revelation was going to have on Spense. His father had died suddenly when he was only eight years old, and he'd idolized his dad—tried to emulate him every way he could. From his obsession with Rubik's cubes right down to the Old Spice aftershave he wore, Spense was all about trying to follow in his father's footsteps. Trying to become the man his father would want him to be. To compose herself, she organized her thoughts and turned her attention to the mechanics of what she'd just learned. How could Dutch be Spense's older brother?

Dutch returned, filled both their glasses almost to the top with straight whiskey, then resumed his place across from her at the desk.

She held the glass of amber liquid up to the lamp, gazing through it, as though it were a crystal ball, wondering how Spense would take the news. She should go easy with this stuff. The world had just tilted on its axis, and the last thing she needed was for her head to start spinning, too. Gingerly, she took a sip, and the potion went down smoothly, relaxing the muscles in her tight throat and warming her cheeks. She resisted the temptation to gulp the rest. "I've been doing the math."

"And."

"You and Spense are three months apart, so obviously, you're his half brother. Your red hair and blue eyes, and your last name, all came from your mother. She's the Dutch one?"

"Yolanda immigrated from Holland when she was sixteen."

"So your father, Jack Spenser . . ."

"Began an affair with her about one year before I was born. She said he was going through some kind of rough patch in his marriage at the time—he told her he planned to leave his wife. I knew something was wrong from a young age—but it wasn't until around first grade that I started asking the tough questions—like why didn't my dad live with us? Why didn't we ever go to the park, or out to dinner when he was around? And the one I asked the most: Who was that other little boy who got to go fishing with *my* father? Jack's wallet was loaded with photos of him and his son— his legitimate son."

"That must've been incredibly hard on you." But her mind was already turning back to Spense and to how hard it was about to be on him.

"It was how I grew up, so it seemed normal at first. But once I started school and began hanging around at other kids' houses, I found my own home life confusing. That's when Mom decided to break things off with Jack. They split up for a few months. He even packed up his *real* family and left the state. He never moved back to Dallas, but the split didn't last. They continued to see each other long-distance, until he had the heart attack—probably the strain of living a double life that killed him." He tossed back more booze. "My mother didn't dare go to his funeral. She's the one who had it rough. I might've been saddled with a Jack-ass for a father"—he smirked as if pleased with his pun—"but at least I had a loving mother."

The whiskey was calling her name. With effort, she ignored its pull. "I think we should table the rest of this discussion until Spense can be in on it. I don't feel right hearing the details before he does. In fact, I think the two of you should talk privately. I feel like I'm intruding on a very personal moment."

"You didn't mind intruding on a very personal moment when I had a gun to my head." Dutch slapped his tumbler on the desk, and the whiskey sloshed out, sending a sticky-sweet smell into the air. "And I'm not going to tell Spense."

Pondering the best approach to take, she dipped her finger into her glass, then let a drop of honeyed liquor fall onto her tongue. Like Spense, Dutch was hardheaded. Maybe she could circumvent his defenses by changing the subject and bring him back on point later. Lull him into believing she'd go along with his plan, wait for him to let his guard down, then tell him *no way in hell*. She wasn't keeping any secrets from Spense. "Like I said earlier, you seem like you don't want me and Spense around."

"No offense, but you got that right."

"So why ask us to come out here in the first place?"

"At the time, I wasn't thinking clearly. Jim—"

"Jim Edison?"

"Yeah. Jim said he thought I should have someone on my side when the cops started in on me. And I wasn't playing out all the possible scenarios in my head then, like I'm doing now. I was confused, so I said okay."

"But why ask for us?"

"I wish to God that I hadn't. Jim thought it was a terrible idea to bring Spense into this. He was adamant I choose someone else. In fact, he offered to step in as my advocate himself, in addition to his duties as SAC."

Spense had told her that Jim Edison had been his father's best friend, and that he'd recruited both Spense and Dutch into the Bureau. Her jaw went slack. Understanding struck lightning fast and probably would've knocked her to the ground had she not been sitting safely in a chair. "Jim Edison knows you're brothers, doesn't he?"

"After our father died, he vowed to take care of both Spense and me. He was there for me when I needed him . . . I got into a tight spot with the Bureau awhile back, but we needn't go into that here. The point is he has my back, and Spense's, too."

Dutch must be referring to that dark history she'd overheard Spense discussing with Edison on the phone, before they arrived in Dallas. Her curiosity was more than piqued by this mysterious incident that no one wanted to talk about. But she didn't press the matter.

"If Jim thought it was such a terrible idea, why did you insist that Spense and I be the ones to act as your advocates?"

"First of all, I figured if anyone would give me the benefit of the doubt, it would be you. Because of your father, I knew you wouldn't rush to judgment."

He'd figured right. She couldn't help drawing the comparison between his circumstance and her father's, no matter how hard she tried not to. Her dreams were still filled with desperate images of her father being led into the death chamber in shackles. Sometimes she still woke with her sheets drenched in sweat and her face streaked with tears. In her heart, she believed in Dutch's innocence. The idea of his being tried for Cindy's murder, in Texas, where the death penalty was no empty threat, knocked the wind out of her.

"Okay, I see why you'd request my help. But why Spense? You two don't exactly get along, and you say Jim, your mentor, was dead set against it."

Dutch picked up the framed photo that rested facedown and turned it over. It was of Cindy in a white sundress, her auburn hair flowing in the wind, a basket of flowers on her arm, and a wide, happy smile on her face. Must've been taken early on in their marriage.

He turned the picture facedown on the desk again. "I have no one left, except my mother, and I don't want to drag her into this.

She's been through enough in her life." His gaze fell on the pistol.

Caitlin had almost forgotten that the gun was still there on the desk. Her pulse quickened in her throat. She understood what it was like to be in a dark place. Her mind went back to her eighteenth birthday—the day her father was executed. She remembered, in a very visceral way, not wanting to wake up the next morning.

"After my father died, I didn't know how to get through even one more day without him." She drew in a long breath. "I've never told anyone this before, but I had a revolver. My mother bought it during my father's trial for protection. A lot of people hated my family back then."

Dutch's hand was inching for the pistol.

She forced herself to continue. "I took the gun into my bedroom, and I locked the door. I turned it over and over in my hands, wanting to make the pain go away. Finally, I raised it up, but just as I brought it near my head, I heard my father's voice in my ear whispering *hold tight, Caity.*" She reached out and covered Dutch's hand with her own. "I couldn't do it. Not when I knew my father would've given anything for the chance to see one more sunrise."

Dutch tugged his hand away. It seemed hard for him to accept even a small kindness. Maybe he thought he didn't deserve it.

"Hold tight, Dutch. And don't forget, you have a brother."

"Half brother." He looked up. "One who can hardly stand to be in the same room with me. Jim was right. I should've never dragged Spense into this." His voice cracked midsentence. "It's just that for one crazy second, I thought maybe he and I could be . . ."

"A family?"

He ripped his gaze away from hers. "We may be blood relations, but Spense and I are hardly family."

"You haven't given him a chance. And no matter what, you have to tell him the truth." She swept her hand over her eyes, not wanting any tears to fall. She needed her strength at a moment like this.

"No. We can't tell him."

"I won't keep it from him. It's not right."

After scrutinizing her forever, he said. "You'll keep this secret." Resting his elbows on the desk, he pressed closer, searching her face. "Because you care too much about Spense not to. Don't try to pretend you don't have a thing for him. You never would've noticed the similarities between us if you weren't so attuned to my little brother. You're a connoisseur of everything Spense, and your detective work tonight proves it."

"I'm not going to make you a false promise, Dutch. I need you to trust me, and I need to be able to trust you. Whatever my feelings for Spense may or may not be, I won't keep secrets from him. He and I have an understanding—that we'll tell each other the truth. If I lie to him about something this important, he might never trust me again."

"That's a chance you'll take, and you know it."

"I don't know anything of the kind. I realize it's not going to be easy for you. We can tell him together if you want."

He shook his head. "You do understand that he worships Jack." His voice dropped lower. "And Jack worshipped him. Spense's whole world is based on a lie. He believes his father was a good man, a great one even."

The very last thing she wanted was for Spense to lose his image of his father. If Jack Spenser had been standing in front of her, she might've punched him in the face. She wanted to stomp the ground and scream at him for the pain he'd caused his sons. But she forced herself to stay rational. "I'm sure Jack was a good man in many ways. One mistake doesn't define his entire life. None of us are perfect."

"One mistake? Jack Spenser was living a secret life, and his wife and son knew nothing about it. I may not have had a perfect father, but Spense did. And now you want to take that away from him for no good reason."

"I'm not robbing him of his perfect father. It's *Jack* who's doing that." Her nails dug into her palms. "Spense has a brother, and he deserves to know."

"Even if it kills him?" Dutch dropped his head into his hands and tugged at his hair. He was drunk.

And she was half-sideways herself. It took a few seconds to process what she'd just heard. Dutch obviously thought he was protecting Spense. But from whom?

"Cindy may have had enemies. I'm not saying she didn't. But over the years, I've made far more. The men I've crossed are ruthless, capable of murder and much, much more. Surely it's occurred to you that whoever did this to Cindy might've been trying to get back at me."

"That's one theory, certainly. But so far the investigation suggests—"

"That I did it." He sighed heavily. "If I were Sheridan, I'd probably think the same damn thing. But I didn't kill my wife, and if someone's looking to take revenge on me by targeting my family . . ."

Her head was throbbing, from lack of sleep, from liquor, and from confusion. "You think if word got out that Spense is your brother, it would put him in danger."

"I might have put you both in danger already. I just don't know yet if this was directed at me, or if Cindy was in fact the real target. But yeah, my worry is that things could heat up fast. Until I figure out who did this, and why, I don't want anyone to know Spense is my brother. Especially not Spense."

The idea of lying to Spense turned her stomach. But what if Dutch was right? No matter how angry Spense might be when he found out, she couldn't risk his life. She took a drink, then another. The issue wasn't coming into clear focus. "We'll tell Spense, then tell him not to tell anyone about it for his own safety."

Dutch arched an eyebrow. "Say that again. The part about instructing Spense not to tell anyone we're brothers—for his own safety."

The lining of her stomach was on fire. She'd had too much whiskey. "Oh, Lord. I see your point." Not half an hour before, she'd been thinking about the fact that Spense was just the type to run toward trouble instead of away from it.

"No one can tell Spense what to do. It wouldn't surprise me at all if he decided to test the theory that someone was after my family by setting himself up as bait. Or suppose he decides his mother deserves to know the truth? Fears for his own safety won't keep him from telling her if he feels it's his duty. Then suppose she tells a friend . . ."

Caitlin nodded. She was beginning to see the wisdom of waiting. The more people who knew, the more likely the word could get out, and maybe Spense's life really would be endangered, all because she didn't have the will to keep a secret a short while. Jim

Edison had kept the secret over thirty years. She at least needed to take time to think through the consequences.

"We have to tell him, Caitlin. But we don't have to tell him tonight, or tomorrow, or before it's prudent to do so."

She swallowed hard, then nodded. "Okay. For *now*."

"Good enough. So here's what I need you to do. You have to convince Spense to leave Dallas. Just go with him to Tahiti, like you planned. Bringing you both here was a terrible mistake. I can take care of things on my own. This is my problem, not yours."

That wouldn't work. "Spense may forgive me, eventually, for keeping this secret—I hope. But if I ask him to walk away from you now, when he finds out he abandoned his own brother, he'll never forgive me. And worse, he'll never forgive himself." She shook her head. "As long as no one *knows* that he's your brother, he's not a target. And if you really are in danger, you need us now more than ever. The police certainly aren't going to watch over you."

He leaned forward, listening intently.

"I think we should compromise," she said.

"What do you have in mind?"

"You promise not to hold anything back from either Spense or me about the case, and I won't tell Spense about Jack until we have a handle on the killer's motivation."

"I guess that's the best deal I'm going to get."

"It's the only one I can offer. And the minute we know it's safe to do so, we tell him the truth about his father."

Dutch grunted.

"I'll take that as a yes. And you need to hold up your end of the bargain, starting right now."

"What do you want to know?"

"Did Cindy keep a diary? You told Sheridan you had no idea, but frankly, I don't believe you. I think you'd know if she kept a journal."

"Yes. My wife kept a diary—she has ever since I've known her. I have no idea where it is." He turned his empty tumbler upside down and set it on the desk with a thunk. "But if I could get my hands on it, I sure as hell wouldn't turn it over to Detective Monroe Sheridan."

Chapter Nine

Thursday, October 17
12:00 P.M.
Austin, Texas

SPENSE TRIED NOT to smile as Caity tiptoed up the steps of the Texas Governor's Mansion. Holding one hand to her forehead and the other out for balance, she looked like pickled death. Just north of Austin, she'd gone green as the rolling hills, even demanded a barf stop—but luckily that turned out to be a false alarm.

"Someone's got a hangover," he whispered, as the door to the impressive Greek Revival-style building swung wide, and the first lady, herself, Heather Cambridge, motioned them inside.

Though they'd never met, she greeted them with a hug, as if they were old friends. "Hope you enjoyed the ride down from Dallas." Her smile was warm and genuine. "The hill country leading into the city is one of my favorite scenic drives."

"Hers too." Spense winked at Caity.

"Beautiful." Somehow Caity managed to sound sincere—and

look gorgeous, despite skin paler than cat's cream and heavy shadows beneath her eyes. She wasn't much of a drinker, so he'd been taken by surprise this morning when he'd caught a faint scent of whiskey on her breath—and on Dutch's. Apparently, the two of them had quite a party last night while he slept. But Caity refused to talk about it, claiming a headache. During the three-and-a-half-hour ride from Dallas to Austin, she'd not only been suspiciously taciturn, she'd barely made eye contact with him.

He'd never seen anyone act so damn guilty over an innocent late-night bender. His fingers curled tightly. If anyone was going to keep Caity up all night, it should be him. But she'd seemed taken by Dutch from the start—and that stuck in his craw more than he cared to admit.

"And here"—the first lady swept out her arm—"is the notable U-shaped staircase." Her smile broadened. "These marks"—she tapped her finger on several imperfections in the wood railing—"represent a fun little bit of Texas history. Governor Hogg pressed tacks into the banister to keep his children from joyriding down it. The scars have never been sanded out." She clapped her hands together in delight. No denying it: Heather Cambridge was a gracious hostess and pretty to boot. No wonder she was one of the most admired women in Texas. But her impeccable manners didn't extend to Dutch. She'd flatly refused to allow him to take part in today's interview, insisting he would never be welcome in her home again.

When Caity protested, Heather had threatened to withdraw from the interview altogether, pointing out that neither she nor Spense had any official standing in the case. Heather said she'd only agreed to talk to them because of their reputation, and because, for Cindy's sake, she hoped they could get to the bottom of things fast.

As they wound down various hallways, the first lady continued to pepper them with anecdotes about the mansion. Then, finally, they entered a library with hardwood floors and walls painted a rich forest green. "We can talk in here."

Spense liked the portrait of a man dressed in fringed buckskin and carrying a musket. Looked like a cool guy to him. "Who's that?" he asked.

"That gentleman is Davy Crockett," Heather responded with a lilt in her voice. It was obvious the she took pride in her state's history. As a governor's wife should.

As she took in her surroundings, Caity's eyes brightened. Either she'd overcome her seasickness after a few minutes on solid ground or she was putting on a very good face for Heather. "Is this an antique?" Caity crossed to a small desk, loaded with cubbyholes and drawers.

"Goodness yes. It belonged to Stephen F. Austin himself. It's been here since 1923."

A number of candles, green, like the walls and carpet, adorned most of the available surfaces in the room. Probably why the library smelled like apples.

"I won't be needing you this afternoon, Brian." Mrs. Cambridge waved away her escort, a brawny, well-dressed man who'd been following them at a respectful distance. One of the governor's protection detail, no doubt.

Now that the tour had ended, and the bodyguard had been given his walking orders, the real fun was about to begin.

The first lady settled into one of the many armchairs—

upholstered in green, of course. Spense and Caity followed suit. "I'm so sorry Matt won't be able to join us, but there's a bill coming up, and duty calls. I'm sure you know all about duty and sacrifice, Agent Spenser."

"Call me Spense."

"If you'll call me Heather." She included Caity with a smile. "That goes for both of you, naturally."

"Not a problem if the governor can't be here. It's you we were hoping to see, Heather," Spense said, hoping to set her off guard by bringing out an informal tone and taking her up on the offer to call her by her first name.

"Oh? Since Matt and I both attended the fund-raiser, I just assumed you'd want to meet with him, too."

"If the governor has anything he'd like to tell us, we'll be happy to arrange a separate meeting at his convenience."

"Separate." She tapped her fingers together. "I'm not sure I like the sound of that." Her laugh seemed surprisingly nervous. "This isn't like on television, where they separate the suspects and try to get them to turn on each other? Surely my husband's not . . . a person of interest."

"We're not trying to pull any stunts. It's just that we already have an accounting of your husband's movements the night of the fund-raiser," Caity reassured her.

A look of relief came over Heather's face. "I see. Well, I'd be happy to list all my movements for you, even though I think I've done so for the police already. Frankly, I don't know where in blazes I was during the party. My husband likes to say I go into *first-lady mode* at these events. I barely remember a thing. But Matt had Brian on me the entire night. He worries too much about me. He left his own men behind in Austin but insisted on bringing my personal guard—when he's the one who needs protection—so silly. Anyway, Brian will know every step I took. I'll call him back in."

"We can get Brian's report from Detective Sheridan. He's already met with the security detail," Spense said.

Caity leaned in, her expression earnest. "Mrs. Cambridge, I'm not sure if you're aware, but Agent Spenser and I are in Texas on behalf of Dutch Langhorne."

Heather's jaw tightened. "You said you were family spokespersons."

"We are," Caity replied.

"Well, then, I'd think you'd be here on behalf of *Cindy*." Heather's posture stiffened, and a small line appeared between her eyebrows. Barely noticeable, due to her Botox, but real nonetheless. This was probably as mad as the first lady was capable of looking. Either she simply didn't care for Dutch, or she was one of the legion of individuals who'd already concluded he had murdered his wife.

"Don't twist my meaning. We're here on behalf of *both* Cindy and Dutch. I simply want to reiterate that the FBI is not officially involved in the case, that you're under no obligation to answer any of our questions. But we do have experience in murder investigations." Caity's tone turned tough.

Did she intend to play the bad cop? That'd be a fun change.

"I know exactly who you are. You're the profilers who worked that Fallen Angel Killer case in Hollywood."

"Spense is the profiler. I'm a psychiatrist. We do work together though, developing profiles for the police."

Heather crossed her feet at the ankles, and that little line between her brows disappeared. She smiled, only a little less warmly than before. Spense had a feeling they'd just witnessed her slip out of *first-lady mode,* then force herself back into it again. "Shall I ring for tea?"

Caity's face went gray at the suggestion. She must still be nauseous, but he was hungry—as usual, and some of those bland finger sandwiches might help settle Caity's stomach. She hadn't touched her breakfast this morning. Also, tea might bring back the earlier collaborative atmosphere. At the moment, Heather was surveying them like a fly circling warily above a spiderweb.

"That would be awesome," Spense said before Caity could object.

Heather walked over to a small desk. The feminine knick-knacks and the neatly ordered boxes—one red, one yellow, and one green, marked the desk as the first lady's personal workspace. She picked up the phone and requested watercress sandwiches, chocolate chip cookies, and coffee. Then she pressed the back of her hand to her cheek. "I forgot the *tea.* I'll call back."

"Please don't bother," Caity said. "I've never once heard Spense complain about a lack of tea, and I'm going to pass on all of it."

"You should eat," Spense said. "It'll help what's ailing you."

Heather returned to her armchair. "Are you ill?"

"No," Caity said firmly.

"Because if you want to postpone . . ."

"Mrs. Cambridge . . ."

"Heather." The first lady shot Caity a saccharine smile.

"Heather, we didn't drive all the way from Dallas to Austin to postpone."

"Then I'm at your service, but I'm afraid I'm not clear what you want from me." She crossed her arms high on her chest.

"Even though Spense and I aren't assigned to the case per se, we've developed certain habits that are hard to break. For one, when a murder's taken place, we like to learn as much about the victim as possible."

"Victimology." Heather dropped her arms. "Don't look so surprised. I watch those crime shows like everyone else. The more you know about Cindy, the more you'll learn about her killer. Have I got that right?"

"Perfectly, and that's where you come in. According to Dutch, you were Cindy's closest friend," Spense said.

Heather averted her gaze. "Best friends since third grade. We used to have one of those necklaces—a heart split in two pieces—but I'm afraid I lost my half years ago." When she looked back, her eyes had grown moist. "I'd give anything to have taken better care of it. How I wish I had that necklace now."

"I'm sure you do, but . . ." Caity softened her voice. She seemed genuinely moved by Heather's emotion. "No one can be expected to keep up with a necklace since the third grade. The important thing is you kept up with the friendship."

So much for Bad Cop Caity. She couldn't maintain a subterfuge of any kind for long—and he loved that about her. He never had to worry about her keeping secrets.

Heather pulled a handkerchief from her pocket and dabbed her eyes. "What a lovely thing to say, Caitlin. That makes me feel much better."

A server entered and set out a tray, laden with goodies, waited for Heather's signal, then quickly disappeared.

"You come from a rich family," Spense said, and by the look on Heather's face, he knew she didn't much like his bringing that up. "Not an accusation. Just stating a fact."

Heather's lips flattened. "I don't see how it's a relevant one."

The press had lambasted Matt Cambridge and his wife for coming from wealth and privilege. They'd dubbed them the spoiled rancher and his princess bride. To her credit, Heather seemed to take it all in stride, laughingly referring to herself and her husband as "the brats." Her easygoing personality played well with the public. She'd one-upped the press and turned their dig in her favor. "I only mention it because Cindy's family . . . wasn't. Her youth was spent in mobile-home parks, bouncing from relative to relative."

"True."

"So, it just seems an odd pairing. I'm wondering how you and she came to be such good friends."

A nostalgic look came over her face. "You want to know how Cindy and I became friends?" Then she smiled, the same way she had just before she'd relayed the story of Governor Hogg pressing tacks into the banister to thwart his children. "We met," she paused, to great effect, "by bobby pins."

Spense leaned forward. "I bet there's a great story behind that."

Heather needed no more encouragement. Her voice was animated, and she gesticulated while she spoke. Spense got the feeling she'd told this story many times, that it was a favorite of hers.

"My parents believed that even though they were wealthy, their children shouldn't be sheltered from the real world. When she met my father, my mother was a teacher, and she believed private schools segregated the rich from the poor. She was quite the advocate for public schools."

"Didn't your mother become school superintendent?" Caity asked. Apparently, staying up drinking last night hadn't stopped her from doing her homework.

"She did, eventually. But she started out her teaching career in Head Start—that's a preschool program for underprivileged students, and it's still going strong." Heather rolled her shoulders back with obvious pride. "Anyway, Mom stayed in that district, even after she moved to a third-grade classroom. I attended the school where my mother taught—so I could see how the other half lived. And that's where I met the best friend I've ever had."

There was something familiar about this story, but Spense couldn't recall what. Caity, on the other hand, got an *aha* look on her face, indicating to him this was a fairly well publicized version of the first lady's history—or at least one easily found on Google.

"How far did your dad go, in politics?" Caity asked out of the blue.

"Started out as a councilman and made it all the way to the lieutenant governor's office. He could've gone much further, I think, if only . . ." Her voice trailed. One thing Spense did remember was that Heather Cambridge's parents had died tragically in a small plane crash. "Daddy had his eye on the presidency."

Like father, like husband?

On the desk that housed the colored boxes, Spense noticed a photo. From where he sat he could see it was actually a framed newspaper article. He approached the desk for a closer look. "May I?"

Heather nodded, and he picked up the frame. The news story included a picture of a young girl with bright blond hair and blue eyes—looked to be around eight years old—boarding a yellow school bus, waving back at a tall, distinguished-looking man. That would most likely be Heather, being seen off to school on the poor side of town by her politico father. Spense quickly skimmed the article and confirmed it. Casting a sideways glance at Heather, who had a faraway look in her eyes, he couldn't help wondering if she understood her parents had used her education to further her dad's career. But maybe he was being cynical. Maybe they would've sent her to public school in any case and simply knew a good photo op when they saw one.

"Tell us about the bobby pins?" Caity rested her elbow on her knee and her chin in her palm, seeming eager to get to the good stuff.

"At the time, my last name was Applegate and Cindy's was Beasley. Back then, they seated students alphabetically, so her desk was next to mine. One day, we were given an art assignment. I think Cindy drew a horse, and I was working on a frog. I was so intent on getting that froggy right, and I was getting quite frustrated. My hair kept falling in my eyes, and I kept swatting it away. I might've said damn." She flushed prettily, but again, Spense sensed she'd repeated the story with the exact same phrasing on many occasions. "Okay, yes, I did. I said *damn*! Cindy giggled, and the teacher said we'd have to stay in from recess if we didn't settle down. I went back to drawing and swatting my hair, and then, Cindy poked me—at great personal risk—but she was like that. Fearless. I looked up, and she opened her fist, and there it was, in her palm." Heather dabbed her eyes with the handkerchief. "A bobby pin! The teacher made us stay inside to clean the chalkboards. After that, Cindy and I became inseparable. It never mattered that I had too much, or that she had too little. What mattered was we had each other."

Despite the rehearsed wording, Heather told the story with an authentic joy that moved even Spense. He pictured two young girls, from such very different worlds, finding a common denominator in something so seemingly unimportant: *a bobby pin.*

A small act of kindness, from one child to the other, had led to a lifelong friendship.

That said something about both women. Whatever Heather Cambridge's current political aspirations might be for her husband, her friendship with Cindy Langhorne had been both real and enduring. She hadn't been stumping for the White House in third grade.

"Sounds like Cindy was kindhearted as a child, and you mentioned *fearless*," Caity said. "I'm wondering what kind of teenager she turned out to be."

"A wild one." Heather folded her hands in her lap. "I guess opposites not only attract, they make good friends, too. Cindy encouraged me to push boundaries, and I helped her see that sometimes those boundaries are there for a reason. I worried about her, but at the same time, I admired her spirit. She had a dazzling personality, and all the boys loved her. She had such a way with people. She sometimes dated several men at a time and wound up marrying too young."

"You knew her first husband."

"I knew everyone in her life, and vice versa. I introduced her to her first husband, and she introduced me to Matt. I certainly got the better end of that deal." Heather took a sip of coffee. "Matt had a big crush on Cindy, but he wasn't her type—too safe and steady. Ethan Eckhart, on the other hand, was far too dangerous for me. So we swapped beaus. Ethan was handsome as sin but a player. To this day, I regret fixing them up. I knew he'd cheat, and I did warn her, but she said . . ." The free-flowing words suddenly slowed, then dried up altogether, as if she was holding something back.

Caity bit her lower lip, probably noticing the change in Heather's speech pattern like Spense had. "You warned her not to marry Ethan Eckhart, because you thought he'd be unfaithful. How did Cindy take your interference?"

"Oh, she took it fine. We had that kind of friendship. Honest and open. Believe me, she got into my business plenty of times." Again Heather's words faltered. She took a deep breath. "Cindy said she'd take her chances with Ethan. She said she didn't love him, but she liked him a lot, and she wanted someone who had the means to take care of her—not that she aspired to luxury. She was just tired of worrying about money all the time. She wanted that part of her life to be over." The little line between Heather's brows fought its way back to the surface. "That's when I realized, that even though I thought I knew her—I really didn't. I only knew the bubbly, smiling woman—the fearless Cindy. That's the first time I understood, that deep down, Cindy was terrified of things I never gave a second thought: going hungry or not having a place to live." Heather laughed nervously. "Anyhow, Ethan took care of her all right. The divorce set her up for life, but you probably already know that. Cindy never worried about money again."

"Did she stay in touch with her ex?" Spense asked. "Any ongoing animosity between them?"

Heather waved her hand dismissively. "You're asking if Ethan might have a reason to want her dead. The guy's a straight-up asshole, but he's no murderer. And no, they didn't keep in touch . . . not as far as I know. He's married to a bunny, last I heard."

A puzzled look came over Caity's face. It took a moment for Heather's meaning to sink in for Spense, too. "You mean a Playboy model."

"Right. And as much money as Cindy got in the divorce, Ethan had plenty more. She wound up with just enough to teach him a lesson about sticking a fidelity clause in a prenup."

It seemed strange to Spense that Heather would laugh off Cindy's cheating ex-husband yet turn hostile on the subject of Dutch. But maybe it was simply a matter of water under the bridge with Eckhart. His marriage to Cindy had ended long ago. "Speaking of fidelity, there are rumors—"

"That Cindy cheated on Dutch? The rumors are true." Heather stuck her chin up. "Doesn't mean she deserved to die."

Spense gave her a minute to swallow her bitterness, then moved her back on track. "I'm wondering if the infidelity was a two-way street. Did Dutch cheat on Cindy?"

"You're his Bureau buddy, why not ask him?" She picked up a finger sandwich, brought it to her lips, but set it down again without taking a bite. "Sorry. I don't mean to snap at you. I'm sure you understand how upsetting this is."

Caity nodded sympathetically. "Take your time."

"The honest answer is I don't know if he cheated. Dutch has always been a mystery to me. And frankly, I've never understood why she put up with him. I would have left a man who treated me like that, and I advised her strongly to file for divorce." She sighed heavily. "Cindy just wouldn't give up on that marriage, though, no matter how bad things got."

"But she was the unfaithful one," Spense turned his palms up.

"Only because she couldn't get his attention. Dutch Langhorne's not a cold fish. He's a *dead* fish. The man's impenetrable. A fortress of secrecy."

"He's *FBI*," Spense said, feeling a rush of empathy for his colleague. It was a rare woman who could tolerate being shut out from a man's daily life. But classified is classified. No way around it. Being a G-man's spouse requires unconditional trust. His gaze fell on Caity. *Marriage* requires unconditional trust.

"Dutch is a jerk." Heather directed her comment to Caity, perhaps thinking a woman would understand better.

"Then why did Cindy marry him? She had plenty of money after her divorce from Ethan Eckhart. No need to marry a *jerk*," Caity fired back.

Heather rolled her eyes. "She claimed she loved him."

"Obviously, you don't believe that. But you just said the two of you were open with each other, and she admitted she never loved Ethan, so why would she lie about Dutch?"

"I-I don't know. Maybe she did love him. It's just hard for me to relate. I don't see how anyone could fall for someone like him. I realize he's good-looking . . . and powerful. He's a special agent and everything. That's a pretty sexy job." Her eyes darted to Spense and back to Caity.

"But?" Spense asked.

"He's a block of ice, at least to me. And you never know what he's thinking—always looking at you funny, like he knows your hidden thoughts. He gives me the creeps. In the beginning, Cindy said he opened up to her a lot about his family. Had some kind of terrible secret from his childhood."

Caity's face lost the little bit of color that had returned to her cheeks.

"What kind of secret?" This was new information and, as such, interested Spense.

"Cindy never told me. And I guess it made me angry that she kept his secrets from me. I told her *everything*—but I'm getting off track." She cleared her throat. "She said Dutch had a warm, mushy center, and that I just needed to get to know him. I tried to like him, but things never gelled between us. Back then, that didn't matter, though, because he made her happy."

"What changed?" Spense asked.

"Again, as the family friend, I refer you to Dutch."

"He's not talking much these days."

Heather cocked an eyebrow. "Clammed up on you, too. See what I mean?"

A rather clever misdirection on her part, Spense thought, since she was the one currently evading his question. She knew something, but she didn't want to talk about it. "I'm asking *you*, Heather. Did something happen to change Cindy's marriage to Dutch?"

"Yes and no."

He waited, giving her a look that let her know he wasn't going to let her off the hook.

"I say no, because the rumor wasn't true. Yes, because Dutch, seemed to believe it. He wasn't used to being in the high-society limelight. He didn't understand that the press exaggerates and sometimes downright fabricates events to sell papers. One summer, word got around that Cindy was sleeping with her tennis pro, and the gossip rags printed the story. It wasn't true—that pro was an oily loser. But the damage was done. Dutch totally withdrew from Cindy. She tried to reassure him it was all a lie, but he wouldn't listen. Whenever he was on the road, he'd go long periods without calling her. And when he was home, he slept in a separate room."

"Did he act jealous? Threaten her in any way?" Caity asked.

"Not at all. At first, it seemed as if he was punishing her with the silent treatment, but as time went on, it began to look like he really didn't give a damn one way or the other."

"How did the rumor start?"

"It could've been any of the women at the club. Most of them are phonies. Nice to your face and ready to stab you the second you turn your back. Cindy had it all. Looks, money, a hot FBI husband. She had a lot of enemies even *before* she'd done anything to earn them."

To Spense, up until this point, Cindy had been a bit of a caricature, painted in broad strokes by the press. But as Heather described her best friend's life story, he began to get a feeling for the real woman. A flawed human being who'd tried and failed, then tried again, never quite finding her happy ending. "Did she 'earn' her enemies later on?"

Heather cast her eyes to the far wall. "She wasn't the hardhearted tramp the press makes her out to be, but she did wreck a home or two. In her defense—not that there's a defense for cheating—they were homes already scheduled for demolition. She had affairs with her friends' husbands, but only those with women on the side already. Cindy started out with so little in life, but she never wanted to take things away from anyone else. She wasn't the envious sort. She never wanted to *keep* any of the men for herself though I suppose one or two of them fell hard for her."

"So what did she want? Fun?" Spense had to admit Heather Cambridge impressed him. Despite her prim-and-proper image, she didn't seem judgmental—at least not as far as Cindy Langhorne was concerned.

"I don't think she had a bit of fun. She put on that big grin of hers for show, but in private, she cried a lot. I think if Dutch had paid her an ounce of attention . . ." Her voice broke at that point, and the handkerchief came out once more. "All she wanted was for Dutch to love her. She wanted him to put his foot down and *demand* that she stop fooling around with other men, but no matter how brazen she was, he never said a word. Like I said before, a *dead fish.*"

Spense tugged at his tie. Dutch had never been anything other than cool to him either. But this wasn't a congeniality contest. It was a murder investigation. Spense looked Heather Cambridge straight in the eyes. "Do you believe he has it in him to murder his wife?"

She gripped the arms of her chair, not shying away from Spense's gaze. "Yes, sir. I sure as hell do."

Chapter Ten

CAITLIN'S BREATH CAUGHT when the door swung open, and a handsome man with aristocratic features and a hint of gray at the temples strode across the field-office conference room. James Edison, the Special Agent in Charge of the Dallas office, wore a perfectly tailored shark gray designer suit—and a grim smile. His tanned skin, bolo tie, and ostrich boots marked him as Texan, while his assessing gaze, and the intelligent gleam in his slate-colored eyes screamed FBI. She'd been eagerly anticipating meeting him, but now something had gone wrong. Dutch wasn't present for today's meeting, as originally planned, and she'd been inventing her own reasons for his absence—none of them pleasant.

Though an appointment had already been on the books for 8:00 P.M., Edison had sent an urgent, and cryptic, message pushing their meeting to ASAP. So she and Spense had driven straight from their interview with Heather Cambridge to the Dallas field office.

The SAC approached, extending his hand. "Jim Edison. You must be Dr. Cassidy."

"Caitlin," she said, the firmness of his grip nearly pulling her to her feet.

He held the handshake a moment longer than usual, a sign of both confidence and friendliness. "I've been looking forward to meeting you. I only wish our first introduction had been under different circumstances."

"I've heard a lot about you, sir. It's a pleasure."

"None of this *sir*, stuff. I'm just Jim." He drew Spense into a brief man hug, and his posture relaxed. "And you can ask this guy—I'm practically family."

Spense nodded, and both men took a seat. "Not practically—Jim *is* family."

"Jack Spenser saved my life back in our army days. He was a great, great man—and now his son is following in his footsteps."

Caitlin realized the SAC meant that as a compliment, but the idea of Spense's following in his father's footsteps soured her stomach. And just when she'd finally gotten over that fermented feeling brought on by too much drink last night and too much time in the car today. "Following in his footsteps . . . I'm not sure . . ."

Jim drew his chair closer to the large glass conference table where they were seated. "I'm trying to say that Spense is a man of integrity, like his father before him."

Clearing his throat, Spense looked away. There was a long pause, then he said, in a voice that sounded deeper than usual, "Thanks, for that Jim. I'm not sure I deserve the comparison to my father, but I appreciate it."

Unease settled heavily over her. Spense certainly did not deserve the comparison—he was a far better man. Scrutinizing Jim's face, she saw no sign of turmoil. He didn't seem at all bothered by the fact Spense had a beast of a misconception about his father. In fact, Jim seemed happy to feed the dragon.

"Sir—"

"Jim."

Caitlin placed her forearms on the tabletop. "You mentioned the unhappy circumstances of this meeting. I can't help wondering why Dutch isn't here."

Jim arched a brow at Spense. "The lady doesn't pussyfoot around, does she?"

"No, she doesn't," Spense said. The approval ringing in his voice made her fidget in her chair. Keeping any secret from Spense seemed wrong, and keeping this particular secret from him took wrong to a whole new level. Yet here she was, colluding with Jim, who didn't even know she knew—and somehow that made her feel doubly dirty. But Dutch's absence had her doubly worried.

The SAC ran both hands through his hair. "I'm afraid I've got some bad news about Dutch."

Her heart sank to her toes.

"I got a call from Sheridan. In addition to all the circumstantial evidence they've gathered against Dutch, the forensics don't look good. You may have heard that blood was found on the shirt he wore to the fund-raiser. Dutch claimed he leaned over Cindy to determine whether or not she was still breathing, and that's how the blood got there."

"I thought he said he didn't disturb the crime scene." Spense's mouth snapped into a tight line.

"I assumed he meant that he didn't disturb the scene further *after* he'd verified Cindy was dead," Caitlin said. "It goes without saying he checked to make sure she was beyond help."

"Does it?" Spense's brows drew down.

"Before we split that hair, let me tell you the rest," Jim continued. "The experts are calling the stain *blood spatter consistent with blowback from a gunshot wound.* And that enabled Sheridan to get a warrant for Dutch's arrest, but when he went to serve it, he found the Preston Hollow house empty. Neighbors claim to have seen Dutch load a suitcase into his car this morning and drive away. That was close to nine."

Dutch had been up and dressed before them. He'd made coffee for Spense and her and seen them off to Austin around eight thirty. He must've packed last night and left the house just minutes after they'd pulled out of the drive.

"I've been trying to reach him by every means at my disposal, all day." Jim's shoulders sagged. "Bottom line—Dutch is nowhere to be found. Dallas PD has a BOLO out on him now."

"I should've never let him out of my sight," Spense slammed his fist into his hand. "But we needed to interview Mrs. Cambridge, and she wouldn't allow Dutch to get anywhere near her. Our trip to Austin gave him the perfect opportunity to bolt. I'm sorry, Jim, I let you down."

"You were called in to help Dutch, not babysit him. Someone let me down all right, but it wasn't you, son."

The vibration in Jim's voice confirmed he was much more to both Spense and Dutch than a mentor. He'd taken on a fatherly role for both men, and this had to be tearing him apart. Caitlin hardly knew how to react herself. Her brain told her the evidence pointed to Dutch's guilt, but her heart—no, not just her heart— her instincts told her he was innocent.

"What was he thinking? Running makes him look guilty as hell—not to mention how it looks for the Bureau," Jim said. "I can just see tomorrow's headline: *FBI agent turns fugitive.* I never thought Dutch would put me in this position."

Caitlin blew out a breath. This wasn't black-and-white. Sure, guilt was one reason to flee, but there were other possibilities. Last night, she'd come to understand that despite his resentments, Dutch was deeply concerned for Spense's safety. It seemed possible he ran to put distance between himself and Spense, thus getting his brother out of harm's way. She couldn't put forth that argument without spilling the secret, but she had another theory that she could verbalize. "Dutch knew Sheridan would be coming for him sooner or later. He's determined to find Cindy's killer, and he knows he can't do that from behind bars."

Spense shook his head. "Doesn't float. Dutch knows the Bureau's behind him, ready to turn every stone to find the murderer."

"He doesn't strike me as the type of man to sit back in a jail cell and let others take the reins," she said.

"He never lets anyone take charge. Which is why this isn't the first time he's gotten himself in real trouble." Spense jumped up, then paced the length of the room and back.

He had to be talking about *the incident.* "Mind filling me in on that past trouble folks keep bringing up? It would help me to help Dutch if I knew—unless, of course, it's beyond my security clearance."

Jim nodded. "Your clearance is high enough to hear about a closed case. It's mostly a matter of public record anyway."

Anything that had made its way out of the Bureau and into the public record must've been serious.

The men exchanged glances. "Go ahead, Spense. You might as well tell it. After all, you were part of it."

Her hands opened and closed at her sides. Spense was somehow involved in Dutch's trouble. That seemed to lend credence to his fears for his brother's safety. All day she'd been struggling with her promise to Dutch, but if someone really was seeking revenge against him for a past wrong by targeting people he cared about, maybe the timing wasn't right to exhume a story that had been buried in the family plot all these years. And Jim must have good reason for keeping quiet.

A troubled look came over Spense's face. "Years ago, Dutch and I were both field agents here in Dallas." He touched his finger to his chest, then pointed at the SAC. "Jim put us together on the counterterrorism squad. Jim, you usually have great instincts, but I gotta say putting Dutch and me together on that squad wasn't your best call."

"Dutch and Spense were two of my sharpest guys," Jim explained to Caitlin, "and even though they didn't seem to be having a love affair with each other, I had the bright idea that if they got to know one another, all that would change."

She couldn't give her honest response, so she kept quiet. Jim had known the men were brothers when he recruited them into the Bureau. Clearly, he'd paired them up in the hopes they'd become friends. It didn't take a degree in psychiatry to figure out his motivation. He was looking out for Jack's sons as best he could.

She didn't fault him for that. But it seemed to her his loyalty should've been to the living more than the dead. It seemed to her, back then, there was no compelling reason to keep Jack's secret—other than misplaced loyalty. It would've been tough on Spense, but if he'd grown up knowing the truth, he would've learned to cope with it. And just maybe, he would've developed a real relationship with his only sibling.

"Jim's plan to turn us into buddies didn't turn out, as you know. But we worked okay together up until the Tesarak case. You ever heard of it?" Spense asked Caitlin.

"Rings a bell." A very faint one.

"Louis Tesarak was a suspect in both a bombing of a day-care center, and the kidnap-murder of a college coed. He'd been on the counterterrorism squad's radar for several years. What we knew for sure about Tesarak was that he'd traveled to Afghanistan for the specific purpose of training with Al Qaeda—and in fact received training at one of their camps. According to his friends, he wanted to stay in Afghanistan to fight alongside Al Qaeda, but they had other plans for him. As a US citizen, Tesarak was a valuable asset to them. While they had plenty of loyal recruits on their own turf, it was much harder to find devotees in the States. So Tesarak came back home, where he could fill a bigger need. After his return, he recruited a few others, mostly young men he met on college campuses, into his inner circle."

Spense leaned forward, placing his palms on his knees. As he recounted the story, the golden brown color of his eyes intensified. She could see the case still affected him deeply. "We didn't have what it would take to arrest Tesarak, but we'd compiled enough evidence against him to go up on his phone. That's how we knew he was about to make a big move."

"Go up on his phone?"

"Get a warrant to tap his cell."

"You can do that?"

"Yeah."

She leaned forward. "How do you tap a wireless phone?"

Spense shrugged.

"Ask the phone company," Jim interjected.

"All I know is how to get the warrant," Spense added, and a quick, self-effacing smile cut through some of the tension on his face. "Anyway, we went up on Tesarak's phone, and tracked his movements to San Francisco. Something big was in the works—another bombing we thought though we didn't have all the details. Somehow, he got wind we were watching him. He jacked a car, making a move to flee. Dutch and I pulled him over and detained him for questioning, but all we had to hold him on were potential charges of possession of a stolen vehicle."

"He would've been out on bail like that." Jim snapped his fingers. The look in his eyes matched the intensity in Spense's voice. "He knew we were watching him, and we were sure he'd go off the grid. So I ordered Dutch and Spense to lean hard on him."

"The guy was a terrorist, Caity." There was no apology in Spense's voice. "We had proof, but most of it would never have made it into a courtroom. We had no authority to hold him long term. We needed a confession." They'd broken rules—and a lot of them. He didn't have to say so because it was written on his face.

"Okay." She went very still, waiting for the shoe to drop. So far she hadn't heard anything that would follow Dutch around like a black cloud and all but ruin his career with the Bureau. Yet that had been the end result. There had to be more to this story. She took a deep breath, trying to prepare herself for what Spense might tell her, not only about Dutch but about his own role.

"We took Tesarak back to his apartment. At one point, we had him in the kitchen, questioning him, and Dutch asked me to go get some food. We hadn't eaten all day, but more importantly,

Tesarak kept saying he was hungry. He seemed on the verge of confessing to the coed kidnap-murder. We offered him Jack in the Box—I know it sounds crazy, but I've seen guys give it up for a cheeseburger before. Feeding them confuses them, gets them thinking you're on their side. So I went to pick up burgers and left Dutch alone with Tesarak."

He lowered his eyes. "Nobody wanted to lose track of this guy—more innocents could die if we did, and that would be on us. I knew Dutch wasn't in tight control—he was pissed out of his mind that our hands were tied. We knew we had to get a confession.

"The honest-to-God truth is both of us wanted to put a bullet in Tesarak's brain. That would've been wrong. We knew it was wrong, and we made sure to keep each other in check . . . until I went out for burgers. I don't know what really happened in that kitchen after I left, but I do know if I'd been there, things might've gone down differently."

"According to Dutch," Jim said, "Tesarak grabbed a knife and went after him. He used lethal force to protect himself. He claimed self-defense."

She folded her hands in her lap to stop them from shaking. "Dutch killed a man while he had him in custody?"

"The case was investigated by the FBI, the San Francisco PD, and the Department of Homeland Security. Dutch was cleared by all—they called it *a good shoot*," Jim said.

"How did Tesarak get hold of a knife?"

"It was on the kitchen counter."

"Why were his hands free?"

"After Spense left, he confessed to the murder of the coed and promised to sign a confession. So Dutch took the cuffs off to get it on paper."

"Do you two believe that's what really happened?" She couldn't read the answer in their stoic expressions.

Jim kept his poker face. "Like I said, Dutch was fully cleared. But frankly, a lot of folks never believed his story. I managed to keep Spense's name off the record, but Dutch was fair game, and the press had a field day with him. Tesarak's family claimed he was an innocent man, shot in cold blood by a corrupt FBI agent."

"I see." And she was, in fact, beginning to get an even deeper understanding of Dutch's concern for Spense. *If* Cindy's death was some kind of revenge for Tesarak, Dutch might be the primary target, but if Spense's name came out, he'd be a close second, and if anyone ever suspected the two men were brothers . . . "Do you think Cindy's murder could have something to do with Tesarak?"

"If you mean could Tesarak's family members, or coconspirators be behind her death . . . ? Maybe. It's always possible a mother or father decided to take Dutch's wife in exchange for a son—that type of thing. Naturally, it's crossed my mind. And we should keep that theory in the mix, but the sad truth is that Cindy Langhorne had plenty of her own enemies. It's a stretch to bring Tesarak, or any of Dutch's old cases, for that matter, into it."

"When you say Cindy had enemies, I take it you're referring to Cindy's reputation as a home wrecker. But according to Heather Cambridge, Cindy hadn't been involved in any extramarital affairs for years. So why would someone come after her now?"

"First, the evidence indicates that she was having an ongoing affair. After all, she was found naked in an upstairs bedroom, where she most likely was meeting her lover."

Caity shook her head. "Not *most likely* . . . more like *possibly.* The killer could've posed her nude to mislead investigators."

"Second, you could put the same question to your Tesarak

theory—why now? Why take revenge after all these years? Cynthia Langhorne's reputation was that of a husband stealer. As far as I can tell, Heather Cambridge seems to be the only woman in Dallas County who didn't hate her. The shredded dress, the word *SLUT* on her forehead, all suggest a very personal motive."

"So for her murder, you like an angry spouse, or a jilted lover or . . ." The end of her sentence hung in the air, unspoken.

A jealous husband.

Caitlin could practically hear both Jim and Spense thinking those words.

"I'll grant you that's the simplest explanation. But then how do you account for the break-in? The tossing of the family's home in Preston Hollow?" she asked.

"It's my understanding there was some kind of diary," Jim said.

Caitlin felt a frisson of surprise, then realized, of course, that Jim had spoken to Sheridan earlier today, and he must've mentioned her theory.

"Did Dutch say anything to you two about Cindy's diary?" Jim bounced an intense gaze back and forth between them.

"Dutch told Sheridan he knows nothing about any diary." One side of Spense's mouth lifted dubiously.

A muscle began to twitch in Jim's jaw. "You don't look like you believe him."

Caitlin avoided Spense's eyes. "Dutch told me that Cindy had been keeping a diary for years."

"When did he tell you this?" Spense's chin jerked up.

"While you were sleeping. After you nearly drowned, I didn't want to wake you up just to tell you about the diary. And then today, I-I . . ."

"You had a hangover, and you forgot." Spense let her off the hook, and she released a pent-up breath.

She hadn't forgotten. She'd been waiting for the right time to broach the subject, and that time was now. She never made any promises to keep quiet about the diary, and it was a relief to tell even part of the truth. "I think the intruder was looking for that diary, and it holds the key to solving Cindy's murder. Dutch agrees."

"Does Dutch have any theories as to why someone would break in to steal the diary? Because frankly, Sheridan thinks the whole tossing of the home, the chase into the neighbor's yard was staged. He thinks Dutch hired the job out in order to lead the cops down a blind alley," Jim said.

"I don't believe that. Spense nearly drowned chasing down the intruder. Dutch wouldn't have deliberately put him in danger."

"And I don't want to believe it, Caitlin. But I'm just laying it all out there. In any other situation, I'd be taking a long hard look at the husband. I'm eager to hear any theory other than *the husband did it*. Maybe there's something in that diary that might implicate someone else. If so, I'd like to know sooner rather than later. Are you absolutely certain Dutch didn't say what was in it? Has he read it?" Jim leaned forward, searching her face for answers.

Did he doubt she was telling him the whole truth? Since she was, in reality, holding something back, maybe her body language was giving her away. "I really can't say. I only know he denied knowing its whereabouts." She hated to betray Dutch, but she wouldn't lie by omission. The only thing she'd keep quiet about, for now, was Jack Spenser's checkered past. "But Dutch also said that if he *did* have the diary . . . he *sure as hell wouldn't turn it over to Sheridan*."

Jim's knuckles went white around a pencil. "And now he's fled—probably with that diary. He waited until he knew the two of you would be on the road to Austin, out of the way, and ran. If he knew the diary existed, he probably knew where to find it." Jim snapped the pencil in two. "And after I've protected him all these years. Every damn time someone brought up Tesarak, I blocked the accusations. I told them that Dutch Langhorne respects the rule of law. That Dutch Langhorne puts his life on the line to protect our freedoms. That Dutch Langhorne deserves our admiration and our gratitude. And now, even after I offer him the Bureau's backing on this thing, he runs."

"I'm sure you're disappointed," Caitlin offered, "but—"

"Disappointed doesn't cover it. Dutch's pulling a stupid stunt like this doesn't just make *him* look guilty, it makes the Bureau seem complicit. It will call up all the old questions about Tesarak and start people talking about conspiracies and dirty cops all over again." He rose to his feet, towering over her. "And I won't have it. The FBI is *not* dirty. I will not allow anyone to sully the reputation we've worked to build with the public. It was J. Edgar Hoover, himself, who first understood the importance of building the public's trust in the FBI." Abruptly he sat back down. "You two are done here. No more looking out for the man who turned his back on the Bureau. You're going to take that vacation you've earned, and I'm washing my hands of Dutch Langhorne. If Sheridan wants him, he can have him."

"He shouldn't have run. No question about that. But we don't know he's guilty. Maybe this is bigger than just Cindy and her infidelity . . ." Caitlin heard hesitancy in Spense's voice and saw warring emotions on his face.

But Jim seemed cool and certain. "I'm ordering you off the case. I can't sacrifice the Bureau's reputation for the sake of one agent. It smacks of a cover-up—even though it isn't."

He pulled his cell from his pocket, then looked down. "Sorry guys, I've got to take this one."

Spense didn't say a word as they left the building, and when he climbed into the car beside her, he left his seat belt hanging out and shut the door on top of it. She could tell he was distracted and struggling to keep his thoughts in order.

"I thought you'd be happier about the time off," she said.

"Me too." He turned to her. "You don't look so thrilled yourself. Wanna tell me what's on your mind?"

She did. But she didn't know whether to follow her head or her heart. She wanted to tell him that Dutch was his brother, but she still wasn't clear if it was the right thing to do. "You first."

"Okay." He put the key in the ignition but didn't start the engine. "I don't like to leave a case hanging like this."

"It's not really our case," she said without conviction.

"Good point. We've been off the books from the start."

"Jim can't order us off a case we were never on. And he certainly can't tell us where to go for vacation. There's no reason we can't take a holiday right here in Texas." Dutch ran to protect Spense. She was convinced of it, and Dutch needed their help, now more than ever. Spense would never forgive her if she let him walk away from his brother when he was in real trouble. But if she told him the truth . . . she couldn't predict what he'd do next. Without a clear-cut reason not to, she decided to wait until they had a handle on who killed Cindy and why—or, at the very least, until they found Dutch, and he could tell him in person.

"Make no mistake, Caity. You're rationalizing. We've been told to back off. And if we don't, Jim isn't going to just look the other way."

"Unless we can find Dutch, and either exonerate him or convince him to turn himself in."

Spense took her hand. "You're willing to risk your career with the Bureau for Dutch Langhorne?"

"I-I don't know." She heard her voice crack. It was more Spense's career she was concerned about. His whole life was the Bureau. But . . . "I believe Dutch is innocent. I know the evidence is piling up against him, but I've interviewed more than my share of killers, and I don't see Dutch as the kind of man who could murder his wife."

Spense turned her palm over in his hand. "I know what you're thinking."

"You do?" Did he feel some connection with Dutch? Was he beginning to suspect the truth? She could hardly breathe.

"You're thinking about your father." He pulled her to him. "And you're right. We can't walk away from Dutch. He may not be a blood relation, but he's FBI, and that means he's family."

"But what about Jim?"

"Like you said before, if we bring Dutch home, or if we prove his innocence, all will be forgiven."

"And if we don't?"

He kissed the top of her head. "Don't worry, Caity. Failure is not in my vocabulary."

Chapter Eleven

Thursday, October 17
11:00 P.M.
Jefferson, Texas

BY THE TIME this case was over, Spense figured, he could write a Texas travel guide.

WELCOME TO JEFFERSON the sign said.

"You sure we shouldn't head out to Mrs. Langhorne's place tonight?" Caity mumbled from her cat curl in the front passenger seat. They'd been on the road all day and half the night, traveling round-trip from Dallas to Austin, and now this side jaunt to Jefferson to interview Dutch's mother, Yolanda Langhorne.

"She's my mother's age. I hate to wake her."

"I thought you wanted to see for yourself whether Dutch was there. If we wait until morning, we might miss him."

"If he's holed up at his mother's place—which I doubt—he'll likely still be holed up there in the morning—hence the expression *holed up*. Although I do want to see whether he's there or not with my own eyes, the other reason I wanted to make the trip is that we have a much better chance of squeezing information out of Mrs. Langhorne in person than we do over the phone. If Dutch warned her not to talk anyone, we're going to have to be persuasive. That means I need to be able to charm her a little, and you'll have to bring out your *you-know-you-can-trust-me* smile. If we knock on her door at this time of night, we'll never get anywhere with her."

Besides, Caity needed sleep. His shoulders tensed. She still hadn't told him why she'd stayed up until the wee hours with Dutch. Reaching across the console, he grabbed her hand. "Do you want to stay at the historic haunted Excelsior Hotel, the historic haunted Jefferson Hotel, the historic haunted bed-and-breakfast, or the yet-to-be-haunted Bargain Bayou Inn? Free continental breakfast at the Bargain Bayou. It's your call, baby."

She straightened in the passenger seat and stretched her arms high over her head. "You're joking."

"Not really. Apparently, just about every room at the Excelsior has its own ghost. There's a headless man, a woman in black with a baby, and get this, Spielberg stayed there. Supposedly he was inspired to write *Poltergeist* after being awakened by the ghost of a young boy in the Gould room. Across the way at the Jefferson, the stairs squeak, and ghosts pull the guests' hair and tap on their toes. At the bed-and-breakfast—"

Caity threw back her head, laughing. A beautiful sound he hadn't heard nearly enough since they'd arrived in Texas and met up with the morosely arrogant Dutch Langhorne. "No. I meant you were joking about the Bargain Bayou Inn. I can't believe there's a bayou in Texas."

"But the ghosts, you believe?"

"I like to keep an open mind when it comes to the paranormal."

Caity had a way of surprising him. He'd never have suspected that from her. She seemed so grounded in science. "I don't know about the spirits, but there really are Texas wetlands—the Big Cypress Bayou. I didn't realize it before, but Yolanda Langhorne's cabin is very near Caddo Lake State Park." A place his dad had taken him fishing more than once. "I don't think we'll have a chance to see it this trip, but I'd like to take you there someday." He'd love to watch her face when she saw those giant cypress trees floating in the wetlands and the fish jumping in between. He'd made plenty of memories with his father there, and he'd like to make some new ones with Caity.

As he drove, he watched her from the corner of his eye. Stretching her arms overhead pushed her chest forward, and from his angle he could see the mounds of Caity's full breasts and the tempting way her nipples jutted against her thin shirt. "You cold?" He'd been running the air conditioner full blast. He switched it off.

"A little. Thanks for noticing."

"My pleasure." God, he wanted her. "So what's the verdict? Headless man, or hair-pulling ghosts?"

"Oh, let's just hit the Bargain Bayou. I wouldn't want to stay at a ghost hotel when I'm this tired. I'd probably sleep right through the chains rattling and whatnot. Maybe we really will come back another time, then we can stay somewhere fun." The hopeful lilt in her voice just about cracked his heart open. She wanted to come back to Jefferson—with him.

"We'll make it happen. I promise." He kissed her hand. "Bargain Bayou, here we come."

"And Spense . . ."

"Yeah?"

"Let's not waste our money on separate rooms—even if they are a bargain."

Visions of Caity, stretched out on a bed, jolted his pulse into overdrive. He stepped on the gas—hard.

Chapter Twelve

THE RACKET AND rattling in Jefferson was enough to drive a man with Malachi's gift of hearing insane. Probably all those damn ghosts.

"Just one night," Malachi addressed the desk clerk at the Bargain Bayou Inn.

Her lips started moving.

"What?"

She pointed at his ears.

Of course, he'd forgotten he was wearing his noise-canceling headphones. He slipped them off.

"That'll be ninety seven dollars plus tax. Sign here, please."

"A bargain indeed." As he handed her cash, he smiled politely. The place was modestly furnished but really clean. The lobby smelled of fresh paint. A picture of a woman dressed like a Southern belle, parasol and all, hung above the front desk. Strange for Texas, but then again, Jefferson was once a river-boat town and quite close to Louisiana. Noting that the Bargain Bayou was relatively quiet compared to the streets of Jefferson, he decided he liked it here.

Good thing Spenser and Cassidy had chosen this place and not one of the haunted hotels—where the cacophony of the dead would've kept him up all night.

Unlike Langhorne, they weren't on his employer's to-do list. But Malachi knew they might lead him to his target, which would save him time and effort. Also, Spenser had seen his face, so on or off the list, he had to be eliminated. Following the pair from Dallas was a good way to kill two birds with one stone.

Or three.

Caitlin Cassidy was a nice bonus.

Ten minutes earlier, while the couple checked in, Malachi had stood at a pay phone in the lobby with his back turned. To pass time, he'd checked the Jefferson phone book and found one Langhorne—Yolanda. Had to be either his target's mother or sister. Whichever, Yolanda would have the information he needed to locate his target and the diary—both of which he'd somehow lost track of. Or maybe Langhorne was with Yolanda now. He smiled to himself. This had been a good plan indeed.

But time was of the essence. He couldn't risk Spenser's arriving first and possibly describing him to Yolanda. He had to get to Cassidy and Spenser before they got to her. So after the couple exited the lobby, he'd followed them to room number 175. The entire way, he'd heard humming, smooth vibrations, two distinct octaves, entwining in perfect harmony.

Two!

His ears vibrated from sheer joy. The couple not only provided him a soothing break from the washing machines of this earth, he knew he'd hit the jackpot. Once he collected these two souls, he was positively guaranteed the magnificent death he longed for.

He watched impatiently while the couple entered the room and closed the door behind them. Then he'd headed back to the lobby to check in. With the noisy strains of useless men assailing him from every direction, he'd been forced to put on his headphones. He had no time to plan the fantastic death Spenser and Cassidy deserved, but he could certainly do better than shooting them in their sleep. So as he made his way back to the lobby, he looked for something useful. Some way to give them a death less ordinary, an ending that would make their families wonder what the pair had done to deserve such a twist of fate.

A freak accident would work.

But nothing came straight to mind. Malachi was just about to resign himself to simply shooting them when he spotted something that gave him an idea. There, on the sidewalk, most likely waiting to be hauled off to the dump, stood the inspiration he'd been looking for.

An old refrigerator.

Chapter Thirteen

Friday, October 18
12:00 A.M.
Jefferson, Texas

DANCING IN PAJAMAS. Caitlin never realized how romantic improvisation could be. Yet here they were at the Bargain Bayou, and she'd never been so swept away. She deeply, *deeply* regretted not having packed sexy lingerie in the little bag she kept ready in the car for emergencies. Spense called his a *go bag*. He claimed he didn't own pajamas, and therefore was currently tripping the light fantastic with her in his T-shirt and boxers.

But she wasn't complaining. The cotton fabric of his shirt felt wonderfully soft against her cheek, and he'd set up her laptop, so that her favorite songs played from the computer's speakers. At the moment they were swaying to the rhythm of Meghan Trainor's "Like I'm Gonna Lose You."

Hopefully, not a portent of things to come.

"My darling, Caity," he whispered in her ear, and the endearment sent little shock waves of happiness through her.

"Mmm hmm."

"This isn't how I imagined our first time together would be."

It wasn't how she'd pictured it either. Then all at once a thought came to her that nearly stopped her heart in her chest. "You're not suggesting we postpone . . ." His thumb stroked her bare skin, just beneath the elastic of her pajama bottoms, and her voice trailed off into a sigh.

"Oh, hell no." He tilted her chin up to meet his gaze. "But, close your eyes. Just for a minute or two. I want you to pretend."

She was bone tired, and dreamily agreeable. Obediently, she closed her eyes.

"Don't open them." He pressed his fingers against her lids. "Take a deep breath, Caity. I brought you a bouquet of wildflowers. I picked them myself," he murmured. "I made sure to get a lot of those purple ones you like so much."

She inhaled long and lavishly. "Lavender. Smells nice."

"Good girl." His hand brushed her cheek, tempting her to gaze up at him, but she forced herself to keep her eyes closed. He wanted to set a lovely scene for her, and she wanted to let him do anything—and everything—he liked. "Your skin is so soft—and in this beautiful candlelight, it's the color of pink pearls. The candles are encircling us. Be careful not to trip on them."

"So many candles." In spite of herself, she grinned. "Hope they don't set off the smoke alarm."

"There are no smoke alarms on the beach, sweetheart." He kissed the tip of her nose.

"Oh, we're on the beach. I should've known as soon as I heard the waves crashing against the shore." Her heart was so full. She grabbed his hands and brought them to her lips. They leaned into each other, moving more to the rhythm of their own bodies than to the music. She knew he was trying to give her more than a night in a cheap motel. But she didn't *need* more.

The music stopped, and she opened her eyes to find him staring at her. "I understand what you're trying to do, Spense, but here's the thing." She'd been waiting so long for this moment. Her entire body was quivering with desire for Spense, and for him alone. "I don't want wildflowers or candles or crashing waves." She tiptoed up and kissed his chin. "I only want *you.*"

"I want you more." His voice came out low and gravelly. Then, to prove his point, he dragged her hand lower, and what she found was gratifying . . . *very* gratifying.

A noise that sounded a lot like purring started up in her throat. It seemed he'd turned her into a domesticated kitten. If she weren't careful, she'd wind up on his lap, begging to be petted.

She nuzzled her face in his shoulder, and the familiar scent of his aftershave triggered a full-body tingle. Funny how a fragrance she'd once found old-fashioned and yes, a little boring, had now become a powerful aphrodisiac—simply because it was Spense who wore it. Something about the way his pheromones mixed with Old Spice turned it into *Spense Spice*, and that was a scent she couldn't get enough of.

Her gaze traveled down to where her hand cupped the fullness in his boxers. She molded her palm around him, knowing she wasn't the only one craving attention. She indulged herself in his hard, warm pleasure, then teasingly pulled her hand away, only to replace it with her hips. "Do you remember the night we met?"

He ground against her, turning her tingles to a fiery ache. "You know I do. It was Baltimore."

They'd sat next to each other at a lecture on spree killers. She'd been sneaking side glances at his distracting profile, wondering who he was, and whether it would be wildly inappropriate to invite a handsome stranger in an unfamiliar city to get a drink, but she couldn't work up the nerve. After the lecture, they both walked out to hail a cab, and he'd asked her where she was headed.

"*The Belvedere Hotel.*"

"*Funny, that's where I'm staying.*"

They'd shared a ride, then a few drinks back at the hotel. It wasn't until after her second gin and tonic he'd told her his name: *Atticus Spenser.* That had been a bucket of ice over her head. They were both in town to testify in the same trial. Caitlin for the defense; Spense for the prosecution.

Special Agent Atticus Spenser was the enemy, and that pull she felt in her belly every time he looked at her only made him more dangerous.

So she'd glared at him and taken her leave with no explanation. The confused look on his face pricked her conscience, but she refused to give in to it, knowing that the next morning in court, he'd have an unpleasant surprise, and that just might give her side an advantage. Looking back on it now, she realized how wrong she'd been. She'd been unkind to one of the best men on the planet—no, better make that the universe.

"I remember what you were wearing the first time I saw you." Keeping his hips in that teasing position against hers, he leaned back enough to catch her eyes. "A yellow blouse with a Peter Pan collar and tiny little raised dots. Swiss polka dots, I think they call them."

At the same moment her body threatened to spontaneously

combust, disappointment seeped into her blissful mood. "Good try. But no, I don't own a yellow blouse with Swiss polka dots."

He laughed. "No?"

"And how do you even know what a Peter Pan collar is?"

"Every Sunday, when I call my mother, she likes to describe to me what she wore to church—in excruciating detail. I consider it my filial duty to let her. Last week she told me all about her pink silk dress with white piping and a Peter Pan collar." He nibbled her ear. "Let's see; so it wasn't Swiss polka dots. Let me think. It was such a hot evening, maybe you were wearing a sleeveless—"

"It was the middle of winter, Spense. It's okay. Forget I brought it up. It's just that I was remembering how handsome you looked that night at the Belvedere."

"I wish you would've let your hair down."

"I had my hair up?" She hated to admit she didn't remember. Or was he speaking figuratively?

"You wore a navy blue blazer with a tailored gray blouse, and a gold locket around your neck. Your hair was up, in one those French twisty things. I wanted to pull it down. I couldn't help picturing how beautiful your long hair would look, falling across your bare breasts while we made love."

"You do remember." She suddenly wanted to kiss him, so she did.

When they came up for air, he said, "How could I forget the first time I laid eyes on you? It was one of those moments when . . . I knew something *big* was going to happen. And I was right. It's taken awhile, but you've changed me, Caity, and now there's no going back."

He'd changed her, too, and she wanted to tell him so, but part of her was still mad about the way he'd teased her. "Swiss polka dots? Peter Pan collar?" She punched him in the chest. "You're cruel for making me think you'd forgotten."

"Then now we're square. Oh, and by the way, I wasn't really staying at the Belvedere. I just said that to get into the cab with you." He dropped a kiss on her forehead before moving on to her eyes and cheeks. "I'm glad we're even, and I can finally forgive you."

"Gosh, thanks." She did her best to stay annoyed, but it was no use. He pressed his hand to the small of her back, urging her closer still. Her heart began to hunt and peck out a rhythm like a child who'd gotten hold of an old typewriter.

"I forgive you, too," she said.

"How's that?" He swept rough fingers across her collarbone, dipping one into her cleavage.

"That's good." She gulped. "Very good."

As he kissed her neck, she could feel his lips curving into a smile against her skin. "No. I meant what exactly did I do that requires your forgiveness?"

"I'm forgiving you in advance because I'm about to break my one steadfast rule, and it's all your fault."

"What rule's that?" His erection ground against her, unmistakable, demanding.

"Never go down on a special agent."

His eyes darkened. "If you ask me, I did you a favor. That rule is begging to be broken . . . eventually. But I wouldn't count on taking the lead, sweetheart. Tonight, I'm in charge."

His commanding tone made her knees wobble, and she forgot all about . . . everything. He cupped her bottom, lifting her slightly off her feet, then walked her backward on her heels until the backs of her knees bumped against the bed. She collapsed onto the tired mattress, and the springs gave way beneath her. Then the creak of the bed disappeared into the thump of her own heartbeat, and the urgent rush of their breathing; the tantalizing words he whispered to her over and over making her crazy and ready.

So. Very. Ready.

"Spense . . ." she raised herself up and tugged his T-shirt over his head, exposing a beautiful expanse of muscled chest. He made short work of getting her top off, and it flew through the air and landed with a soft thud, somewhere across the room. He reared back, admiring her.

"God, you're beautiful," he murmured, and sank his mouth onto her nipple. Sucking and teasing, he headed lower. With his hands, he yanked away whatever pieces of clothing stood between them—her panties, his boxers. With his forbidden, sexy words, he stripped away the deeper barriers between them, taking her some-place secret, and intimate—a place meant only for the two of them. He used his mouth in other ways, too, and by the time he nudged himself between her legs, she was already so close she could have soared to climax just from the pressure of his entering her.

But she wanted more.

More time, more touching, more *Spense*. She wanted to tease and taste—to put her mouth on him as he'd done with her.

She flipped on top and heard a satisfying moan below her. Reaching for him, she stroked him, kissed him, whispered in his ear what she wanted to do to *him*. Her world tunneled down until there was nothing left but the two of them, and the pleasure they brought each other. Her head was light, and she tried to force her-self to focus. She wanted to remember every sensation, so that she could detail it all later in her fantasies. But each thrilling touch made her forget the one that came before, until she heard a soft curse and the sound of a wrapper tearing. He must've had the condom at the bedside, but in her haze she hadn't noticed until he was already slipping it on. Now he grabbed her by the hips, pulled her up, and guided her onto him. This time, she surrendered to his urgent need. No more thinking. No more talking. She became impossibly lost in this journey she was taking with him. Closing her eyes, she gave herself up to the moment. There was no longer any past, and the future would have to wait.

CAITLIN KNEW SHE was dreaming because no way can little girls roll uphill—and because of her sweet, thick brain fog that made it impossible to lift her head off the deliciously warm object lying beneath her cheek.

A guttural moan floated in on the haze. *Spense.* Her face was buried in his chest, and the wiry hairs tickling her nose made her want to sneeze. Again, she tried to lift her heavy head, with no success. A spring from the worn-out mattress that had made its way up and out poked her butt. Which just might explain her dream: She was a young girl rolling up and down soft, fragrant green hills when suddenly, her old pediatrician, Dr. Dan, ran up behind her and stabbed her with a shot in her gluteus maximus. *It's for your own good*, Dr. Dan said, with an unholy gleam in his eye.

Ugh. With great effort, she pulled away from Spense and the offending mattress spring that had so rudely awakened her. But her brain fog remained inexplicably heavy, and that rolling sensation hung around, too. She was going to be sick. As predicted, nausea attacked in full force, driving her into a sitting position. She heaved only air—nothing in her stomach, thank goodness.

"Spense." Bending forward, she put her throbbing head between her knees and literally fell off of the bed. The thump of her head against the carpet knocked her fully awake, but still the weird cloudiness in her thoughts, the heaviness in her body continued. She crawled over the carpet to Spense's side of the bed. She shook him and noticed she'd somehow snagged her sleeve—luckily they'd slipped their nightclothes back on after making love. When Spense didn't respond, she shook him harder, panic stopping her breath.

Something was off. Her crippling grogginess made no sense. She hadn't had a drop to drink last night, but she felt far worse than she had the morning after her bender. She swatted hair off her forehead and noticed it was damp with sweat. It was hot as the devil in here, yet the room had been cold enough to make her reach for her pajamas before she fell asleep.

She didn't remember turning on the heat.

"Spense!" she croaked, through a scratchy throat. "Wake up! We have to get out of here now!"

No response. Summoning her strength, she slapped him hard on the face. "Get up!"

Finally, his lids crept open. He frowned at her, "What the hell did you do that for?"

"I'm sorry, but we have to hurry. I think there's something wrong with the ventilation system." An idea was winding its way through her brain. She could taste terrible words on her tongue. She spit them out. "Carbon monoxide." She rubbed her pounding temples. "Maybe." Whatever it was, they needed fresh air.

Spense shoved himself up on his elbows, then he, too, fell out of bed.

Dammit.

"Can you stand up?" No way could she physically drag him out of there. Then she slapped her own cheeks, trying to get oriented, and it hit her. All she had to do was open the door and let the life-saving oxygen flow into the room. With adrenaline reviving both her body and mind, she wobbled to her feet and made her way to the door.

Jammed.

She turned the dead bolt and tried again with no luck. "It won't open," she shouted.

To her relief, Spense got to his feet and made it to the door.

He tried the knob. No luck.

Together they went to the window. Spense jerked the curtains aside. Nailed shut. Fighting the urge to scream, she took his hand.

He turned to her, shaking his head. "I thought I could break it, and we could crawl through, but it's completely blocked by that damn refrigerator."

Could it be coincidence? Someone just happened to push a full-sized refrigerator in front of their window? Maybe. But . . . then the door to their room accidentally got jammed from the outside? Not a chance.

She found her cell, lying on the floor and dialed 911. "Bargain Bayou. Carbon Monoxide. Send help." No voice answered back, not even a dial tone. She was talking into a dead phone. No bars. No service.

"Call the front desk." Spense shattered the glass in the window with the butt of the fire extinguisher. He pressed his face up against the sill, sucking in the air leaking in between the back of the refrigerator and the broken pane. Coughing, he doubled over.

The phone on the nightstand was dead, too. The receiver fell from her hands. Her knees gave way, but Spense dragged her to the window, lifted her to the source of the oxygen. It might be enough to restore her fading consciousness, but she knew it wasn't enough to keep them alive.

Spense had his arms around her, holding her tight. "Hang on, Caity. Stay with me."

They were going to die.

Eyeing the old air-conditioning vent in the ceiling, they both said, in unison, "We're not going to die." She was grateful for the fresh burst of energy, and the way the small bit of oxygen had revived their brains. And she was even more grateful for that old mattress, whose sharp, broken spring had saved their lives—she hoped.

The next thing she knew, Spense had hoisted her onto his shoulders. His height allowed her to grab hold of the grate, and her will to live enabled her to squeeze herself into the grimy vent. "Window!" she called back down. "Go back for air. Stay there until I open the door."

The musty vent was too shallow and narrow to get up on her knees. With darkness all around, she combat-crawled ahead. Her pajama top climbed toward her neck, offering little protection from the smooth metal beneath her that chilled her aching chest. She stopped a time or two for more dry heaves. Her lungs burned, and her muscles gave way, but the thought of Spense, still locked in that room, wouldn't let her give up. Each time she collapsed, she willed herself to plant her elbows out front and drag herself another foot forward.

Keep going.

But where? Who was waiting for her on the other side? The stale air in the vent gagged her with its rotten-egg smell, but she desperately needed to keep breathing. Her thoughts jumbled into a confused mass of images. She became a worm, burrowing deeper and deeper into the earth. Her fingers went cold and numb. She could barely see through the darkness.

Keep going.

There. Up ahead.

A light!

Crisscross shadows in the form of a grate.

She'd made it to another room.

"Help!" she screamed, then "Look out below!"

With her bare foot, she kicked out the grate, then stuck her legs through before dropping like a crash dummy into the room below. She didn't know what she'd find waiting for her there—a monster or a savior.

She thudded onto the carpet. Her back popped and one leg turned beneath her. A cigarette dropped from the mouth of a rail-thin woman, who leapt out of her bed, screaming at the top of her lungs.

Caitlin smiled.

A savior.

Chapter Fourteen

Friday, October 18
7:30 A.M.
Jefferson, Texas

DR. BORDEN KEPT his eyes down, and his brows formed a deep V, as he flipped through the papers on his clipboard. Spense didn't know if that meant bad news, or if the Jefferson ER doc's face always looked like he'd just dripped spaghetti sauce onto his favorite necktie. When he looked up, finally, he managed a half smile. "The blood work confirms the presence of carbon monoxide, but the levels are low. You two are very lucky."

"I wouldn't say lucky, exactly." Not in Spense's view. Someone had tampered with the ventilation system at the Bargain Bayou in order to poison Caity and him with carbon monoxide. The window, blocked by an old refrigerator, and the jammed door lock left no doubt in his mind—someone was trying to kill them.

"The nearest hyperbaric oxygen chamber is over one hundred

miles from here. You're *lucky* you don't need to be air-evaced for treatment. You're *lucky* you didn't succumb to the gas."

In other words, they were lucky to be alive. Spense reached for Caity's hand. She leaned her head on his shoulder, and cobwebs in her hair, acquired during her crawl through the inn's air vents, triggered a sneeze.

She ran her fingers through her messy hair. "Sorry. Guess I need a shower."

He shot her a no-worries smile.

"So we're good to go?" Caity pulled her oxygen mask away from her face to speak. Red marks appeared from where the elastic band had cut into her cheeks, then the mask snapped back into place.

Dr. Borden shook his head. "I'd prefer to keep you overnight to monitor your breathing and your carbon monoxide levels."

He'd said *prefer*, and to Spense that meant there were other options. Like getting the hell out of here. But Caity looked pale. It was one thing for him to go against the doctor's advice on his own, but quite another to tow Caity away from needed medical care. And he didn't dare leave her here alone. Being in a hospital was no guarantee she'd be safe from whoever had done this.

Caity reached over to a gadget on the wall and shut off the flow of oxygen to her mask, then jumped to her feet.

On the other hand, Caity liked to call her own shots.

If she thought it was safe for them to leave . . . he tended to trust her judgment. Sure, she was a psychiatrist, but she had a medical degree, just like the guy standing in front of them.

"There's no reason to expect our carbon monoxide levels to rise from here," she said to Borden. "We're away from the source of the gas, and we've been breathing supplemental oxygen for nearly an hour. Aside from a bit of a headache, I feel fine. You said yourself that we're lucky. The levels are low—so we don't need a hyperbaric chamber. Looks like we got out pretty quickly after the gas leak started." She tugged her mask over her head, then dropped it onto the bed.

"I'm surprised you woke up. Most people who are exposed in their sleep . . ." He left the rest unspoken.

"I'll have to send the Bargain Bayou a thank-you note. A spring poking out of the mattress woke me up." Caity drew her bottom lip between her teeth. "You filed some kind of report, right?"

"It's taken care of. The inn will be shut down until the source of the leak is found."

"Good," Spense said tersely, jerking his own mask off. As long the hotel was going to be shut down for inspection, to ensure the safety of other guests, he wasn't about to go into the details with the doc or anyone else. He suspected the phone lines had been cut, and the maintenance man who'd gotten Spense out of the room would probably get around to telling someone, sooner or later, that the door lock had been jammed from the outside with a small nail. But with all the chaos surrounding the EMTs' arrival, no one had called the police.

Everyone seemed to be operating under the assumption this was a freak accident, and he and Caity were happy to leave it at that for the moment. The last thing they needed was to have to bring the Jefferson cops in on this. Sheridan had a BOLO out on Dutch, and they'd gone against Jim's direct order not to interfere with the case. The situation was getting more complicated by the minute—and nothing seemed to add up. His hands clenched at his sides as the unpleasant, but inescapable, thought came to him that Dutch himself just might be behind this.

Dr. Borden plopped down on a gurney facing them, as if they were about to have a heart-to-heart. "You really should stay twenty-four hours. It won't hurt to get a little extra oxygen in your systems, and if everything looks good, we'll get you out of here first thing in the morning. What's the hurry?"

The concern on the doc's face was genuine. Spense looked to Caity—this was one call he was going to leave to her. But if it was medically safe to go, they should. Someone was out to get them, and at a small-town hospital . . . they'd be sitting ducks.

"You were locked in the room longer, and had the greater exposure . . ." Caity sent him a questioning look.

He held out his hand, and Borden gave him the clipboard. Spense passed it to Caity. "I feel fine. I can't read this gibberish, though."

She leafed through the labs. "Your carbon monoxide levels are even lower than mine. I guess it pays to be a big guy."

He grinned. "So you're giving me the thumbs-up to get us out of here, Dr. Cassidy?"

She nodded. "We'll sign out AMA—against medical advice," she reassured Borden. "That way you won't be liable if we croak."

The doc's face went white as his coat.

"I'm joking about croaking." She offered him a broad smile. "Really, it's okay. I promise if our symptoms return, we'll get help."

Back at the inn, a jittery, apologetic clerk had their things packed and waiting for them. After loading the car, Spense pulled out his GPS and mapped a new route to Yolanda Langhorne's cabin near Caddo Lake State Park. They were no longer just looking for a fugitive. They were now on the run from a cold-blooded killer.

Best to keep off the main roads as much as possible.

They'd likely been followed to Jefferson, and they didn't want that to happen again, both for their own safety, and for Mrs. Langhorne's— assuming, of course, Dutch himself wasn't the would-be assassin. One thing was sure—Spense would be on high alert for a tail from here on out.

Caity hadn't yet clicked her seat belt into place. Reaching over, he did it for her. "Tell me everything you remember about your private conversation with Dutch," he said. "If this is about Cindy's diary, and the killer thinks Dutch has it, he may suspect that we know what's in it. Otherwise, I don't see the killer's motive for coming after *us*." He turned to her and took her by the hands. "I know you care about Dutch. And I know this case is bringing up feelings of helplessness about your father."

He waited for her to protest, but she didn't. She kept her gaze steady, listening intently.

"But we have to be smart about this. We have to consider every angle without personal prejudice. And that means we have to admit the possibility that Dutch killed his wife. And that he might've orchestrated that carbon monoxide leak. I'm tempted to call Jim, fill him in on what's happened, and send you back to Dallas for safekeeping . . ."

Her face flushed. He was glad to see she had enough oxygen in her system to turn pink, even if it was because she was pissed. "While you continue to put your life in jeopardy –and your career? Absolutely not."

"Take it easy. I said I was tempted. But I won't send you back. Until I know who tried to kill us . . . and why . . . there's no way I'm letting you out of my sight. You're stuck with me, Caity." He lifted her hand and brought it to his lips. "I'm just reminding you to stay alert. Right now, I don't trust *anyone*. Not even Dutch."

She cast her eyes down to her lap, and the healthy pink in her cheeks drained away. He wished it'd been safe to stay at the hospital longer. "You don't look so hot."

She waved off his concern. "I'm fine."

"Let me rephrase. You make warmed-over death look like the *after* picture."

"I promise I'm fine—physically."

He squeezed her hands then released them. "I don't know what that means, babe. Are you upset about something else? Does this have anything to do with what happened between us last night? Because if you're having second thoughts . . ."

She leaned over and pressed her fingers against his lips. "Shh. No second thoughts."

He let out a relieved breath.

"It's just . . . there's something I need to tell you."

He didn't push her, but the apprehension in her voice, the way her pupils had dilated set his pulse racing.

"We can trust Dutch," she said at last.

"I disagree. I understand you like the guy. More than I do, for sure. But don't be naïve. His wife cheated on him. He knew about it, and now she's dead. He was among the last to see her alive, *and* he discovered the body. Forensic experts say the blood spatter on his shirt is consistent with blowback from a gunshot. He fled town just when he was about to be charged. He lied to the police about Cindy's keeping a diary, and he probably has it with him now. You can't tell me that if you didn't know him, if he weren't with the FBI, that you wouldn't like him for Cindy's murder. I'm sorry to say it, but you have a blind spot because of your father. But this isn't the same thing at all. No one is framing Dutch."

"You don't know that. You said yourself, this could be about something much bigger than marital infidelity. I don't believe he killed his wife." She unhooked her seat belt and turned to him, placing her hands on his shoulders. "And I *know* he didn't try to kill us."

"Then you must know something I don't, because . . ." The look on her face made him stop midsentence. "You *do* know something I don't. What the fuck aren't you telling me, Caity?"

Her lower lip trembled, but she made no answer.

"For God's sake. Someone just tried to kill us. I'd think that if you had any information at all, you'd have told me already."

She looked away, then back again, with moist eyes. "You're right. And I was wrong." Her throat worked in a long swallow. "Spense . . ."

"I'm waiting." He tapped his fingers on the steering wheel, suddenly fed up. There was no excuse for her withholding anything about this case from him.

"Dutch is your half brother."

She was looking at him so intently, for a second he thought she was serious. Then he shook his head. "That's the strangest attempt at a practical joke I've ever heard." Not to mention the timing sucked. Then a thought occurred to him. Confusion was one symptom of carbon monoxide poisoning. He touched her forehead with the back of his hand. "You sure you feel okay? No headache or nausea? You don't seem feverish."

She just stared at him, as if expecting some sort of delayed reaction. "I'm not crazy or confused. Your father had an affair with

Yolanda Langhorne that started before you were born and continued until the time of his death."

His throat tightened ominously, but his mind fought back. "Caity, that's ridiculous. I'm not sure what's going on here, but I'm thinking maybe we should go back to the hospital and have your carbon monoxide levels rechecked."

Her eyes didn't drop. They seemed clear, not confused. His head, on the other hand, felt fuzzy. He reached in his pocket for his Rubik's cube. It wasn't there. He took a deep breath and closed his eyes, focusing on her words, stripping away all the emotion that was getting in the way of evaluating them. "You're serious."

"I'm sorry."

"You're telling me that Dutch Langhorne is my brother—and that my father was a-a . . . lying, cheating bastard."

Her eyes widened, and she grabbed his hand.

He shrugged. He'd evaluated her statement calmly, and it still made no sense. "That's impossible, Caity."

"I don't think it is." She folded her hands in her lap, finally dropping her gaze.

"If Dutch told you that—"

"He did."

"Then he was lying—and you just swallowed his story hook, line, and sinker. What proof did he offer you?"

"I figured it out on my own. I'm the one who asked him how you two were related. I didn't ask for proof."

"You figured it out, how?" He narrowed his eyes, concentrating, wondering what the hell she could mean. He and Dutch were polar opposites. That's why they didn't get along.

"The two of you are so similar . . . you're both brilliant and stubborn. You're built the same, your features are almost identical. Your mannerisms . . ."

"We look nothing like each other. We *are* nothing like each other."

"It's hard to notice at first, because of his red hair and blue eyes. But if you look past the coloring, you'll see it. The similarities are striking. Didn't you ever notice anything familiar?"

His jaw clamped down. "No."

"Because I sure did. And I couldn't quit thinking about where I'd met Dutch before until I suddenly realized the two of you had to be related somehow. Spense, he has the same birthmark on his ankle that you do."

Anger flooded his system, replacing his initial astonishment. She actually believed Dutch was his brother, and yet she'd kept it to herself. The whole idea was preposterous, and clearly a lie, but if she believed it to be true, she should've come to him. "When did you have this epiphany of yours? Wait, don't tell me. It was the night the two of you had a private party and got rip-roaring drunk."

"Yes. Except, we were only a little drunk. I'm not denying the whiskey, but don't misunderstand. We had our wits about us. That night, I found him in the study—holding a pistol to his head. An empty one, but still, he was grieving. He truly loved Cindy, in spite of all their issues. I cannot believe he killed her. I *do not* believe he killed her."

"If he loved her, he sure had a piss-poor way of showing it. And even if he did, love is a fantastic motive for murder—in fact, it's the most common one."

"No, Spense. You're confusing obsession with love. But I didn't get that feeling from Dutch. I believe his love for Cindy was genuine, and I don't think he would've ever hurt her. Real love requires forgiveness and selflessness."

He didn't know how much longer he could keep sitting in this car without punching the windshield. "Get the stars out of your eyes, Caity; they're blinding you. And more to the point, you're avoiding the real issue. If you honestly believe what Dutch told you about my father is true, then why the hell haven't you told me before now?"

"I was wrong not to tell you."

"You're goddamn right you were wrong." He laid his hand on the center of the steering wheel, and the horn blared. "Everything about this is wrong. All those hoops I jumped through for you, proving myself to you, waiting day after day, week after week for you to trust me—to take me at my word. Now I come to find out, *after we made love,* Caity, that you're the one hanging on to a big fat earth-shattering secret. It's not true, but the point is you think it is, and you damn well should've told me."

Silent tears poured down her face, and any other time they would have softened his heart, but not now. Not today. He'd trusted her, believed in her, and she'd betrayed him. "If this really were true, Caity, just think of the consequences of not telling me." His heart squeezed painfully.

She looked at him, and he could read the anguish in her eyes. "If someone is avenging a loved one by attacking Dutch's loved ones, then if it came out that the two of you are brothers, it might put you in danger. That's the main reason I didn't tell you. But I was wrong."

His lungs stung from breathing the air in the car. He got out and jogged toward the trees, faster and faster. From behind, he heard Caity running after him, calling his name.

Dammit, <u>it was hard to breathe.</u> The carbon monoxide had weakened him more than he'd realized. And if it was hard for him to breathe and run, it might be flat-out dangerous for Caity. She was smaller, and her carbon monoxide levels had been higher than his. She was chasing him, and that had to stop now.

It wasn't safe.

He pulled up short, and she slammed into him, almost knocking him over. He put his arms on hers and shoved her away, keeping her at a distance, but still supporting her, not letting her fall.

"I'm sorry. So, so sorry. I wanted to tell you. But I was afraid, and I didn't think it was my place. I thought it would be better for Dutch to tell you himself when the time was right."

"That doesn't play with me, sweetheart. Your loyalty is supposed to be with me, not Dutch."

"My loyalty *is* with you. And that's exactly what I told Dutch. But he convinced me that someone might be out to get him. That Cindy's murder had something to do with his past. Maybe someone was seeking revenge or . . . he wasn't exactly sure." She pushed his hands away. "You can believe me or not. But I think that's why Dutch ran away. Not because he's guilty but because he's trying to protect you. To keep you from being dragged into this."

Spent, he dropped down on the ground and rested his arms across his knees. "If you think this information will somehow endanger me, why tell me now?"

"Because we're already in danger. Someone just tried to kill us. Now I understand the real risk was in *not* telling you. I was afraid of how you'd react, but I should've trusted you. You didn't have a complete set of information, so how could you hope to predict the killer's next move? I wanted to tell you so badly, but I-I didn't think you'd be willing to keep up the lie, and that would make you a target. I was wrong—but I can't undo my mistake."

He couldn't swallow, and his chest was tight. His breath came out in short, wheezy spurts. And something besides Caity's betrayal was gnawing a hole in his gut. Someone wanted them dead, and he didn't have a reasonable explanation as to why.

A small voice whispered in his head that this was possible.

Maybe an old enemy from Dutch's past was seeking a twisted form of revenge. Stranger things had happened.

"It's not true," he muttered, but this time, he knew he was convincing himself, not Caity. "It can't be true. My father was a good man. A good husband." He paused and spit bile from his mouth. When he was a boy, his father was his world.

Jack and his shadow his mother used to call them.

"Dad taught me right from wrong. He was my conscience, my moral compass. How could he teach me to stand up for the truth if his whole life was a lie?"

Caity reached out her hand to him.

He turned his face away. "And how can I ever trust you again when you've lied about something this important?"

"I-I don't know. And I understand you want proof. I suppose, if I hadn't seen that birth mark, if I hadn't sensed the connection between you and Dutch so strongly, I would've asked for some kind of evidence." He heard her breathing heavily. "There's someone else who knows the truth. Someone you trust."

"Not my mother. I'm not going to her until I know for certain this isn't some crazy scheme to make me . . ."

"To make you what?" she asked. "If Dutch is trying to manipulate you with false information, why would he swear me to secrecy? But don't worry, I'm not talking about going to your mother with a question like this."

"Then who?" His head felt so heavy, he didn't know how much longer he could hold it up.

"Jim Edison. If you don't believe Dutch, I'd suggest you ask your father's best friend."

"I can't ask him now, and you know it. Not when I'm going directly against his orders to stay out of the case."

He let out a low moan.

There was someone else who knew the truth.

And they were headed to her ranch right now.

Chapter Fifteen

Friday, October 18
8:00 A.M.
Near Caddo Lake State Park, Texas

THE WIND CARRIED the smell of manure to Malachi's nostrils. The nearby wetlands infused their soggy flavor into the east Texas air, and there was no way to stop it from landing on your tongue. Even if you kept your lips shut tight, the stuff would make its way down your nasal passages and eventually wind up in your mouth. Some said it tasted like earth, but the plain truth was the air here tasted like shit. He didn't mind, though, because it was that same dankness that made everything here green and fertile. Looking around, he thought about how this spread would make good farmland. But from what he could tell, Yolanda Langhorne wasn't much of a farmer. He'd seen an old cow or two in the pasture, and some chickens, but no crops. He wondered what a woman was doing out here on a washed-up ranch in the first place. Maybe she'd moved out here with her man, and he'd left her high and dry—or around these parts, you might say high and wet.

His shoes made a slurping noise with each forward step.

He smiled. Though Malachi didn't enjoy killing—he didn't enjoy anything, really—he found satisfaction in doing something the right way. So he was looking forward to his work today. He wiped his palms on his slacks, leaving red-brown mud streaks on the sides. He could tell by the color, that stain would never come completely out of the fabric. No matter. These were his killing clothes, so he was going to have to burn them anyway. He'd come prepared with a change of outfit in the car.

The natural-wood ranch house up ahead had a ground-hugging profile, long low roof, and attached garage. The place was old but kept up. That and the cows in the pasture meant there would likely be a ranch hand around somewhere. Malachi scanned the horizon and spotted a barn about one hundred yards back from the house.

Despite the early hour, the sun was blazing, and perspiration dripped down his forehead and stung his eyes. He wiped his brow with a hankie he got from his jacket pocket. Today's job required him to dress the part. Normally, he liked to make a good appearance, but it was too hot out for a suit. He was definitely on the right track. He'd find Dutch Langhorne and the diary soon enough. He only wished he didn't have to sweat to do it. Stuffing the soiled handkerchief back in his pocket, he passed the house and headed for the barn. He arrived at the entrance, pressed his back against the open door, and carefully edged over until he could peek inside. A Hispanic man, probably in his early thirties, whistled as he mucked out a stall.

Malachi let the door swing open and stepped squarely into the entrance. He could feel the warm light of the sun pouring over his shoulders, spotlighting him, and he imagined that from the perspective of the ranch hand, who'd now turned to face him, he must seem like one of those apparitions people were always claiming to run into around here.

"You lost, mister? Can I help you?"

Mild disappointment rippled through him at the man's unfazed reaction. Malachi listened intently, and heard a rickety, unpleasant sound coming off the ranch hand. No special treatment needed here. Reaching beneath his jacket and behind him, Malachi gripped the butt of his pistol, which he'd stuffed in his waistband. He drew, aimed, and fired. For obvious reasons, his pistol was equipped with a silencer, so only a faint pop accompanied the muzzle flash.

The man's expression froze in confusion, as if he literally didn't know what had hit him.

No reason not to be polite to the target. "I shot you," Malachi explained.

The man grabbed his gut, sank to his knees, then fell sideways.

Malachi turned around and headed back toward the house.

By the time he'd retraced his steps, he was feeling content again, despite the heat. Maybe he did enjoy killing after all. The front door to the house stood open. He tried to pull open the screen door, but it was locked. He knocked on the frame.

"Be right there, Francisco," a female's cheery voice called out.

Then a blond woman appeared. She shaded her eyes, and looked hard at him, and that same look of confusion Francisco had worn came over her.

"I'm afraid I'm lost, ma'am. May I come in and use your phone. Get out of the heat a moment."

He could feel perspiration wetting his shirt around his armpits.

"Why don't you take off your jacket?" she asked, a hint of wariness in her voice.

"Quite right. I certainly will, but may I come in?"

"Don't you have a cell?"

"Can't get service."

"Mine works fine out here. Tell me the number, and I'll make the call for you."

He scratched his head. She wasn't as daft as he'd expected.

"Look. I haven't been completely honest with you. The truth is I work with your son, Dutch—Alex. I'm with the FBI." He pulled out his wallet and flashed his driver's license, counting on the fact she couldn't see well enough through the screen and sun to tell the difference. And if she could tell the difference, then it would be too bad for her.

"You work with Alex?" She opened the door and motioned him inside. "Come on in. Sorry to leave you standing in the heat, but I'm sure you know Alex has me trained to be careful. Let me get you some tea. Or would you rather lemonade? I've got fresh, I just squeezed."

"Water would be fine, Yolanda."

"Got that, too." She eyed his jacket, and he thought a hint of suspicion had returned to her face. He shrugged out of it, and laid it across the back of one of the sturdy, living-room chairs, taking care not to turn his back to her. He didn't want her to spot his pistol, which he'd returned to his waistband.

Apparently satisfied he wasn't hiding anything under his jacket, she turned and headed into the kitchen. He followed, leaving enough space between them to keep her comfortable. He leaned his hip against the counter and watched her turn on the faucet, allowing the first bit of water, which was brown from the minerals, to flush away before filling his jelly-jar glass.

That was thoughtful of her.

About then, he noticed a pleasant vibration, though it did not rise to the level of a hum, coming off her. He accepted the water and gulped it greedily. It was damn muggy in this unholy swamp town. "What's a cultured woman such as yourself doing in place like this?" He was curious. Despite her selection of drink ware, the woman looked classy, like an aging supermodel: platinum hair, high cheekbones and a statuesque, hourglass figure. She had the same piercing blue eyes as her son, Dutch. Certainly didn't look like she belonged on a ranch in the middle of Nowhere, Texas.

"My parents immigrated from Holland when I was sixteen."

So she was raised in Europe. That explained the cultured air she had about her . . . and the slight accent.

"My dad worked as a cook when we arrived in the United States. Eventually, he saved enough to buy this place. It kept us fed and clothed and even turned enough profit for my parents to send me to UT Dallas. Anyway, about ten years ago, when they died, I decided to come back here and keep it going as best I could." She pulled back her shoulders. "I may not look like it, but I have a degree in animal husbandry. The place still turns a living—a small one—but it's enough for me. You said you work with Alex." Her smile suddenly faded, and she placed her hand on her heart. "Nothing's happened? I mean nothing else . . ."

He took three full breaths before answering, letting her squirm and worry. He wasn't sure why, since she'd been perfectly nice to him, letting the dirty part of the water rinse down the drain and all. Then he made a show of reassuring her. "No. No. No. Not to worry. I'm not here with bad news . . ." He rested his chin in his hand. "Not really."

Her complexion paled, and she leaned back grabbing the counter for support. "What do you mean, *not really*?"

"I have a message to deliver—from the Bureau. Is he here?" He doubted Dutch would be foolish enough to come to such an obvious place as his mother's ranch, but he didn't doubt he would've been in touch with her. And Spenser and Cassidy had thought it worthwhile to make the journey. Too bad they were dead.

"He's not here. But you can leave the message with me, and the next time he gets in touch, I'll give it to him."

"When was the last time you heard from him?"

"Yesterday morning. What's the message?"

"Classified."

Yolanda straightened her back and walked past him, careful not to touch him as she sidled around him in the cozy kitchen. "I'll see you out then."

He went to the living room and sat down, still keeping his pistol from her view.

"Alex isn't here." She held up her hand. "I'm sure your next question is do I know where he is?" She shook her head. "The answer is no. So, now that you've had your water, and your answers, since you don't want to leave a message, I'd like you to get back in your car and drive away." A flush crept up her neck. "I know why you're here. You think my son murdered his wife."

"And you don't? Your son is capable of murder—he's killed in the past, after all." Malachi meant Tesarak. It paid to do research because it made you believable. It was one of the things that separated him from all the other, mediocre hit men out there.

"That was self-defense."

"Of course it was." As if that mattered. But obviously Yolanda Langhorne was one of those fools who believed every life held value. "I guess it's time to stop with the half-truths. You're far too intelligent to be fooled."

"Spit it out or be on your way." She planted her hands on her hips.

"I'm sorry to tell you, but Alex is going to be charged with his wife's murder. The Bureau wants him to turn himself in, but now he's fled. That makes him *look* guilty. You understand?"

She nodded.

"So if you know where he might've gone . . ."

She closed her eyes, thinking, then opened them again. "Not a clue."

"You must have some idea. Some sense of where he might go when he's in trouble."

Her gaze arrowed to a photograph on a side table. Malachi rose, walked over to the table and picked up the picture. "Where was this taken?"

She shook her head again. "I-I can't recall. It was so long ago."

"Try."

"I-I can't remember." She reached in her pocket and pulled out a cell phone. Her finger poised on a button. 911? Somehow, she'd realized he wasn't FBI—even though he'd mentioned Tesarak indirectly and worn a polyester suit. He thought he'd done a good job of acting. But now he'd spooked her, and she wasn't going to give him anything more.

The good thing was the way she trembled when he picked up that photograph told him everything he needed to know. All he had to do was figure out where the photo was taken, and that was where he'd find his target.

Yolanda whisked her hand toward the door, gesturing for him to go.

He grabbed the butt of his pistol, and then, remembering the drinking water and the pleasant sounds coming off her, he changed his mind. He'd had a nice chat with Yolanda. He'd enjoyed her hospitality. She didn't quite hum, but he didn't feel right just shooting her. He slipped his hand off his gun.

For Yolanda, he needn't go hog wild, but something more personal than a bullet would be appropriate. He bent down, lifted his trouser leg, and unsheathed his knife.

Chapter Sixteen

Friday, October 18
8:30 A.M.
Near Caddo Lake State Park, Texas

SPENSE KILLED THE engine, and Caitlin unhooked her seat belt. They'd made most of the short trip from the Bargain Bayou Inn to Yolanda Langhorne's ranch in stony silence.

"Why does Jim Edison, who kept your father's secret all these years, get a free pass, but I, who only kept it two days, became a pariah?" Caitlin understood Spense's resentment toward her, that wasn't the source of her confusion. What she didn't get was why he didn't seem angry with Jim. It was clear from the few words Spense had muttered that reality was beginning to sink in. He'd even made the comment that Jim's loyalty to his father would be understandable—since Jack saved his life in the war.

Spense opened his car door.

"Answer the question, please. Why does Jim get a pass?"

He turned to her and lifted one eyebrow. "You really want me to answer that?"

"Yes."

"Because Jim didn't fuck me last night." Spense climbed out of the car and left her sitting there with the stuffing knocked out of her.

A minute later, he came around and opened her door like a perfect gentleman, apparently preparing to put on his company manners for the woman who'd had a decade-long affair with his father.

Screw that.

She slammed her door and pushed past him, trying to beat him to the porch, then suddenly stopped short, sensing something wasn't right. Maybe *sensing* wasn't precisely correct, since she could *see* fresh tire tracks in the dirt drive, Yolanda's screen door flapping in the wind, and an overturned rocking chair on the front porch.

She exchanged a glance with Spense, and he immediately took the lead, motioning her to stay back. He crept around the perimeter of the house, Glock drawn, systematically clearing the outdoor area. Caitlin noticed a barn in the distance, but understood they'd have to deal with the house first. When she tried to follow him into the home, Spense shoved her back. That wasn't about their argument. She knew no matter what, he'd protect her with his life. Whatever issues they had between them would be dealt with . . . or not, at a later time.

"Clear!" Spense called out. Then yelled again, "I need you in here."

Not good. The only reason she could think of that would make him call for her help was a medical emergency. Barreling through the door, she caught sight of him kneeling on the floor in a side room. A woman's body lay supine, blood pooling around her neck and shoulders.

Spense pressed a scarf to her neck. "Throat's cut."

Caitlin squatted on the other side of the woman. She recognized her from photos as Yolanda Langhorne. Touching two fingers to Yolanda's neck, she looked up at Spense.

"She's got a pulse. Breathing, too."

Barely.

And she was unconscious. Beside Yolanda's hand, lay a cell phone and a shattered photograph. Caitlin saw bars on the phone. Picked it up to dial 911. Then heard approaching sirens. "Good work, Yolanda." Somehow, the woman had managed to call for help. "She's a fighter," she told Spense.

Caitlin ground the base of her palm on the woman's breastbone, and was rewarded with a moan—a good sign. She saw a question in Spense's eyes. "That's a sternal rub," she explained. "To check her response to pain."

Spense nodded. "What do I do?"

"Keep pressure on the wound—like you're doing now. We don't want her to bleed out before the paramedics arrive."

On cue, footsteps thundered up the porch steps, and two uniformed men burst into the house.

"Her throat's cut, but the wound is shallow. Whoever did this left her to bleed out slowly. She's breathing on her own. Pulse is present but weak. I'd estimate GCS at 6. We need to tube her now."

"You a doctor?" The bearded one dropped his equipment and got down on the ground next to Yolanda.

"Psychiatrist."

He shook his head, and Caitlin recognized his disappointment.

"Can you start a line?" he asked.

Nodding, she rummaged in his bag for an Angiocath. The second man tossed her a pair of latex gloves. She snapped them on. Luckily, she'd always been good at procedures. A moment later, she saw blood flash in the hub. "I'm in!" They had their IV.

"Nice." The second man raised a bag of fluids overhead.

"I'm in, too." The bearded paramedic had been busy inserting a breathing tube, while Caitlin and his partner tended to fluids. "Somebody wanna listen for placement?" He hooked up an Ambu bag and used it to pump air through the tube.

Caitlin grabbed a stethoscope, checking for the sound of air moving through Yolanda's lungs while the paramedic squeezed the bag.

Silence. Not good.

She saw Yolanda's abdomen rise and fall. "You're in the esophagus. Try again."

He yanked the tube. "Suction!"

A bloody field could obscure the view of the trachea, making proper tube placement difficult. He dropped the tube a second time. "How about now?"

She held her breath, listening. This time she heard the air moving evenly through the chest. "Bingo." She smiled up at him and glanced at her watch.

"Three minutes," she told Spense, as the paramedics hefted Yolanda onto a backboard and raced out the door. "I think she's got a good chance."

"We'll follow behind," Spense said.

Then Caitlin's gaze returned to that photograph, which lay shattered on the floor. She lifted it up and tapped it to clear away the glass. Her heart, already racing in her chest, picked up speed while her mind tried to process the image. The proof about Spense's family could be right here, in her hand.

She climbed to her feet. "Spense," she whispered urgently. "Look—"

He grabbed the photo from her hand, and his face went ghostly pale.

FROM THE MINUTE he'd seen that photograph, he'd known that Dutch had told Caity the truth. Now Spense stood, with his gut twisted into a hard knot, gazing at Yolanda Langhorne. Even lying in a hospital bed with bruising to the face and a bulky bandage covering her neck and shoulder, she had an air of refinement about her. She fixed crystal blue eyes on him, and he could tell she'd been a beauty in her youth. He could see that she'd be a great temptation for any man, but that didn't excuse his father's infidelity. And from what Caity had told him, Yolanda had known full well Jack Spenser was a married man.

He forced himself to relax his shoulders and steady his breathing. This woman in front of him had betrayed the principles he held dear—the ones his father had taught him. Just thinking about the pain that was about to rain down on his mother, thanks to Yolanda and, of course, his dad, made the blood pound in his head and tightened his hands into fists. And yet . . . Yolanda needed his help, and so did Dutch.

Her chin trembled, and her vulnerability tugged at his heart. She appeared close in age to his mother—another factor that made it hard to hold on to his resentment toward her. "Yolanda, do you feel well enough to talk? It's important, for Alex's sake."

Her eyes darted away from his face and back, as if his voice had startled her. She lifted a frail arm and stretched out her hand to him. "Jack. My darling, Jack."

Bile burned his throat. She'd mistaken him for his father—her lover. His father had died young, and no doubt Spense resembled him—maybe sounded like him, too. The doctors had pumped Yolanda full of morphine, so it wasn't hard to understand her mistake—but it still sickened him.

Yet no matter how hard he tried, he couldn't hate her. Stepping close to the bed, he accepted her outstretched hand. "I'm not Jack. I'm his son." He cleared his throat and with difficulty, corrected himself. "I mean, I'm his youngest son—Atticus."

"Atticus!" She clung to his hand, and a myriad of emotions braided through him. This might not be easy on him, but it had to be just as hard for her. He was the son who bore Jack's legal name, the one who'd stolen time from her own child, and yet, she seemed genuinely happy to see him. What kind of man would he be if he turned his back on her?

He looked at Caity and saw her eyes glistening. She nodded her approval, and he knew she knew: Yolanda Langhorne was about to become a part of his life. He wouldn't abandon her. That would make him just like his father. And his father was exactly the kind of man Spense never wanted to be. Not anymore.

"Yolanda, I want you to rest. But this is important. I have to ask for Alex's sake, and for your own—do you know who did this to you?"

"He said his name was Will Thresher." Her voice came out scratchy, but they were fortunate she could speak at all. The wound to her throat had been surprisingly shallow, leading Spense to agree with Caity's theory that her attacker wanted her to die a slow death. He must've believed she'd exsanguinate long before anyone found her in such an isolated spot. "But I don't think Thresher's his real name."

"Most likely not," Spense said. But he would run it through the database from his laptop. "Can you describe the man?"

She pressed her hands to her temples and winced. "I have a terrible headache."

"For Alex's sake, Yolanda," Caity said softly.

She grimaced, then offered, "He was tall, but not as tall as Alex or Atticus. He had blond, or maybe light brown hair. And . . . he said he was with the FBI. He showed me his credentials."

"Did you get a good look, or did he flash them?" Spense leaned in. He didn't believe for a minute Yolanda's attacker was FBI, but if he'd gotten hold of official credentials, that might mean he had some kind of connection with law enforcement.

"I could hardly see the card. But it didn't look the same as Alex's ID. I thought he put the card away too fast on purpose, and that it might be a driver's license. I think he lied about being FBI, just to get inside. As soon as I let him in, I was sorry. And when I saw those horrible eyes of his, I knew I'd made a terrible mistake," A tear drifted down her cheek. "And now he's after Alex."

"Do you know where Alex is? Did you tell this Thresher where he went?" he asked.

"I told him *nothing*. I would die before revealing that Alex went back to the scene of the crime." She closed her eyes and fell back on her pillow.

The scene of the crime.

At first, he thought it was just the morphine talking, and that no doubt had something to do with the odd phrasing. But Yolanda's words triggered a head rush, and he dropped into a bedside chair. He could visualize odd moments of his life, falling into place, like puzzle pieces that had never quite fit, now suddenly turned the right way.

Caity pulled the covers up to Yolanda's shoulders. "She needs rest, and I think we should wrap this up."

"I need another minute." Spense pulled the photograph they'd found on Yolanda's floor out of an envelope. He stared down at the little group pictured: his father, then him—around age seven, and next to him, a boy with bright red hair . . . and a beautiful, young Yolanda. "I don't remember this photo being taken, but I definitely remember the trip to Fort Worth—and meeting this boy and his mother."

Yolanda opened her eyes and motioned with her hand. Caity cranked the bed into a more comfortable position for her. "Your father and I both thought that trip was a terrible idea. But Dutch had seen your picture in Jack's wallet, and he kept begging to meet you. He just wouldn't give up on it. So, finally, your father agreed. I took Dutch to the stockyards, and your father brought you. We stayed in separate rooms at Miss Molly's."

"I remember," he said. They went down to the dining room. And a woman came up to the table, saying she had a boy who was going stir-crazy to be around someone his own age. Then his dad invited the woman and her son to join them for lunch. "We spent the day together at the stockyards. Watched the cattle drive through the streets. Rode rides, ate a lot of cotton candy. I'll never forget it . . ." Because he'd had such fun with that other boy—even though they'd gotten into a bundle of trouble. He'd had no idea that playmate was really his brother.

"We looked away for one minute, and you dared Alex to climb into one of the bullpens."

When the bull starting chasing the boy, Spense went in to save him. Then his father jumped in and pulled both boys out. Afterward, whenever Spense begged his dad to take him back to the stockyards, his father always gave the same answer, "No way. We're not going back to the scene of the crime." Dutch must've begged, too, and gotten the same answer.

"Your brother's in terrible trouble. He needs you, Atticus." Yolanda could barely lift her head to speak.

"You hang on to this." He pressed the photograph into her hand. "I'll get a copy when I come back with Alex. I'll find him. And you have my word, Yolanda. I'm going to bring him home safe."

Chapter Seventeen

Friday, October 18
4:00 P.M.
Fort Worth, Texas

UNTIL THEY ARRIVED at the stockyards, "Cowtown" seemed, to Caitlin, like any other major metropolitan city in this part of the country. But here, Fort Worth history came alive—especially as far as the cows were concerned. Over the centuries, this historic district might have evolved into a tourist trap, but in addition to the drugstore cowboys strolling the sidewalks, tipping their Resistols and Stetsons to the ladies, real cattlemen were still in business. Over at the exchange building, livestock auctions and big Texas-sized deals were taking place right alongside the fake shootouts, bank robberies, and saloon shenanigans.

Every day, just about this time, authentic cowhands drove an impressive herd of cattle right down Main Street. Any other time, this would've been a treat, and even in spite of present circumstances, she couldn't help feeling a rush of excitement when she noticed the crowd thickening up. The show was about to begin.

Beside her, Spense strode wordlessly. Though he wasn't giving her the silent treatment . . . exactly. On the three-hour drive here, they'd called a détente. Because of the recent attempt on their lives, the near-fatal attack on Yolanda Langhorne, and the fact that Dutch remained a fugitive from both the police and the bad guy, agreeing to temporarily table their personal beefs seemed the only sensible thing to do.

Given the urgency of their situation, Spense's razor-sharp focus on the business at hand—searching the crowd for Dutch— was appropriate. But while Spense might've been to his fair share of rodeos, the closest she'd come to witnessing an actual cattle drive was watching *City Slickers* on her DVR.

As a woman waving a giant ear of corn on a stick passed by, Caitlin's stomach gurgled. She turned her head to admire a pair of hand-tooled leather boots, stamped with pastel flowers in a store widow. But boot shopping wasn't on the list. If Dutch was here at the stockyards, as they hoped, they needed to concentrate on finding him.

Though she felt certain they'd not been followed, who was to say Yolanda's attacker—presumably the same man Spense had chased back in Preston Hollow and the same individual who'd flooded their room at the Blue Bayou with poison gas—hadn't gotten the same idea they had about where Dutch might be hiding. Yolanda hadn't told him, but it wasn't impossible he'd figured things out. She pulled her gaze off the boots.

Spense smiled at her—and that was a sight for woebegone eyes. "You like those boots?"

She shrugged. "Just assessing the environment. Looking for likely places Dutch might've gone."

"Right. He could be anywhere, including inside one of these gift shops." Spense cupped his hand over his eyes and began peering into every store they passed.

As the density of the crowd increased, it became harder to stay together, or to recognize one Stetson from another. She realized this was actually a decent place to hide in plain sight. Some of the cowboys even had bandanas pulled over their mouths and noses. Not to mention the proximity to Dallas would be very convenient if Dutch had ideas about conducting his own inquiries into Cindy's murder. He really might be here. And even with the costumes and crowds, it was a relatively small area to search. A flicker of optimism lifted her spirits. This was a hell of a mess—the police were looking to arrest Dutch for murder, she and Spense had put their jobs at risk, and a ruthless killer was after all three of them. But if only they could find Dutch, she had to believe that, together, they could figure a way out.

In the distance, she heard hooves thundering against brick. Lots and lots of hooves. She stepped back to let a family pass and came face-to-face with the fangs of a cottonmouth snake. She shuddered. She'd accidentally sidled into the doorway of a taxidermy shop. The shop gave her the creeps, with its wide display of snakes, buzzards, and cow skulls.

Then Spense reached back and took her by the hand. For a moment hope leapt in her heart, but then she realized why he'd grabbed her hand—he simply didn't want to lose her in the crowd. He yanked her out of the shop and dragged her down the street. When he picked up his pace, she had to trot behind him through a throng of not-so-pleasant people. "Sorry. Sorry!" she called back as she jolted her way through the crowd. "Do you see something?" she yelled, winding up to a full-on jog.

"Red-haired cowboy at nine o'clock." With her in tow, Spense zigzagged his way into the street.

A street full of cows.

"Spense . . ."

"Don't worry," he said, gripping her hand tighter. "They're docile unless you rile them up. Just keep moving."

Mooing, mingled with shouts from the crowd, filled her ears. One of the longhorns bumped her arm with its coarse, damp face, and she tried to put thoughts of a stampede out of her head. They made it to the other side of the road without being trampled to death, and she thanked her lucky stars. As they followed the red-haired cowboy, Spense slowed to a brisk walk, finally giving her a chance to draw a good breath. Then the scent of the herd put a damper on her will to breathe.

Keeping a low profile, they slowed up some more, hanging back until the cowboy was barely in sight. Even without the red hair, she would've recognized Dutch. His build, the way he carried himself, his posture—were uncannily like Spense's. And she would've recognized that backside anywhere. Not that she'd spent time studying Dutch's ass, but given the family resemblance, and the hours she'd logged admiring Spense from behind, she had no problem making the call. They were indeed on Dutch's tail.

A few yards later, Dutch turned and walked off road. They passed some straggling cows and cowhands, and she wondered if they were headed toward the pens. Soon they found themselves trudging across a dirt path with no one else in sight. Apparently, the jig was up, assuming it'd ever been down to begin with. No telling how long Dutch had been onto them.

He whirled around. "Get the hell away from me, will you?"

"You're welcome." Spense pulled up short and spit in the dirt.

Caitlin dropped back, giving the men their space.

"I told that one"—he raised his arm and pointed accusingly at her—"that I don't need any damn Bureau advocate. This is my problem, and I'll handle it on my own."

"Well, you're doing a swell job so far. Sheridan's got a BOLO out on you, and everyone this side of the Rio Grande is convinced you murdered your wife."

"Including you, so why not get the hell away like I asked you to do?"

"I never said I thought you killed Cindy."

"It's written all over your face, and I can hear doubt in your voice every damn time you speak."

Spense's mouth twitched from side to side. "I have some questions, yes, but that doesn't mean I've made up my mind you killed her."

"So you think I *might* be innocent. That gives me the warm fuzzies. Now take Caitlin, who's far more woman than you deserve, by the way, and go back to Dallas or to Tahiti or anywhere I'm not. I don't care, as long as I don't have to keep staring at your ugly mug. Unless, of course, you want to put a big fat target on your back, and Caitlin's, too."

"You're a little late with the heads-up." She suspected Spense's accusation was directed as much to her as to Dutch.

Dutch swept off his hat and threw it on the ground. "What happened?"

"Long story, and one I don't care to go into in the middle of a cattle drive. We'll talk back in your room. Assuming you've got one. Assuming you're not hiding out in that hole you dug yourself."

Dutch kicked his hat. "I'm staying at Miss Molly's. I'll save you the trouble of tailing me back there."

"So you really did return to the scene of the crime. That's where we stayed that weekend . . ."

Dutch rubbed his eyes with his fists, then glared at the ground. "No idea what you mean."

"That photograph your mother kept brought back a lot of memories, brother."

Dutch transplanted his glare from the dirt to Caitlin. "*She* told you."

"Didn't have to."

Why Spense felt the need to protect her, she didn't know, but she was sick of lies. No need to toss another one onto the pile. "I had to tell him, Dutch. When someone tried to kill us, I realized keeping secrets was no way to protect anyone. I know you wanted to be the one—"

In the distance, she heard a clap of thunder. Spense put out his hand in warning. He wanted her to stay out of this. *Message received.* She shut up.

"Someone tried to kill you." Air hissed through Dutch's teeth, making it sound more like an accusation than concern. This could get out of hand fast. She itched to step in and try to mediate between the two brothers, but the black look in Spense's eyes told her she'd crossed him enough for one day.

"Let's go back to Miss Molly's, and I'll tell you everything. There's a lot more you need to know." Spense's jaw clenched, and his voice sounded tightly stretched—like a rubber band about to snap.

"I don't want you hanging around." Dutch's eyes narrowed to menacing slits. "You're deadweight."

Spense came up on his toes, making him seem even taller than usual. "I'm your *brother*."

"Not hardly."

"As in not hardly my fault." The thunderclouds forming overhead were nothing compared to the lightning flashes in Spense's eyes. "I just found out a few hours ago, but seems you've known all along—and for years you've made it clear how you feel about me. So if you wanna hate me, go right ahead, but don't you dare put it on me that we never bonded over . . . over . . . whatever the hell brothers bond over."

"I don't hate you." Dutch stepped closer to Spense. He reached his hand up, and Caitlin held her breath, hoping he'd offer a gesture of friendship. Instead, he jabbed Spense in the chest. "Go back to Dallas."

Then Spense poked Dutch, and she saw his finger bend from the force. "I don't hate you either. Not leaving you here."

"Don't give a damn." Glaring at one another, the men began circling like boxers in a ring.

"Since you don't give a damn, why pick Miss Molly's? Why hide out here—in the one place we ever got to be brothers?"

"I don't want you around." Dutch stopped circling and ground the toe of his boot into the dirt.

Spense pointedly looked at a pile of manure. He inhaled a long, drawn-out breath. "I smell bullshit."

"Bullshit?"

Another clap of thunder sounded overhead, but no one seemed to care. The air was charged with so much electricity, Caitlin half expected the tumbleweeds to burst into flames.

"Bull. Shit."

Dutch slammed his fist into Spense's jaw, knocking him back a step.

Looking away, Spense rubbed his face. "I didn't pick you for my brother." His body swung back, then forward, gaining momentum. His arm came around like a wrecking ball. He punched Dutch in the nose, and blood sprayed the air.

Adrenaline fired up her muscles and sent heat rushing to her face. Spense didn't want her to interfere? Well, too damn bad. Her blood was up enough to make her want to throw a few punches herself. She wasn't going to stand by and watch Spense and Dutch beat each other up. They had a chance to be a family, and they were throwing it away like it meant nothing. "Stop it! Both of you." She tried to step between them, but it was too late. They grabbed each other by the shoulders and fell to the ground, cursing each other, and rolling around like kids in a schoolyard.

"Jack never took me fishing."

"He was always gone on business. *You* were the business."

Fists connected with guts. Bones crunched. Heads cracked.

She tried to grab Spense's collar, but he and Dutch rolled at her, and she had to jump sideways to keep her feet under her. Planting her legs wide, she pulled in a deep breath and yelled loud enough to be heard above the din of slamming fists. "Stop it! You're breaking my heart!"

Suddenly, Dutch climbed to his feet. "Get up, brother. I won't hit you again." He bent, offering Spense his hand. Spense grabbed him by the arm, yanked him down in the dirt, and let out a yelp of triumph.

Then Spense catapulted to his feet, grinning. "Get up, brother, and I won't hit *you* again." He jerked his bloodied chin toward

Caitlin. "You heard the lady. We're breaking her heart." Reaching down, he extended his hand to Dutch, this time, without tricks.

Thunder rumbled in the distance, preceding a few drops of rain, then, from nowhere, both men began to laugh. Spense and Dutch clapped each other on the back and took off in the direction of Main Street like this had been nothing more than one of the fake fights put on for the tourists, like they hadn't just kicked the tar out of each other in earnest.

Caitlin's breath whooshed out in relief. A bubble of happiness rose in her throat. It was only a small miracle, perhaps, but a miracle nonetheless. Running to keep up with them, she narrowly avoided slipping in the mud.

Minutes later, they arrived back on Main Street, where the cattle drive had now ended. The threat of rain and the lack of cattle had most people scurrying toward the parking lots. Still trailing behind, Caitlin passed a building with a big picture window. MISS MOLLY'S according to the sign.

"Hey, guys . . ." She felt a lot like a third wheel, but she couldn't help the pang of happiness that resulted from seeing the brothers ambling side by side, identical gaits, arms gesticulating wildly as they talked. They had years to catch up on, and there would be hard conversations, she knew. Spense looked over his shoulder at her and grinned, and she could see that his lower lip was split and swollen. Dried blood caked the corner of his mouth. Dutch turned, and she noted a nice shiner already forming under his left eye and a cut below his nose.

She scavenged in her purse for wet wipes, then managed to catch up with them. "You gentlemen might want to clean up a bit."

Halting, they touched their faces, then clapped each other on the back again—whole lot of that going on. Soon, they'd be bringing out the man hugs.

"You should see the other guy," Spense said, then roared back laughing. "Oh wait, you are the other guy."

Caitlin absolutely did not believe in violence as a way to solve problems, but she had to admit this fight had been like knocking the lid off a pressure cooker. If she wasn't mistaken, Spense and Dutch were bonding—like brothers should. A bittersweet sight, since at the moment, Spense had to force himself just to be civil to her. A left-out feeling came over her, but she shook it off. Spense and Dutch were getting along, and that was the important thing.

That, and staying alive.

Chapter Eighteen

Friday, October 18
4:00 P.M.
Near Fort Worth, Texas

MALACHI DIDN'T MIND a setback. He'd learned through the years that most problems were actually opportunities in disguise. He'd learned many things from his profession, both about living and about dying. Given the amount of wisdom he'd accumulated, it was really too bad he didn't have time to write one of those self-help books.

The point was, however, when he'd circled back to the hotel and learned from a chat with the desk clerk that Cassidy and Spenser had survived his hurried attempt to give them a meaningful death, he saw opportunity—not failure. It meant he got a do-over. Unfortunately, his employer didn't view the situation in the same light.

"What do you mean Cassidy and Spenser survived? I told you

to get rid of *Langhorne* and bring me the diary, not chase those two around," Hawk shouted at him in a distorted voice.

Malachi switched his phone to speaker and held it a good distance from his ear. "I thought they might lead me to Langhorne, and in a way, I was right."

"So you know where Langhorne is."

"Not exactly."

"But you do know where Cassidy and Spenser are. Because as of now, they've become my problem, too. You'll take care of them—and not for a penny more."

"Understood. But I don't know their exact whereabouts at the moment." Before Hawk could yell at him again, he added. "But I have a plan to recover the diary."

He suspected the pair would be with Dutch, and, so much the better. With all three of them together, it would be easy to secure the diary for Hawk, then eliminate them all one by one.

"Tell me where Langhorne is. Obviously, you have some idea."

It had been quite simple to deduce the location of Dutch's hideout once he'd noted Yolanda Langhorne's reaction to that photograph. In the background, he'd seen a sign that read: MISS MOLLY'S. The place turned out to be a famous old whorehouse down at the Fort Worth stockyards. One that had been converted into a bed-and-breakfast. But he wasn't ready to share that information with Hawk. Hawk was just as likely to hire someone else to do the job and maybe even try to have *him* eliminated. "As soon as I have a lock on the targets, I'll be in touch."

He heard a hiss over the phone and disconnected before his employer could object.

At the Bargain Bayou, Malachi had acted impulsively, but that had taught him a valuable lesson. This time he'd be more careful. He wouldn't let Hawk rush him. He'd take the time to plan out a truly magnificent death for his targets—starting with Caitlin Cassidy. That would give Spenser and Langhorne a chance to appreciate the Thresher in action.

It was unfortunate to be so skilled in your craft as he and yet never have anyone witness your greatness.

Almost to Fort Worth, now, he stopped his car on the side of the road, near one of those ubiquitous barbed-wire fences. He removed a pair of shears from his tool kit. Then he took the barbed wire in hand. The twisted metal made pleasing impressions on his fingertips, as he held it securely in place for clipping. Satisfied with his work, he held up the length of wire, then measured it against the radius of his right thigh.

Caitlin was fine-boned and delicate. Still, he wanted to be sure he had enough length, so he measured out a second strand, with a bit of extra tail. Next, he propped his shoe on the fence post and studied the width of his calf. A strand measured against the bulk of his lower leg would be just about the right size for his purposes.

Perhaps he'd cut a spare, in case he wanted to repeat this method. He never knew when he'd run into another soul who'd earned the right to a meaningful death.

Malachi tightened the barbed wire around his calf and observed the angry welts forming on his skin and the blood sliding in fat drops down his leg. He twisted the wire again and again, until the pain became unbearable.

Good to know about how many turns that would take.

He worked on his leg until he had the technique honed to maximum effect, then left the wire in place as he hobbled back to his car. He didn't mind the pain. He liked knowing how it felt to be on both sides of the fence. *Ha-ha.* Someday, he thought, he wouldn't mind knowing how it felt to die. He only wished his end could be as magnificent as the one he had planned for Cassidy.

As he thought about his own death, an even more brilliant idea for hers came to him. He was missing one item, but no matter, he could stop by a Home Depot along the way.

Friday, October 18
4:20 P.M.
Fort Worth, Texas

"Guys, we passed Miss Molly's already. Where are we going?" Caitlin asked, still hurrying to keep up with Dutch and Spense.

"To grab a bite and a beer. We haven't eaten all day in case you forgot. We want to see some bull riding too," Spense answered.

"So are we going to see bull riding, or are we going to grab a bite?" She didn't quite get the plan. Except that obviously it had something to do with hiding in plain sight. She understood they were really no safer shutting themselves away in the room, but she couldn't help thinking that if they could hide among the crowd, the killer could, too.

"Both," Dutch said.

She noted the way both his and Spense's eyes darted around as they walked. No matter how casual they might appear, she knew their guard was up. For them, however, being on high alert was second nature. And then the light dawned. They weren't just going to dinner, they were sniffing out the area.

The killer wasn't the only one on the hunt.

A rush of adrenaline hastened her steps. They turned the

corner, and suddenly, there, before her eyes, the world's largest honky-tonk appeared. She'd always been curious about this place. They were going to Billy Bob's.

The men had just brawled, and they looked the part. She passed out the wipes she'd pulled from her purse, but they didn't seem interested in cleaning up.

"Around here, nobody cares if you've been in a fight. Just shows you're not a damn tourist," Dutch said.

Spense put his hand on the small of her back, guiding her inside the honky-tonk. She could almost believe he'd forgiven her, but she knew that wasn't so. He was in a good mood, now that they'd found Dutch, and he would honor their détente for however long it took to get out of this jam.

Blinking hard, she waited for her eyes to adjust to the dim light inside the honky-tonk. She noticed a band set up on stage. Mixed in with the sound of too many voices talking at the same time, she heard the bray of bulls. It seemed the bulls at Billy Bob's were the real, live, fire-breathing kind.

While they waited for a table, they walked over to the arena and watched some cowboys take a ride. For a few wonderful minutes, they hadn't a care in the world. Dutch smiled—more than she'd seen him do. She suspected this was probably one of the few times since Cindy had died that he hadn't been thinking of his wife.

And Spense—his face came alive when he talked. She'd never seem him engage with another man like this. It occurred to her that as devastating as it was to learn of his father's secret life, Spense had been an only child and had probably wished for a sibling many times. Now he had a brother. She was in no hurry for the hostess to seat them. She wanted this moment to last as long as possible. Too soon, the beeper went off, and a young woman, dressed in skintight jeans and red boots, led them to a table near the dance floor.

Dutch ordered a pitcher of Lone Star and a rattlesnake appetizer for the table. The snake tasted like chicken. Caity had melt-in-your-mouth ribs. Spense and Dutch both started in on their T-bones like it'd been years, not hours, since their last meal, Spense, apparently suspending his heart-healthy diet in honor of the occasion, or because, given the menu, it was that or starve.

Then the band came back from break. As they made adjustments to their setup, a few couples made their way to the edges of the big, sawdust-covered dance floor.

"By special request for Beau and Jen's thirty-third wedding anniversary." The gravelly voice of the lead singer battled with feedback from the microphone. He plucked a few strings of his guitar to ensure it was tuned to his satisfaction, and the other band members joined in with their instruments. The lead man began to croon "Lookin' for Love" in a deep bass tone that sounded as though it had been seared with a Texas branding iron.

Tilting his head toward Caitlin, Dutch elbowed Spense. She smiled and tried to make eye contact with Spense, but he refused to look up from his plate. He carved out a bite of steak and brought it obliviously to his mouth.

Whatever.

She shouldn't expect him to get over this so easily. He'd been deeply hurt. But he seemed to be madder at her than at anyone else involved. She pulled her shoulders up. He was funneling his anger for his father into a bucket, then dumping it all on her. She might be a psychiatrist, and she might be familiar with *displacement* as a psychological defense mechanism, but that didn't make it fair, and it didn't make it hurt any less.

Dutch squinted at Spense and threw down his napkin in apparent disgust. "Care to dance, Caitlin?"

"I'd love to. But I have to warn you, I don't know the two-step."

"No worries. It's really easy . . . just two steps." His grin was wide. "Let's give it a whirl." Reaching over, he pinched Spense's shoulder. "While I dance with this beautiful woman, you stay here and keep a lookout."

Despite Dutch's joking manner, she knew he was serious, and he pulled the brim of his Resistol lower, obscuring his face.

As she thought about the trouble Dutch was in—the trouble they were *all* in—that momentary feeling of safety vanished. No doubt they'd made some missteps, not the least of which was lying to Spense. But there was no going back now. From here on out, the three of them had to stick together. And if the men could keep up the appearance of a happy trio out on the town, so could she.

She and Dutch elbowed their way to an open spot on the dance floor. With his hand low on her back, he easily led her in time with the music.

"You're a good dancer," she said.

"My mother taught me." He pulled her in and dipped her. "Spense might've had more time with Jack, but I was the only apple of Mom's eye. And Jim was around a lot when I was growing up, too. Dad asked him to look out for me when he was away— which was most of the time, I guess."

"I'm sorry."

"Don't be. I am who I am, in large part, because of the weirdness. Made me tough. Opened my eyes to the fact most people, sooner or later, are going to let you down. Doesn't mean you don't love them."

She nodded. Wondering if that was how he felt about Cindy. She'd let Dutch down, but he loved her anyway.

"And for the record, I understand why you told Spense the truth. I'm not mad, and now that the hand's been played, I'm glad it's all out in the open. I do wish I hadn't put you in the middle, though. I can't help noticing that things are a little tense between my brother and you."

"He thinks I betrayed him."

"Then he's a fool." He twirled her beneath his arm. "He won't stay mad forever, Caitlin. Mark my words." Dutch pulled her close and gave her a quick kiss on the top of her head, and then he spun her—around and around and around, until breathless, she begged him for mercy. Her gaze landed on Spense, who'd pulled his chair out from the table and was watching them. She shot him a big smile, but his expression didn't alter. Her knees threatened to buckle, and Dutch had to shore her up.

What if Dutch was wrong?

What if Spense never forgave her?

Chapter Nineteen

Saturday, October 19
10:15 A.M.
Fort Worth, Texas

Spense pulled up a chair close to where Dutch hunkered on the edge of a bed covered by a red velvet spread. Miss Molly's décor paid tribute to its early days as a one of the most popular brothels in the Wild West. Dutch's room was named for its former "hostess," Miss Josie.

Spense and Caity had bunked in with Dutch last night. Caity had scored the bed, while Spense and Dutch made do with pallets on the floor. Spense was less than thrilled with the accommodations, but when he asked Dutch why he hadn't selected the "Gunslinger" room, Dutch explained that since he was on the lam, he'd thought it best to book the only room with the private bath—even if it did have lace curtains and floral wallpaper.

Last night, Spense and Caity had relayed the whole story to Dutch of what had happened in Jefferson, and they'd been going round and round the same argument ever since. Arguing with Dutch was exhausting, but on the bright side, it didn't leave Spense much time to dwell on Caity's betrayal, which was proving harder to deal with than Jim Edison's or even his father's. "I didn't just promise Yolanda I'd bring you home, Dutch. I promised her I'd bring you home *safe*."

"Yet you expect me to just leave her lying alone in some hospital room. What if she were your mother?"

"She's not *lying alone* in a hospital room. I called in some favors and arranged a couple of private bodyguards to stay with her. And to answer your question, if she were my mother, I'd hope I'd have the level head to do the right thing. And the right thing, at the moment, is biding our time. Right now, you're in trouble from all sides. Sheridan is hell-bent on locking you up, and now that you've 'fled,' Jim's washed his hands of you." He cleared his throat. "He doesn't know we're looking for you."

"You mean he doesn't know you found me." Dutch tugged a thread on his shirtsleeve. "You're sure you want to stick? You're willing to risk everything to help me—a guy you don't even like? Just because I'm your brother doesn't mean you have to flush your future alongside mine."

Spense squared his gaze with Dutch's. "Good luck getting rid of me." He was now absolutely convinced of Dutch's innocence. Just as he was, now, absolutely convinced that Dutch was his brother. He didn't need a DNA test for proof—in either matter. But there was one thing still bothering him. "They say there was blood spatter on your shirt, consistent with blowback from a gunshot wound. Any idea what that's about?"

Dutch raised an eyebrow. "When I first found Cindy, it was obvious she was dead, and beyond help, but I couldn't stop myself from checking her anyway. I remember leaning over her, listening for breathing and feeling for a pulse. I'm guessing that's how the blood got there."

"Then the experts are wrong about the 'blowback spatter.'" Certainly wouldn't be the first time. Unlike DNA, blood-spatter analysis was highly subjective.

Dutch looked away, then said, in a low voice. "I don't know what changed between us, but . . ."

"I know," Spense said. "I'm glad, too." He wasn't an emotional guy. But finding out he had a brother was testing his equanimity. One minute he was pissed as hell and lashing out at Dutch, the next, he was planning a brothers' fishing trip in his head for when this was all over. There was a long, awkward pause, and he changed the subject. "Yolanda's description of her attacker fits the man I chased out of your house in Preston Hollow. And that's a good thing. Surely, even Sheridan will have to admit you didn't stage the attack on your own mother."

"One thing that doesn't point to my guilt. I guess it's something," Dutch agreed.

The bathroom door opened. Then Caity, looking fresh as the petunias on Miss Molly's front porch, emerged, bringing the scent of jasmine soap into the room along with her. "Thanks for loaning me your shower," she said to Dutch as she pulled a chair up to join them.

Steeling himself against the sweetness in her smile, Spense brought her up to speed on the conversation. Every time she walked into a room, he wanted to wrap his arms around her and say *sorry*, tell her he understood why she'd done what she'd done . . . but the truth was he didn't understand, and he couldn't seem to let it go. For months now, every time he'd looked at her, he'd imagined what a life with her might be like. He'd even pictured kids and a big house, a family dog—the whole nine yards. But never once had he pictured her deceiving him. Caity was the most straight-up, honest person he'd ever met. And maybe that was the problem. Caity had been the one and only person he'd thought he could count on unconditionally.

"As far as the mystery man," Caity jumped right into the conversation, making it easier to put his conflicted emotions aside and focus on business. "Yolanda gave us a name, but we haven't had a chance to run it yet."

Dutch's posture straightened. "He told her his name?"

"Not likely," Spense said. That was one reason they hadn't rushed to run it—it was almost certainly a fake. The other was that logging onto the Bureau's databases might alert Jim to their whereabouts. "But he claimed he was FBI and said his name was Will Thresher."

"The guy said *Thresher*?" Dutch got to his feet and prowled the perimeter of the room, running his hands through his hair as he did. "Something about that name is familiar." He came back and sat on the bed again. At last, he jerked his chin up. "Got it. Back in the day, even before I got put on counterterrorism, I was assigned to violent crimes. Not for long, just a month or two. But there was a local guy on the squad's radar. Sort of a jack-of-all-trades badass—hired himself out for all kinds of crap. Everything from petty theft to murder." Dutch pressed his fingers to his temples, as if concentrating hard. "I'm almost certain he called himself the Thresher."

"Could be coincidence, but I'm not much of a believer in those." Ideas rapid-fired through Spense's brain. This could turn out to be their first real break in the case.

"So then, you're saying this guy who's after us is just the hired help—the tip of the iceberg." Caity seemed to be working to keep her voice steady.

If she was scared, she had a right to be. There very well might be a monster behind the monster. "Even if our guy is not this *Thresher*, he's likely to be a hit man." Nothing else really made sense at this point. At least not to Spense.

"All the more reason for you two to go back to Dallas and let me handle things from here. It's too dangerous to hang around me," Dutch said.

"Well, it's a little late for that now. I've seen this guy's face, and he's seen both mine and Caity's. The three of us are in this for the duration, whether we like it or not." And Spense didn't like it one bit. "Believe me, if there was any way I could safely send Caity packing, I'd do it in a heartbeat."

The look on her face said it all. Just about every time he opened his mouth, he hurt her. But he couldn't think about that. Right now, he had to pull his attention back to the case.

"I've been answering your questions all morning, Dutch. So now I've got one for you. Your whole life, you've been keeping secrets to protect other people. Your mother, our father," he hesitated. "Me. So I'll tell you what I think. I think you're holding something back now. Trying to protect Cindy. You think that by keeping what's in that diary a secret, you're looking out for her. When the truth is, if you don't tell us what's in it, we can't help you find her killer. And I'm assuming you want to find the bastard—or else you'd be lying on a beach in Mexico, not hanging out in Fort Worth, just thirty miles from the scene of the crime."

"Did you miss the part, back in Dallas, where I told you that I do not have Cindy's diary?"

"You also told Caity if you did have it, you wouldn't turn it over to Sheridan."

"But I don't have it. And at some point, you have to start trusting me. It's a crying shame that I know where I stand with Caitlin better than I do with my own brother."

"I believe you didn't kill your wife. Isn't that enough?"

"No. It's not. And I'll give you sixty seconds to decide if you can trust me from here on out. Otherwise, I don't want you on my team."

He dragged a hand over his face, trying to cover his indecision. "You've lied to me for what, let's see, all our lives, but now you expect me to believe every damn word you say. Have I got that right?"

"Damn straight."

Caity raised her eyebrows and checked her watch. "Looks like you still have thirty seconds on the clock, Spense." She put her hand on his shoulder.

The first time she'd reached out to him since the blowout over his father.

"I get that it's hard to believe someone who's lied." She cleared her throat nervously, and he knew she wasn't just talking about his brother. "But put yourself in Dutch's place. Do you really want to go back to the way the two of you were before, or do you want to suck it up and decide to trust him?"

Still unsure of his response, he went for his pocket, then stopped himself, remembering he no longer had a cube to help him think. Suddenly, the room was too damn small. He had to get out of there, but there was nowhere to go. He looked up, searching his brother's face for answers.

"I don't have the diary. I'm not lying to protect Cindy, or anyone else. I did a piss-poor job of protecting her while she was alive, and yes, I intend to find the fucker who did this, and when I do . . ."

Caity showed her watch. "Ten seconds."

Spense knew she didn't want Dutch to dwell on what he'd do to Cindy's killer. He'd have to keep a close watch over him to be sure he didn't do anything that would land him in jail when they found the guilty party—but first, they had to smoke that guilty party out.

He closed his eyes, then opened them to find both Dutch and Caity staring at him. His throat worked in a dry swallow. It was time to give his answer. In truth, he had absolutely no way to know whether or not Dutch was still withholding information from him. The only thing he had was his word . . . so he guessed it was just like Caity said. This was a decision, plain and simple. It was his choice to believe in his brother or not. He let out a long, relieved breath. "I want to stay on your team, Dutch." He paused to collect himself, then added. "I trust you."

Then Dutch, too, heaved out a breath. It was like looking into a very strange mirror.

Caity put one hand on each of their shoulders. "Good. We're all on the same team. But, I also have issues." She leveled a hard gaze at Dutch. "We know you don't have the diary, because you told us, and we believe you. But Jim thinks you ran off with it, so it's not a big leap to think others think so, too—like Sheridan and our mystery man. The man who tossed your house and went after your mother took no valuables. He was almost certainly looking for Cindy's diary. So I have to ask . . . have you read it? Do you have any idea what might be in it that would make someone willing to kill just to get his hands on it? Because it seems that whoever is after us, is after the diary—or maybe it's vice versa—whoever is after the diary is after us. Not sure which is the chicken."

Dutch leaned forward earnestly. "That's my operating assumption, too—someone wants Cindy's diary. And if they're chasing you chasing me, they must believe I have it, or at least that I know what's in it." Dutch fisted his hands. "I wish to hell I had read it. Part of me wanted to know what was in it so badly that I went on a search for it one day. And I found it, too, hidden under her mattress. But I couldn't bring myself to read it. So I just walked into the kitchen and handed it to her. I told her she needed to find a better hiding place if she were going to keep a secret from an FBI agent. Then I suggested she get it out of my sight before I changed my mind and read every humiliating word aloud to the cook."

"You did that in front of the cook?" Caity's eyes widened.

Dutch cast his gaze downward. "Yes. Cindy got so upset, she ran out of the kitchen crying. And I didn't go after her. I didn't do a lot of things I should've done." He sent Spense a meaningful look.

Obviously, Dutch was alluding to something he thought Spense needed to do with Caity. But again, he couldn't process that now.

Caity sorted through some items in her purse and came up with a tissue. Dutch waved her off, then used his shirtsleeve to blot his eyes instead.

Spense didn't understand why women always had Kleenex and wipes on them. The only thing he carried around that consistently was his Glock. "You thought the entries would be humiliating."

"I assumed the diary contained the sordid details of her affairs."

Unfortunately, that seemed like a good assumption to Spense. "If that's the case, then the most logical suspect would be someone who had an affair with Cindy, and who didn't—who doesn't—want the information in her diary to get out."

"Maybe Cindy threatened to blackmail one of her lovers, then, in a fit of rage he killed her. But now he needs the diary." Caity sounded unconvinced.

"Then the blackmailed lover slash killer hired a hit man to steal the diary?" Spense didn't like the theory much. He still thought there was something bigger going on.

Caity shrugged as if she really didn't believe the blackmail theory either even though she'd proposed it.

"It's not that far-fetched." Dutch tugged at his chin. "Let's suppose, for the sake of argument, Cindy was involved in some kind of blackmail scheme. Anyone she hung around had money, so it's plausible. And if her lover killed her in a fit of rage, he'd know the diary would not only reveal the affair, but now it would implicate him in her murder. Suddenly, the stakes have been raised. This individual is not, by nature, a killer, and it would be much harder to come after me, a special agent, than it was to murder my wife. He needs help. So he hires a jack-of-all-trades bad guy to get the diary and eliminate anyone who *might* have read it—meaning me—and now, unfortunately, the two of you."

Spense liked that only slightly better. Something about the blackmail idea seemed half-right. He just didn't know which half.

Dutch tilted his face toward the ceiling, staring for a few seconds. "Only . . . Cindy didn't have a mean bone in her body. And she certainly didn't need cash. She's not the type to blackmail anyone, so I guess we're back to square one."

"Maybe not." Caity looked from one to the other of them with obvious excitement. "Dutch may not know what's in the diary, but he's seen it. He knows what it looks like."

"So?" Spense asked, intrigued, but not following.

"So, if our hired gun is after the diary, maybe we should give it to him." She looked at them expectantly.

They looked back at her, blankly.

"What color is the diary, Dutch?"

Dutch gripped the bedspread. "It was a pink cloth journal with one of those cheap locks that would open if you even looked at the key from across the room."

Spense smiled. Oh yeah. Caity was right on the money.

"I'm going shopping in a bit." Caity smiled. "You think if I bring back a few pink diaries, you could pick the one most similar in size and appearance? Then I'll write some entries, so they'll be in a feminine hand."

"I've got a tracking device in my go bag," Spense said.

"We can fix that under the binding somehow, shouldn't be hard," Dutch added. "But if this is the Thresher, he's not stupid. He's been evading the FBI for years. We can't just leave the diary sitting around in our room, or he'll never believe it's real."

"We have to make him believe it's real," Caity said. "We'll hide it somewhere we'd put it if we never wanted him to find it. And then, we'll find a way to lead him to it."

"What if he opens it?" Spense was thinking aloud.

"He won't," Dutch said.

"How can you be so sure?"

"Because the Thresher isn't the type who cares. He's not curious—he's calculating. But even if I'm wrong, and he opens it, we'll make sure there are enough entries that it could pass for Cindy's journal. I'll give Caity the names of Cindy's friends and the details of her routines. We'll make him believe it's real, then . . ."

"We follow the diary," Spense said.

"And it leads us straight to the puppet master." Caitlin spread her hands wide.

"A decoy diary. Not a bad idea for a civilian." Dutch reached out his hand to Caity. "You can play on my team anytime you want."

Spense shook his head. "Except she's not going shopping for diaries."

"Why not? I thought we were hiding in plain sight," she said.

"Who told you that?"

"It's obvious. When we found Dutch, he was walking around town like he owned the place."

"She's right." Dutch said. "I'm a firm believer that it's better to blend in than to hide. That's how you become truly invisible. And if I do get caught, I want to be able to say I wasn't trying to evade arrest. I was just taking a break. Having myself a little fun down at the stockyards."

"No one's looking for a woman on her own. Both of you are well over six feet. I'll blend in a lot better without you men guarding me, and the shop I have in mind is literally next door. I can do this."

Spense folded his arms. "I'm sure you can, Caity. This isn't about your ego, though. There's no reason to risk you going out on the street on your own. You stay here with Dutch, and I'll get the diary."

She looked to Dutch for help, but he just turned his palms up as if to say he was going to stay out of this one. "Okay, but I think you're being overly cautious."

"How is that a bad thing?"

"I guess it's not." Caity shrugged.

Dutch got to his feet. "The real problem may be getting the

Thresher, if that's who he is, out to the stockyards. No one knows we're here."

"Last night, we used cash because we didn't want to leave a trail. Now we want to lead our assailant to us, so, I'll use my credit card at the shop next door. If this guy is worth his salt, he'll be able to track us. It might take a few days, but he'll find us. And when he does, we'll 'accidentally' lead him to the diary," Spense said.

Dutch frowned. "I'm the one going shopping, though, and I'm using my own card. I don't want you two in any more trouble with the Bureau, in case Jim's watching your transactions."

"You do realize your purchase might not just lead the Thresher to us. Sheridan could pick up the scent, too," Spense warned. The plan was good but risky. They were baiting a killer and leaving a trail of breadcrumbs for Sheridan at the same time.

"That's a chance I'm willing to take. From what I've seen of Sheridan's investigative acumen, my money's on the Thresher to find us first." Dutch turned to Caity. "Start thinking up some believable entries. Because if this doesn't work, we're going to be in even more danger than before."

Chapter Twenty

MALACHI STOOD FROZEN on the sidewalk, blinking in the bright sunlight. It was too noisy for him here in the stockyards. Even with his headphones on, he could hear disharmonious sounds wafting off the passersby. He pulled his headphones off, checking to see if the batteries had gone dead.

Ah. Yes, that was the problem.

Relieved, he dug in his pocket for his spares, replaced the batteries and was good to go. He smiled at a lady in a blue dress, and she smiled back. This wasn't such a bad place after all. He strolled up one end of the street and down another, looking for just the right spot but not finding what he needed: someplace quiet. Not just for the sake of his sensitive ears, either. The location had to be near enough for convenience but far away from prying eyes. If not soundproofed, it should at least have thick walls to cover the screams—just in case.

In addition, he'd need electricity.

He walked long enough to grow sore feet and was thinking of sitting down. But the benches were crowded, and he didn't like the idea that someone might try to speak to him. Most people's voices were unpleasant. Then, off in the distance, he spotted a building with boarded-up windows, set well back from the thoroughfare with an alleyway behind it.

Just might work.

It took him ten minutes, walking across a field to reach the place. Then using a bump key, he entered via the back door. He tried the lights. Excellent. The electricity was on. He flipped the lights back off. Based on the saddles and ropes strewn about, it looked like an old tack shop that had gone under. He headed back to his Escalade, whistling all the while. He'd found the perfect device for Caitlin's magnificent death at the home store, but it was far too heavy to carry to the abandoned shop on foot.

Chapter Twenty-One

Saturday, October 19
1:45 P.M.
Fort Worth, Texas

THREE HOURS LATER, Caity laid the finished diary on the desk in Dutch's room. "How did I do? You think this will work?"

Spense flipped through the pages. "Definitely looks like a woman's handwriting."

"Glad to hear it." She wrinkled her nose at him, and he realized how lame his compliment had been. She passed the diary to his brother. "I wanted Dutch to look at it, not you. He's the one who would know if it will pass muster."

Dutch took a minute with the entries, then nodded. "Looks like you got her schedule right. Wednesday's bringing breakfast to the senior center. Friday's volunteering at the Boys and Girls Club . . ." His voice dropped off. "She was a good woman. I know what everyone thinks, but I'm telling you, Cindy had a big heart."

Caity gave him a hug. "I had that feeling when I was composing these entries. Thanks for trusting me with them."

A long, sad silence followed.

"We'll get him, Dutch. We're not going to rest until we do." Spense looked to Caity for help. He didn't know what else to say to comfort Dutch. But as it turned out, his brother wasn't going to give him a chance to offer sympathy.

Dutch was already pulling on his Resistol and tucking the journal beneath his shirt. "I'll go bury this thing now, while I have the chance."

Spense nodded. "I'll come with you. We just need to stop by the car. I've got a bag with a tracking device in the trunk. It's faster for two to dig a hole than one, and, frankly, you might look suspicious burying the thing. Just in case this Thresher is smarter than we think and has made his way here already, I'd rather stick with you while you're wandering around in the boonies."

Caity pulled on her shoes.

Spense looked to his brother. "I think she'd be better off here."

"Agreed," Dutch nodded. "As long as she locks the doors and doesn't leave the room, it's probably safer. We have to go off the main streets to bury this thing, so there's not a lot of blending in with the crowds for cover."

Caity slipped off her shoes, then said emphatically, "You're going with Dutch, Spense. I promise not to open the door."

She must've read his mind. He didn't like leaving her here alone, but using his head, not his heart, it seemed like the best plan all around. Dutch needed him for backup in case things went south. It was broad daylight, and Caity would be locked in a bed-and-breakfast with plenty of people around inside and out. Surely, that was safer than if she came with them to the deserted areas of the stockyards where they planned to bury the decoy.

SATISFIED WITH HIS setup, Malachi closed the door to the abandoned shop and headed over to Miss Molly's. He didn't know for sure that's where his targets would be, but he had a good feeling about it.

He parked his truck behind the bed-and-breakfast and strolled inside.

"We're full up." A pretty young thing, about twenty, and wearing booty shorts told him.

"Oh, too bad. My wife had her heart set on this place. But maybe I could look around, in case we want to come back sometime."

"Where's your wife?"

"She's down the street with the little one. Took him for ice cream."

"Won't that spoil his lunch?"

"We already ate."

The pretty young thing smiled. "Well, you can look around if you like, but I can't show you the rooms. They're occupied, like I said."

"No worries. I'll just check out the lay of the land." He headed past the lobby and dining room over to the guest rooms, then paced up and down the hallway, listening for the sound of humming. When he reached the third door on the left, he heard the music of souls.

Perfect.

They were here, or at least they'd been here.

He exited by the front, thanking the hostess on his way out.

Then he planted himself behind a hitching post and waited. As long as he had his headphones, he could be out here all day. No problem.

But he didn't need all day.

Moments later, he saw Dutch Langhorne and Atticus Spenser amble out of Miss Molly's, and Caitlin Cassidy wasn't with them. This was going to be far easier than he'd thought. He had to make a fast choice between following the men and grabbing the girl, but securing Caitlin first made the most sense. Even with his skills, he'd need an advantage to take on two FBI agents at once.

He'd been prepared to wait however long it took for the trio to separate, and maybe even to create a diversion, like pulling a fire alarm. But it wasn't necessary. Caitlin was alone. He could nab her, then use her to get the upper hand on the men before ending her—magnificently.

The small bed-and-breakfast was all but empty of tourists. This time, he went around to the service entrance, found a maid's cart, and pushed it down the hall like he belonged. Excitement trilled within him as he tapped his knuckles on the third door from the left. "Maintenance."

Good thing he'd been careful enough to invent a cover. A woman who was definitely not Caitlin Cassidy opened the door and said she didn't need him.

A quiver of doubt assailed him but dissipated after a moment's consideration. The humming must have been transmitted through the thin walls from the room next door. There was no other way to account for his error.

Sure enough, in the neighboring room, he hit pay dirt.

There was a brief pause, then Caitlin's distinctly sweet voice came through the door. "I didn't call for maintenance. We're fine here."

No matter. He'd anticipated she'd be too clever to open the door and that she'd pretend she wasn't alone.

He knocked again. "There's a leak coming from your bathroom into the basement. I need to get in there."

"I'm sorry, but you'll have to come back."

His fingers twitched at his sides. "It's a bad leak. I need to fix it now."

Another pause, and then, "I'll call the front desk to verify first. And I'd like the clerk to come inside with you."

"No problem," he said, smiling as he slipped his bump key into the lock. Lucky for him this old building kept to tradition and used good old-fashioned keys.

A minute later, he was inside.

Caitlin Cassidy had her back turned, standing at the bedside, holding the receiver to an antique dial-up phone—another throwback to a previous time.

The humming in the room made his blood pump ferociously through his body. He jetted across the carpet, grabbed her from behind, and stuffed a medicated rag into her mouth.

"Fuck!" He took an elbow to the gut, and crammed the rag deeper into her throat with his fingers until only gurgling sounds came forth.

She slammed her heel into his instep, and pain shot up his leg.

Oh, my, she was a fighter. Better for him this way. Much more magnificent.

Somehow, she twisted around and looked at him with hellfire in her eyes.

The humming got louder, and his dick got harder.

Hers was no ordinary soul.

She head-butted him. Tried to hit him in the face with the phone, but missed. Then her arm went limp. He heard a dial tone as the receiver fell from her hand. Her wild, roving eyes told him she knew she was losing this battle. Spurred on by her panicked breathing, he got his hands around her neck.

Squeezed.

The humming undulated sweetly around the room.

He was the maestro, and she was his Stradivarius.

At last, her gasping ceased. He'd taken all her air. She struggled only a moment longer. He squeezed one last time, inhaling the pungent smell of her fear. She released her urine, and her body went limp.

He yanked the sheets from the bed, doused them with chloroform, then laid her on top, bundling her like dirty laundry. He searched the small room, but of course the diary wasn't there. He knew it wouldn't be. But no matter. He had Caitlin, and that would be enough to get both the men and the diary.

He stuffed her into the cart that waited in the hall and wheeled her to his Escalade. On his way out, the woman next door peeked from her room.

He gave her a jaunty wave.

Chapter Twenty-Two

Saturday, October 19
2:30 P.M.
Fort Worth, Texas

It WAS LIKE those first few, disoriented moments when you waken from a bad dream. Only this time, as Caitlin blinked hard, no familiar objects came into focus. No relief chased away the shadows in her brain, and she had the terrible sense that when she came fully awake, things were only going to get worse.

Her lids closed heavily over her eyes.

The world tilted.

A seasick feeling in her gut told her she was going to heave up her stomach contents, but she couldn't for the life of her remember what she'd eaten . . . or where she was. She sucked in air through her mouth, trying to calm the storm in her stomach, but it was too late. A robust wave shook her body, and a violent spasm overtook her belly. She was dry heaving. Her brain sloshed in her skull like mush in a bowl. She'd been through this before—her first thought was carbon monoxide poisoning. Was she back at the Bargain Bayou?

Where am I?

"Open your eyes, Caitlin. I know you're awake."

She couldn't place the man's voice though she recognized the drawl as Texan. His tone was friendly, though impatient, like a child waiting for his playmate to come out and join him in the day's games. Another wave of nausea rolled over her but dissipated without realizing its full potential.

"Dr. Cassidy, can you hear me?" The voice grew sharper, more impatient.

She nodded, then, with great effort, battled her eyes open again, to find herself looking through a filmy layer of goo.

She felt a light touch on her hand.

Then cold fingers quickly pulled away from her skin. "It's okay. I put some ointment in your eyes to keep them from drying out."

What the fuck?

Through the haze, a fat orb bobbed closer and closer. At first she saw only colors, like an impressionist painting, but eventually a man's face came into focus. Kaleidoscope blue eyes, dirty blond hair—just like the man Yolanda had described.

The Thresher.

A scream rose in her throat but died at her lips. He'd taped her mouth shut. Thank God nothing came up out of her stomach, or she'd have choked on her vomit. She lifted her hand to yank away the tape, but couldn't move her arm more than a few inches. Her shoulders ached. She turned her head from side to side and realized her hands were hooked behind her body. Cold metal pinched her wrists.

Handcuffs!

A thick rope wound around her body, securing her to a chair. The room was empty save for the Thresher's chair, a worktable with tools scattered on top, and some contraption behind and to the side of her that she couldn't quite make out.

Panic knocked the cobwebs off her brain.

She might not know where she was, but at least she knew who she was. And Caitlin Cassidy was not about to do whatever some hired hit man ordered her to do, simply because he'd drugged her—obviously—roped her to a chair, and cuffed her hands behind her back.

Defiantly, she raised her eyes.

"That's better." He had a tissue in his hand and swiped her eyes, removing the excess ointment. "Sometimes people don't fully close their eyes when they're unconscious. I didn't want your corneas to dry out."

He seemed to be expecting a thank-you.

And those crazy eyes of his. Something was definitely off with this hit man. She had the distinct feeling she was more than just a job to him.

"If you give me your word not to scream, I'll take the tape off your mouth. No one can hear you in here, but I'd rather not have to deal with a shrieking woman. I'm rather sensitive to noise."

A pair of headphones hung around his neck. He must have some serious noise aversion.

"Do I have your word?"

Another wave of nausea hit. Maybe the next time, something would come up. She needed to get this tape off her mouth. She nodded.

"All right. One quick"—he ripped the tape from her mouth—"pull."

"Th-thank you," she managed in a scratchy voice. She needed to make him think she was docile, cooperative, everything he hoped for in a victim. Then when he least expected it, she'd turn the tables.

"Would you like some water?"

She nodded again, saving her voice—for screaming later.

"Just take a few sips, I don't want you to get sick."

Neither did she. As he held a paper cup to her parched lips, she swallowed cautiously. The cool water soothed her burning throat. "Where are we?"

"Curious little monkey, aren't you?" He smiled, as if pleased. He wanted to talk to her. Why else would he remove the gag? He really had been waiting for her to come out and play. And that was good. If he wanted to interact with her, he'd have to keep her alive to do it. He seemed to like her, and that meant she had leverage.

"We're somewhere safe. Has anyone ever told you, you have a positively mellifluous soul?"

No. And she didn't have time to focus on his crazy. Her heart contracted at the thought he might have Spense and Dutch, too. "Are we . . . *alone*?"

"Your friends are close by." His Adam's apple bobbed. "Perhaps they can save you."

So he *didn't* have them. If he did, he'd be crowing to her about it. She worked to keep the relief from showing in her face.

"Don't look so happy. I said they *might* be able to save you."

She waited.

"If they have Cindy Langhorne's diary, and if they're smart enough to cooperate. Otherwise, I wouldn't want to be you."

She didn't play coy with him, pretending not to understand. She wanted him to believe they had the journal, and that they'd hidden it carefully from him. "I'll take you to the diary, myself," she tried. Though, unfortunately, she didn't actually know where Spense and Dutch had concealed the decoy. Then another spasm swept over her, this time it was of involuntary laughter. All that effort to use Dutch's credit card, trying to create a trail for the Thresher to follow, and he'd been there all along. He'd found them on his own. He'd played right into their hands—in his own horrible way. She neared hysteria.

He covered his ears with his hands. "Stop it!"

She gasped, trying to regain control of herself. If she made him too angry, he'd tape her mouth again. "I-I'm sorry. I laugh when I'm nervous. Just give me a second. I won't do it again."

He shook his head. "I suppose you might know where the diary is, but I don't trust you."

Another peal of laughter assailed her. "But you trust those two? Then you're a fool."

His fist slammed into her cheek, cracking against the bone. She tried to pull in a breath but couldn't. She closed her eyes, anticipating the next blow.

Boom.

There it came, but this punch knocked the breath back *into* her.

You son of a bitch. "I only meant that you can trust me because you have complete control of me. What can I possibly do when I'm in your custody?"

"If I untie you, you can lead me on a merry chase, or straight into a trap."

"What makes you think they won't?" Part of her wanted him to find the men because they had laid him just such a trap. But she'd much rather be the one who led him into it. If only there were a way to keep Spense and Dutch out of it, and safe.

"They'll take me straight to the diary. Because if they don't, you'll die." He leaned in, and she could smell mint on his skin. "And what a death it will be." Smiling, he spread his arms. Then like a magician, pulled something out of his sleeve.

A long strand of barbed wire.

She recoiled in the chair as much as her bindings permitted.

"Your outfit is a bit drab. I think you could use a few accessories."

Her heartbeat rocketed into outer space as he approached, then draped one long piece of barbed wire around her waist, in between the ropes that bound her to her seat. He wound it just tightly enough to stay in place. The sharp barbs scratched her skin like brambles on a bush.

"There, that belt looks quite nice on you, don't you think? But it's not enough. We need one more thing."

He stroked the hollow of her throat with his thumb, and she had to fight off another retch. "A pretty barbed-wire necklace would be just the right touch."

She forced herself to remain perfectly still while he wound another length of barbed wire around her throat. Again, just enough to stay in place, and this time the barbs, pricking her bare skin, drew blood. Looking down, she watched a drop make its way from her neck to her chest.

Don't move.

Any resistance might anger him and make him tighten the "necklace." She didn't know what kind of game he had in mind, but by now, she was absolutely certain he was a sadist. Her hysteria replaced itself with a deadly calm.

He snapped a picture of her with his phone.

Light cracked through the boarded-up windows, but the

semidarkness had a terrible effect on her spirits. The man placed his headphones on his ears. He stepped behind her, fumbling with the belt and necklace, then a soft, mechanical whir echoed through the room.

"What's that?" she asked, fighting to keep the bile down and her voice calm.

He walked to the door, and she saw he held a remote control in his hand. He pressed a button on the remote.

The whirring grew louder.

He stepped outside, and she heard the door lock behind him.

MALACHI RUBBED MORE of his special mint ointment onto his hands, then raised his palms to his nose, inhaling a cleansing breath. He'd resumed his position behind the hitching post in front of Miss Molly's. A few minutes later, the men popped out of the bed-and-breakfast, waving their arms around and scanning the area in apparent agitation.

He smiled.

It seemed the gentlemen were looking for someone.

The two men walked into a shop with a pair of boots in the window, then came back out, still scanning the horizon. He followed them from a distance, keeping within range of the humming coming off their bodies. As long as he could hear them, he didn't need to see them—but oddly enough, it turned out the ideal range for listening and seeing was about the same. He followed them into a sweets shop and lounged near the doorway until the noise of children gave him a headache. Apparently, Spenser and Langhorne believed Caitlin was a fan of boots and candy. He went back outside and waited on the sidewalk for their return.

After a while, they left the tourist area, eventually arriving at a pasture, where several longhorns were on display behind iron fences. He had to stay far back, to keep from being spotted. But then he decided, now that they'd left the crowd, it was time to show himself anyway. Pistol drawn, he stepped out into the open, a pace or two behind them.

In his pocket, something buzzed. Ah, that would be Caitlin's phone—her beau was calling again. He kept his pistol aimed straight for Spenser while he answered, "Hello."

The men whirled on him.

"Hands in the air please. Stay right where you are," he said over the phone.

He thought the men had given each other some sort of signal with their eyes, but no matter. He had the advantage. Both men raised their hands in the air. Spenser still held a cell phone. "On your knees. I'm coming for your guns."

The men nodded, again looking at each other with crafty eyes.

Malachi approached and cautiously removed both men's side-arms. Nobody put up a fight, which made his confidence waver a moment. This seemed almost *too* easy, but then again, by now they'd surely realized he had Cassidy.

Good.

That meant a little less explaining for him to do. "Keep your hands in the air, but you may rise."

The men climbed to their feet.

"Now then, let me tell you how this is going to go. You two are going to do exactly as I say. If either one of you so much as takes a sideways step out of line, I'll shoot the other one dead. But your troubles won't end there. You see, I've got your girl." He was gratified to see angry red splotches appear on Spenser's neck and face. "If anything happens to me, I've got a real party planned for Dr. Cassidy. So you're going to take me to Cindy's diary, and quick."

"We haven't got it," Langhorne answered with a funny look on his face. Obviously, he was lying.

"What a shame for Caitlin." He almost felt sorry for them, the way they exchanged worried glances. "But if, upon reflection, you decide you do have your wife's diary, you only need to take me to it, and I'll let Cassidy go." The Thresher had never failed to deliver. Not once. And he didn't intend for his spotless reputation to be ruined. Of course, he also didn't intend to let Caitlin Cassidy go. Not when he'd planned such an exciting death for her. It would be one of his finest productions ever.

She should be very, very grateful.

The truth was he envied her. Because she was being granted a truly magnificent death. Then a pleasant thought came to him. Suppose these two special agents put up a fight. Suppose instead of cooperating, they captured him, or killed him. Cassidy would still die her magnificent death, her soul would be added to his roster, and his own death would be elevated.

Win-win.

There were so very many ways to win in this scenario.

The man who knows how to embrace death will always emerge the victor.

WITH THE WINDOWS boarded up, and so little light in the room, it was difficult to judge how long the Thresher had been gone. But Caitlin's bladder throbbed, and her dry throat clamored for water. Had it been hours or merely a few minutes? She must've been dozing off and on because she had no sense of the time that had passed.

However long it'd been, though, whatever drug he'd used on her seemed to have cleared her system and left her quite the hangover. Her head ached from the inside out, as if Zeus had taken up residence in her skull and was using its walls for target practice. When she shifted her upper body, even a little, the barbs on the wire ripped into her skin. But it was that mechanical whirring that really had her worried.

She swiveled her head, trying to see the source of the mysterious sound, and again the wire dug deeper into her skin. Due to her squirming, her shirt was now fixed to her skin by the barbs of her "belt."

The noise sounded like some kind of motor. A generator maybe. She could barely distinguish one motor from another if she was looking right at them. How was she supposed to identify this machine by sound alone?

Whatever it was, she had to know.

She exhaled and held it, succeeding in making her chest smaller. That in turn made her bindings looser by the width of a breath . . . literally. Finally, she was able to twist her head, along with one shoulder. And that's when she saw them.

Two giant red reels enclosed in a metal base. A steel cable extended from each reel. One cable hooked to her barbed-wire "belt," and though she couldn't see the end of it, the other appeared to be running to her barbed-wire "necklace."

This contraption looked like the kind of thing she'd seen used to reel in garden hoses. But she didn't see any hand crank. These must be automatic winders, like the kind used in industrial shops.

Oh dear God.

Her stomach quivered. Her pulse pounded so hard in her ears, she thought her eardrums would burst.

She allowed herself one split second of sheer terror, then shut it down. Shut it *all* down. She didn't have time to panic. Gritting her teeth, she jerked her cuffed hands back and forth until she located a cold twist of wire coming off the belt. She gripped it between her thumb and forefinger and set to work.

SPENSE SHOT DUTCH a quick glance, an involuntary reaction to the Thresher's insistence that they lead him to the diary. Spense could only hope the hit man hadn't understood the meaning of the look that passed between him and his brother. They'd been trying to figure a way to lead him to that decoy, and he was playing right into their hands—in some respects. If Spense hadn't been out of his head over the fact this son-bitch had Caity, he might've smiled and given away the whole plan.

It was just like Caity to come up with a scheme that would wind up saving the day. Only . . . she was never supposed to be bait. The Thresher's taking her hostage had never been part the plan. A plan that had better work because now it wasn't only about getting to the man who'd killed Cindy and about clearing Dutch's name. Now Caity's life was in immediate danger. So as much as it galled Spense not to jump this bastard and kick the life breath out of him, he had to stay in control.

The best thing for Caity was for him to stay sane and keep to the original plan as much as possible. At a moment like this, sanity was a tall order, and one he'd never have been able to fill without his years of training in the Bureau. He hauled in a breath and drew on that training now.

With another fast glance, he checked in on Dutch and got a brief nod that let him know his brother was on the same page.

They would stick with the script as far as possible. But Spense knew adjustments would have to be made.

They'd lead the Thresher to the diary. Then, if he didn't release Caity, they could track her via the device implanted in the diary's binding—assuming he'd go back to finish what he started or to cover his tracks. With a little bit of luck, though, the Thresher might keep his word and set Caity free. Then they could track the decoy all the way back to the monster behind the monster per the original plan.

If all else failed, there was always plan B: Beat the living hell out of the guy until he gave it all up.

Spense counted to ten, then forced a cold calmness into his voice, allowing just a hint of his rage to come through. This guy was too smart to believe they trusted him. He had to know Spense would rip his heart out of his chest, barehanded, if he could and still get Caity back unharmed. "If we take you to the diary, what guarantee do we have that you'll keep your word? That you'll let her go?"

"Guarantee?" The Thresher smiled, revealing a row of orderly white teeth. This was no ordinary thug. This was a thug with a dental plan. "I can guarantee *this*. If I don't have the diary in hand within twenty minutes or so, Dr. Caitlin Cassidy is going to experience an excruciatingly beautiful death." He pulled a snip of barbed wire from his pocket. "I've strung a length of this fine Texas fencing around her waist and throat. I've also attached steel cables to the wires." He put the barbed wires in his pocket, casually waving his gun with one hand.

It took all Spense's willpower not to jump the guy and choke him until he turned black and swallowed his tongue. He guessed

Dutch might be having the same struggles but he didn't dare look at his brother again.

"I don't suppose you know what a RoboReel is?" the Thresher asked.

The adrenaline coursing through Spense had his heart pounding against his ribs and sweat dumping out his pores, but his voice came out cool and dry. "No."

"It's a common device found in many automotive shops. Mine is state-of-the-art. With the flip of a switch, it reels in up to fifty feet of cable. Swiftly, smoothly, efficiently. Takes about sixty seconds. Now, if you were at all familiar with these machines, you'd know they have a safety device. If the cable becomes obstructed, or meets with resistance, it automatically shuts off."

"Get to the point. I'm tired of your strutting."

"In addition to my other gifts, I'm quite mechanical. I've made a good device even better by disabling the safety feature. No matter what, it will keep reeling and reeling and reeling . . . are you getting a visual yet? Oh, and the best part is I've added a timer. So you see . . ." He checked his watch. "I don't really need to hold this gun on you boys, because in precisely twenty-eight minutes and forty-six seconds, the barbed wire around Dr. Cassidy's neck and waist will tighten, steadily and painfully. It'll take only a minute before she's decapitated and cut in half by barbed wire. It's going to be my most magnificent death ever."

Spense wanted to lunge for the bastard, but he couldn't give in to his rage. He turned his back on the Thresher, and at the same time, on any weakness within himself. Caity needed him, and he wasn't going to let her down. He took off running toward the last pen in the row.

"Slow down, sir. I don't want anyone who might happen to pass by to think there's something wrong. They might stop to inquire what's happening, and that would waste precious time. Hopefully you gentlemen haven't hidden the diary so far away I won't have time to get back to Dr. Cassidy."

Spense stopped running and started racewalking. He'd turned off the sound of the wind in the trees, the braying of the bulls, and yes, the sound of his own heart beating far too fast. He focused every ounce of energy on one thing, and one thing only. Getting Caity back. He assumed Dutch was following, but he didn't have time to verify. He had to get this asshole to Big Red's pen fast.

Minutes later, they arrived at *the scene of the crime*. The very pen where he and Dutch had once taunted a champion bull and been rescued by their father.

There in all his glory was the winner of this year's longhorn competition.

Big Red weighed in at just under a ton, with horns measuring over eight feet from tip to tip. His dappled skin was freshly washed and shimmered in the sunlight. Around here, this bull was king. His pen was the size of a barn, and his handlers pampered him like a star athlete. But this bull would never carry a rider on his back. He was meant for breeding, not the sting of a spur.

Spense swung a leg up, then vaulted into Big Red's pen.

"That's quite a bull," the Thresher said admiringly.

"Stay back. I don't want you to get hurt," Dutch ordered, following Spense into the pen. "And like you said, no need to hold a pistol on us. You've got something much more dangerous hanging over us."

"Worried for my safety, are you?"

"For the next thirty minutes, yes. But after that, if I were you, I'd watch my back."

Spense had always found that honest answers were the most believable, and far easier to keep track of than lies.

"You hardly seem worried about that fellow. You've got your back to him now." The Thresher shrugged one shoulder.

"We've got experience with these animals," Spense answered, picking up one of the shovels they'd just used to bury the diary a short while ago. "'Longhorns in particular are relatively docile."

The Thresher climbed up on the fence and looked as though he were about to jump right in.

Spense held up his hand. "Stay put. I said *relatively* docile. If provoked, any animal can be dangerous, and frankly, I wouldn't want to be on the wrong end of this one's horns."

Ignoring Spense's warning, the Thresher loped over the fence. Damn idiot. "Don't spook him, then."

Again, not listening to good advice, the Thresher approached Big Red. "Would you look at those," he cawed. Pointing at the big bull's bright red testicles. So that's where he gets his name."

"Probably a safe bet," Dutch answered while he dug.

"This is a fine bull. I think it would be an honor to be gored by such an animal. It would be what I like to call a magnificent death."

Spense couldn't keep watch over the Thresher and dig at the same time. He had to make a choice. He chose to keep digging.

In the distance, a wrong noise, the kind Spense was trained to listen for, broke through to him. Like firecrackers popping off in the distance. Just the kind of noise that would spook an animal.

Spense fell to the ground, started digging deeper with his own hands. "Got it!" He raised the decoy diary high in the air, then handed it over.

The Thresher squinted at the journal with obvious indifference. He seemed far more interested in Big Red than the diary.

"I suppose you want to look it over," Spense said, hoping the Thresher would pass so they could get straight back to Caity. He was fetching it for a price and had no personal stake in what was inside.

The Thresher turned back to the bull in an almost obsessive way. For whatever reason, he seemed fixated on Big Red.

"You got what you wanted," Spense reminded him.

"Don't worry, she's not far away. There's plenty of time."

"Still, we've kept our end of the bargain, and you gave your word. You wanna tie us up or something, we'll make it easy. Just let her go."

The Thresher pursed his lips. "Gave my word? Do you think this is some kind of honor-among-thieves scenario?"

Spense had had it with playing games. He'd marshaled his self-control and stuck to the script. But it was becoming apparent the Thresher was in no rush to get back to Caity and wasn't likely to keep his end of the bargain. The trouble was, they needed him alive. Otherwise, they might not find her in time.

The popping noises he'd thought were firecrackers got louder and closer. It finally registered with Spense—they weren't firecrackers at all. This was one of those fake gun battles or bank robberies, with the sheriff chasing the bad guys through the stockyard's streets.

Big Red snorted, and in true, champion-bull fashion, stamped his front hooves. Watching three men in his pen, digging up his yard seemed to make him nervous. The fake gunfire might put him over the top. Sure enough, Big Red, began loping around the perimeter of the pen.

"We need to get out of here," Spense said.

The Thresher stood rooted to the ground, mesmerized by the longhorn's antics. Spense jerked his head at Dutch. They both clambered over the fence, betting the Thresher would follow. Surely he wasn't planning to just let them go. If anything could pull his attention off the bull, their impending escape should do the trick.

"Leaving so soon, gentlemen?" he barely turned to look at them.

What the fuck was going on in this guy's head? "Where the hell is Caity?"

"I got what I came for, so why should I tell you?"

In a flash, Spense drew his backup weapon from his boot. On the opposite side of the pen, Dutch mirrored his actions. "Are two pistols trained on you good enough reasons?"

The Thresher raised his gun, swinging his aim back and forth between Dutch and Spense.

Spense growled. "You can't shoot both of us before one of us shoots you."

"But if I die, you'll never see that girl of yours alive again. So who wants to die first?"

Spense's thigh muscles contracted, ready to pounce. Dutch would back him up, and this guy was soft and stupid. Spense could easily take him. But the Thresher was right about one thing. They had to take him *alive*. "I'll go first." He gave Dutch the side eye. "Just give me *three* seconds to say good-bye to my brother." That was the signal. On a silent count of three, they go.

One . . . two. . .

The sound of fake gunshots peppered the air.

Pop. Pop. Pop.

Big Red pawed the ground, swung his horns, and brayed loud and long.

Instead of getting out of the bull's way, the Thresher clapped his hands over his ears.

"Look out!" Too late, Spense leapt into the pen.

Head down, Big Red charged, an otherworldly noise trumpeting out his flared nostrils. There was a blur of motion, followed by a terrible cry. The scream coming from the Thresher didn't sound human.

The long, curved horn of the bull jammed into the Thresher's neck, then up and out his mouth, straight through his tongue. Big Red had impaled the hit man on his prizewinning horns. Enraged, the bull flailed, beating the Thresher's limp body against the fence. Blood spewed up and out of his mouth like a fountain, drenching his face and clothes.

Spense rushed Big Red—in spite of his fear. If there was any chance to save the Thresher's life, he had to take it. If the Thresher died, Caity's hopes died with him.

Somehow, he got his arms around the bull's neck. Spense made soft, soothing sounds and held on tight, as the bull reared, lifting Spense off the ground, bucking against his ribs, raging against the world. Spense locked his arms and dug his fingers into the soft fur, hanging on for the ride. Finally, the bull managed to dislodge the hit man from its horn. The body flew like a rag doll through the air.

The popping stopped.

The gunfight had drawn to an end. Big Red let out a long bray, then quieted. As Spense's feet touched ground again, he continued to soothe the bull while Dutch rushed to check the Thresher, lying prone in the pen.

"He's gone." Dutch threw his hat in the dirt.

Spense let out a long wail.

The tracking device and the decoy diary were of no use to them now. It wouldn't lead them to Caity, or to Cindy's killer. Spense released Big Red, and the bull began trotting around his pen as if calming himself.

Spense fell to his knees, exhausted.

His brother wrapped an arm around him in a half hug, then lifted him back to his feet. "We have to get out of here."

"We'll kick down every door in the stockyards," Spense managed to choke out as they dragged each other out of the pen.

They had to find Caity.

She only had minutes to live.

Chapter Twenty-Three

CAITLIN WAS NOT going to sit back quietly, waiting to be sliced and diced. She hadn't heard a single set of footsteps pass by, so wherever the Thresher had taken her, it must be well off the main path. With the windows boarded over, screaming would be a waste of time and energy—though she vowed to let loose at the top of her lungs if she heard someone approaching. For now, she wasn't going to simply hope for someone else to come along and rescue her.

The old expression, *do or die,* had never been more true.

It didn't matter that her every breath was constricted by her bonds, or that dread floated like sewage in her blood, contaminating every part of her with fear. Nor did it matter that her handcuffs had already chafed the skin right off her wrists, or that the barbed wire she'd been manipulating had punctured the delicate pads of her fingertips.

None of that was important.

It didn't seem so terrible to die. Everyone did—circle of life and all. It wasn't even the anticipation of the slow agony of being lacerated into pieces that drove her to work the wire between her fingers until she nearly fainted from the pain. No, it wasn't the fear of a horrible death that drove her.

It was the fear of an unfinished life.

All those moments that would never be. If she succumbed to death, here in this darkened room before she'd really lived, really *loved*—that would be a tragedy. She didn't want to miss out on the days of studying Spense's profile, watching his sudden smile when he hit upon the solution to a puzzle; or the Thanksgiving she'd promised her mother. The one where they would not sit stiffly at the table, making strained conversation, like they had every year since her father's execution. This year was to be their new beginning. She ground her teeth and twisted the wire another turn. The Thresher wasn't going to take those things away from her.

With the next turn of the wire, she felt it snap, piercing her finger to the bone. Pain rose in her body, but she tamped it down, not allowing it to distract her—not now. Not when she'd finally managed to free a strand of wire. If she could just get her hands close enough . . . The cuffs scraped and stung the raw flesh on her wrists.

Good.

They were slipping lower. She strained harder.

Then her breath stopped in her chest. She heard several clicks.

The whirring sound, coming from behind her, changed to a loud buzz. Looking down, she saw coils of cable snaking toward the machine. Something had activated the autowind feature. A timer?

She had no idea if she had seconds or minutes left, but her brain split each moment into a million parts. Then she filled each one of those parts with work.

With *hope*.

The very wire her captor would use to decapitate her, was the same instrument that could save her . . . if she could only pick the lock on her handcuffs with it. Her tears stung her eyes like acid, blinding her. The cable uncoiled at her feet, relentlessly disappearing into the autoreel. She kept working, kept hoping. She bit down on her cheek when she found a notch in the handcuffs, and then shoved the wire in with all her might.

Click!

She jerked her wrists apart. The handcuffs jangled as they hit the floor.

She'd done it!

She'd picked the lock on her handcuffs with wire from her "belt." But she was still bound to the chair. Then she smiled, realizing she didn't need to get free of the chair. All she had to do was get free of the barbed necklace and belt. Three loops of cable remained on the floor. Once they uncoiled, the slack would be gone, and it would be mere seconds until the wires cut her in two.

Her father's voice sounded in her head.

Hold on tight, Caity. I won't let you fall.

If her father had had even a sliver of a chance, he'd never have wasted it. He'd had no chance at all. But she did. She had *seconds*, and right now those seconds amounted to a lifetime.

Yes!

She'd unhooked the belt. It dangled across her lap in one straight piece, scraping her thighs, but no longer dangerous.

At her feet, one coiled loop of cable remained.

And that meant she had more seconds. Another lifetime.

She tore at the necklace, trying to release it. Dear God. She'd been twisting it the wrong way.

I want you, Caity.

She imagined Spense whispering words of love, low in her ear, his warm breath on her cheek. She opened her eyes, blinking away the moisture.

She couldn't give up. The thought of never hearing his voice again was far worse than the pain and far more potent than her fear.

There!

The necklace opened, jerking across her throat, grazing her skin as it was sucked into the beast behind her. But she was *alive*. Now, all she had to do was get these damn ropes off, and get the hell out of here before the Thresher returned. She looked at the thick lines that bound her to the chair . . . took a deep breath . . . and then cried out as a long, booted leg kicked open the door to her torture chamber.

THAT RUSH OF sheer joy when he first spied Caity was enough to keep Spense on his feet—despite the full-body trembling that overtook him. She was bound to a chair, her hair wrung with sweat. She had the feral look of a trapped animal preparing to chew off its paw. His heart stopped in his chest, but then her smile brought its beat back with a vengeance.

"I'm here," he heard a calm voice say, and realized he was speaking. Somehow, he'd crossed the room, and his hands had set to work loosening knots. Other hands were busy, too. Together, he and Dutch freed Caity from the bindings.

He picked up her hand, and the sight of her delicate fingers with broken, bloody nails, her wrists ringed with red, the flesh torn from them, made his heart stutter yet again. He bent his head near hers. "I'm here."

"We have to hurry," Caity tried to stand.

Her legs gave way, and Spense lifted her in his arms. Holding her close, he came back to himself, and only then did he remember Caity didn't know that the Thresher was dead.

"It's okay. He's not coming back." He sat down in a chair near the table, with Caity still in his arms. "He's dead."

The quick flash of relief on her face was soon followed by a frown. "So he didn't take the decoy."

"We tried to stick with the plan." Dutch came closer, resting his hand on Caity's shoulder. "But I'm afraid a longhorn bull had other ideas."

Spense let Dutch do the talking. He didn't want Caity to hear his voice shake. He was usually cool in the face of trouble, no matter how terrible. But the sight of Caity, bound to that chair, had been almost more than he could bear.

Dutch relayed what had happened in the bullpen. Caity listened and asked a few questions. Keeping remarkably calm, even through the description of the goring.

When the story was over, she climbed off Spense's lap, steadying herself with one hand on the table. "What are we going to do now?"

Hoping he was composed enough to speak in a normal tone of voice, he took a deep breath, and said, "We're going to get you to a hospital."

She shook her head. "Absolutely not. If I go to an ER, that might alert Sheridan to Dutch's whereabouts. Injuries like mine are bound to trigger a police report, and we're supposed to be in Tahiti, remember? If I suddenly show up at Harris Hospital Emergency, even someone as thick as Sheridan might make the connection to Dutch. And Sheridan would absolutely run to Jim."

"It's not worth risking your health, Caitlin," Dutch said.

"You need a doctor," Spense added, holding up her raw, abraded wrists.

"I *am* a doctor. I can keep an eye on these wounds myself. I've got antiseptics and bandages in my go bag, and if they show signs of infection—I've got antibiotics, too."

"I'm going to turn myself in. I won't endanger the two of you any longer." Dutch paced the small room.

"It's no use, Dutch. I'm sure the Thresher reported in to his boss on a regular basis. The monster behind the monster probably assumes that if we're with you, we know too much. Turning yourself in won't keep any of us safe."

Caity was right. Crazy to think they could lose their lives over information they didn't even have. Not a single one of them really knew what was in that diary, and the hit man's insistence that they produce it eliminated all doubt that the diary was the key to everything. "Now that the Thresher is dead," Spense said, "the plan of following the decoy diary to this mastermind is no longer an option. That's the bad news."

"What's the good news?" Dutch sighed heavily.

"When the Thresher's body is discovered, it's going to look like a freak accident. No one will know we were even there."

"It *was* a freak accident," Dutch said.

"And the press will be swarming the stockyards to cover the story. We need to get out of here fast," Caity said. "Once the 'puppet master' finds out his hired help is dead, it won't take long to find a replacement assassin. And this time, we'll have no idea when or where he'll strike."

Spense could hardly believe the way she was able to shift gears and focus on the problem at hand after what she'd just been through. "Is there anywhere safe to go?"

There was a moment of thoughtful silence.

"Back to my place in Preston Hollow," Dutch said. "We can regroup and figure out our next step. We'll have everything we need there. Caity can rest, and frankly, it's the last place anyone will look for us."

"Seems risky." Caity frowned. "If I were Sheridan, I'd have surveillance on your place."

"But you're not Sheridan, and since unlike you, he assumes I'm guilty, he probably believes that given my personal resources, I'm out of the country by now."

Spense knew from experience that it took more than twenty men to keep twenty-four hour surveillance on just one terrorist. "He's right, Caity. Absent a specific reason to believe Dutch is about to return, it's not likely the Dallas PD has surveillance on the house. They can't afford to tie up that kind of manpower indefinitely." He turned to his brother. The plan sounded reasonable enough, only . . . "Without the decoy diary, we're up a proverbial creek, unless you have some sudden insight into who might've killed your wife."

"That's funny, because I was hoping the two of you would tell me."

"How's that?" Spense turned his palms up.

Dutch grinned. "Last time I checked, the two of you were profilers. And sitting on top of quite a winning streak. Short of finding the real diary, you and Caitlin are the best chance I've got."

Chapter Twenty-Four

Saturday, October 19
5:00 P.M.
Preston Hollow, Texas

AFTER CLEANING CAITY's wounds and bandaging her wrists, Spense had driven everyone to Dallas in his Bucar. They'd taken the back roads into the city and parked out of sight in Dutch's private garage. Now they'd settled into the basement of Dutch's Preston Hollow home. They didn't dare stay in the main part of the house for fear the neighbors might spot them.

"Check out what I brought along in my go bag." Caity produced a small whiteboard and Dry Erase Markers. Spense had to smile at her forethought. She'd come prepared with everything: medicine, bandages, Kleenex . . . and she'd brought the tools of their trade, ones that in some ways were every bit as important as his Glock.

"So you were planning on profiling the killer all along," Dutch said. "I can't wait to watch the two of you work your magic."

"First, you're not going to sit back and watch us *work our magic*. You're going to get down and dirty right alongside us. At the moment, you're our most important resource. And second, we're not going to profile Cindy's killer. Not in any traditional sense, because this case doesn't really fit the model." Caity held up one finger. "But I do think some of the same principles apply, which is why I brought the board. In particular, I think we can learn a lot about the killer's motivation by 'profiling' Cindy herself."

"Unless Cindy wasn't the target," Dutch said.

"In case you're the real target, Dutch, we'll have to consider two entirely different paths. And you know what that means."

"I don't."

Caity grinned. "It means we need more colors. We'll use blue for Cindy and green for you."

Spense uncapped a marker, and the scent of a fresh puzzle, itching to be solved, filled the room. Even Dutch seemed to be getting into the spirit of things. The Thresher's death was a blow, but that didn't mean they were going to wait for the next hired hit man to come strolling through the door. They had work to do. And they had better get to it. This was their window of opportunity.

The monster behind the monster might've already found his new assassin. But just as they had to start from scratch to find him, his henchman had to start from scratch to find them.

The playing field was even, and the race was on.

He and Caity still couldn't report in to Jim. Spense hated withholding information, but if they told him they'd located Dutch, Jim would either have to turn Dutch over to Sheridan or risk disciplinary action for concealing a fugitive. And judging by all those meetings with the boys from D.C., Jim was being groomed for bigger and better things. Spense would rather not put his mentor in an untenable position with the Bureau. For now, they had to keep Jim in the dark—but that didn't mean Spense couldn't rely on some of his other contacts at the Bureau. He was tight enough with a few agents to ask for help on the down low. Plenty of folks knew he and Caity had been assigned as off-the-books advocates for Dutch, and Jim was too discreet to have advertised the fact he'd taken them out of that role.

SECRETS.

Caity scrawled the letters with a heavy hand, in all caps giving them a bold, important appearance.

Spense wasn't sure where she was going with that. It was a departure from their normal methodology—but then again, they weren't looking for a serial killer.

"I realize this isn't how we usually do things, but both Cindy and Dutch had more than their fair share of secrets. It seems likely to me, that if we turn over all those secrets, we're more likely to find the motive for Cindy's murder, and if we know the motive . . ."

"The killer will be obvious," Spense said.

Dutch arched a skeptical eyebrow.

"Obvious might be overstating," Caity rushed in to qualify his statement, and a warm feeling spread through his chest. He was being arrogant; she was trying to tone him down. That meant things were getting back to normal between them, and that was good. Very good.

Dutch rolled his personal marker between his palms. "Are we all in agreement that the Thresher did not kill Cindy?"

They'd only discussed this possibility once before, back at the stockyards, but Spense was glad to see Dutch remembered. His brother would not require spoon-feeding.

"Probably. The events at the ranch, and the attempts on our lives, were well planned out—and those were committed by the Thresher. But in Cindy's case, although the killer escaped detection, the murder appears to have been either unplanned or poorly planned. There were hundreds of guests at that fundraiser, making the scene extremely high-risk. And the shredded evening gown suggests the crime was highly personal." Caity wrote the word *LIPSTICK* in blue on the board. "And the killer made a rookie mistake—using lipstick that wasn't Cindy's on her forehead."

"It's also the only indication we have that the killer might be a female," Dutch said. "All other signs point to a man: the use of a firearm, the posing of the body—of course, men leave lipstick notes, too. For me, the killer's gender is still in question."

"But if we're correct that Cindy's murder was impulsive, then we could all but rule out the idea that someone killed her in order to get to you, Dutch." Spense wanted to get that out early, because it was true, and because he knew it would alleviate some of Dutch's guilt.

"Not entirely," Caity said, almost apologetically. "Someone with a grudge against Dutch could've taken advantage of an unforeseen circumstance."

"A crime of opportunity." Dutch nodded. "I've been thinking along those lines."

"I say we travel both paths to see if there's any point where they intersect." Caity had an artificial lilt in her voice, and Spense figured she was trying to stay upbeat for Dutch's sake.

This was the first time they'd ever boarded a murder with the victim's husband in the room. It was tricky, but Caity was right. Dutch was their best resource. They needed him here, no matter how painful it was for him. "We should start with Cindy's secrets."

Dutch's complexion went gray, like he was about to be sick.

"Do you need a minute?" Caity asked.

"No." He sighed. "I need my wife back. But that's not going to happen, so the least I can do for her is have the guts to face the truth. I can't help thinking that if I'd been more involved in our marriage, she'd still be alive. Now I can't even tell you much about her affairs—that's what you meant when you said *secrets*, I'm sure. Because of my indifference, I'm practically no use to you."

"You were not indifferent. You loved her," Caity said. "If you practiced denial, it was a survival mechanism. But I bet you know more than you think you do. Remember what you told Cindy about the diary—that she'd better hide it well since she was married to an FBI agent? Think about it, Dutch, a man with your background and observational skills had to have picked up on clues."

He rubbed his forehead. "I can tell you more from the early years . . . before I checked out of our marriage. The first time I heard rumors, they were about the tennis pro at the club. At first, I didn't believe they were true. I waited for Cindy to come to me and explain things, but she never did. Then at some point, I started to think where there was smoke, there was fire, so I buried myself in my cases. And I left her to her own devices. Either the affair ended, or maybe it never happened to begin with. I was never really certain.

"Then a few years later, I traveled to the coast of Somalia to negotiate the release of hostages. When I returned, it was like déjà vu. Whenever I entered a room, people would suddenly stop talking, and when I left, they would start to whisper again."

"So you thought she'd taken another lover?" Caity asked in a soft, but businesslike tone.

"Yeah. I guess I knew she was cheating. No one ever told me who the man in question was, but I had a pretty fair idea. Before I left for Somalia, Cindy had become very friendly with Sue Ellen James. A woman she had met at Junior League. They worked a number of charity events together. But when I returned, Sue Ellen and Cindy had had some sort of falling-out. Then, a few months later, Sue Ellen and her husband, Peter, divorced. The reason, according to the Dallas grapevine: Peter was sleeping with one of Sue Ellen's best friends."

"Sue Ellen and Peter James." Caity wrote their names in blue—to indicate this was Cindy's secret. "Had motive to kill Cindy."

"You know where the tennis pro is now?" Spense asked.

Dutch shook his head. "It wasn't him."

"You sure about that?"

"He got behind the wheel, drunk. The creep took a family of three with him to the grave."

"That's one off the list of suspects then. Who else?"

"Kip Keiser. I think his wife's name is Georgia."

While Spense asked the questions, Caity scribbled the information on the board.

"They're still married?"

"Yes. Georgia was pregnant at the time, this one I know for sure, because Georgia brought it to my attention. She called me and begged me to intervene with Cindy."

"And did you?"

"No. I suggested she speak directly to her husband. But I never asked Cindy about it."

Caity stopped scribbling. "Forgive me, Dutch, but I'm trying to understand this. It seems you had something like a don't ask, don't tell policy in your marriage. Did that go both ways? Were you having affairs, too?" Expectantly, she uncapped the green pen.

"Not unless the FBI counts as a mistress. I guess in Cindy's eyes, it did. You two are very fortunate to be able to work together. You both understand the demands of the job. If you weren't colleagues, how would you have time for a relationship? In fact, in a way, working together *is* your relationship. That's why there are so many couples in the FBI."

"Not to mention it smooths the issue of security clearance," Spense said, only half joking.

"I'm determined to use this green marker, Dutch." Caity wrote *the Bureau* on the board. "You did say she was your mistress." Next she got the blue pen out and used it to write *Georgia and Kip Keiser*.

"Not as high on the list, because they managed to stay together," Spense said. "Maybe put an asterisk by those names."

Caity shook her head. "You're kidding? Right?"

"You disagree, that the motive is less? It was a long time ago. Water under the bridge," Spense said, then thought better of it. Was his father's affair water under the bridge? Just because something happened in the distant past didn't mean it couldn't still hurt like hell.

"I absolutely disagree. In fact, I'm adding an exclamation point by Georgia's name." And she did. "Georgia was pregnant at the time of the affair. I can tell you, from a woman's perspective, there are very few crimes worse than that. Anything that could affect the children, ups the pain. And not only that, because Georgia took the initiative to contact Dutch, we know she's a woman who doesn't sit back on her hands. She's a woman who acts. A wound like that could've been festering for years, then something, an anniversary, or a found memento, for example, triggered a sudden rage."

"Okay. You can keep your exclamation point," Spense conceded before turning back to Dutch. "Who else?"

"I really don't know."

"But you believe there are more."

"I'm not aware of anyone, but the rest of the world seems to think so. And the rumors have been swirling faster than ever these last months. It doesn't take much to become notorious in Dallas high society. If you're guilty once, you're guilty forever. Mistakes are never forgotten, and definitely not forgiven."

"According to Heather, who you say was Cindy's one true friend, Cindy hadn't had an extramarital affair in years." Caity capped her green marker and sent Dutch an empathetic look. Like Spense, she seemed to wish she could rewrite history and posthumously turn Cindy into a faithful wife. "But here's something I don't get. Heather knew about all of Cindy's past affairs. So if she had taken a new lover, how is it possible that Heather doesn't know about that—assuming it's true? And even more confusing, Heather keeps pointing the finger at you, Dutch. In all the *Dateline* episodes I've ever watched, it's always the victim's best friend who guides police in the right direction. The best friend always knows."

Dutch knit his brow. "Caitlin, it sounds like you're saying you think I did it."

She shook her head. "Not at all. What I'm saying is I think Heather Cambridge knows more than she's letting on. She's lying . . . to protect someone."

Subject Unknown, Caity wrote in blue, and put two exclamation points by the label.

"If Cindy had a new lover and held true to her pattern," she said, "he would be a married man. And thus, either the lover or the lover's wife, would have the strongest motive of all, since that affair was ongoing."

"Dutch, you really have no idea who that man might be?" Spense asked.

"I'm trying to think, but I just don't know. Cindy spent most of her time with Heather, scheming to put Matt in the White House. I really don't see how she had time for an affair unless it was with Heather herself."

Caity and Spense exchanged glances.

Dutch shook his head. "I know my wife's sexual tastes, and they don't swing that direction."

The marker bounced between Caity's fingers. "Okay. We'll have to trust your judgment on that one. Cindy's lover was male. I'd like to move on to your list, now. Can we come up with some names of people who might have it in for you?"

He laughed, but it wasn't a happy sound. "That list is long. We'd have to go back into the files and find everyone I've ever locked away. Narrowing that group down would be difficult to do in a short amount of time. It can be done, but not quickly. We'd have to find out who's in prison, who's dead, or out of the country, etc."

"Technically, that may be true. But here's where a profiler thinks differently than a field agent. We like to work by *inclusion* rather than by a process of elimination." Spense wasn't sure he was making himself clear.

"Not following."

"Instead of ruling people out, we'll try to rule them in. Let's start by noting the characteristics of Cindy's death. Brutal, designed to humiliate. Personal. This doesn't seem likely to be revenge taken against you for locking someone away. For that, a person would've come after you directly. If this is aimed at you, it has to be by someone who cares more about making you suffer than about seeing you dead. Let's *include* names of anyone like that."

"Maybe Cindy was just an easier target."

"At a fund-raising ball, no one's an easy target," Caity contributed. "What about Tesarak? Sorry to bring it up, but you shot and killed the man. I can see a family member wanting you to know how it feels to lose someone you love." She added *Tesarak* to the green column. "And according to the reports leaked to the press, Cindy was killed with a revolver, not a pistol. So this was probably someone with no military or police experience. That fits with a family member."

Dutch nodded. "Cindy's killer didn't behave like a professional. I think we can lock down the idea that whoever killed her later wised up and hired someone with *experience* to get the diary and come after me. Spense became a target the moment he saw the Thresher's face. Caitlin is probably just collateral damage. Or maybe the killer figured she knew too much . . ."

"About what?" Caity drew a big circle on the board between Cindy's long blue column and Dutch's short green one. "Where do your secrets intersect with hers?"

The silence ticked loud and hard in their ears.

"Sorry, but I don't see any connection—between Tesarak or my work at the Bureau and Cindy's affairs."

Neither did Spense. Though if there was one, that would blow this case wide open. "Okay, what else then? Which of Cindy's paramours had the most to lose if word got out about the affair."

"They were all powerful men, and wealthy, except of course for the tennis pro, and he's got an airtight alibi—otherwise known as a coffin."

"Cindy told you she was going to meet the governor that night," Caity said. "And you said she'd been spending all her time working on his campaign . . . but Matt Cambridge had a DPS security detail on him. He couldn't possibly have killed Cindy, according to them. I wish we had the diary because then Cindy could talk to us, and if we listen well enough, she would very likely lead us to the truth."

"But we don't," Spense said. They'd given the whiteboard a solid chance and come up with very little. "I think the only option we have left is good old-fashioned police work, and yes I'm talking about shoe leather. I'll start by setting up an interview with Georgia Keiser and Sue Ellen James—the women scorned. Dutch, you hang out here in the basement and keep a low profile. Caity, would you care to join me in interrogating the Dallas housewives?"

"Of course, but first, I want to review the file Sheridan gave us when we did the walk-through at Worthington Mansion. I think the statements from the governor's security detail are in there, and I want to see them with my own eyes."

"Why do I have to stay behind while you two take all the risks?" Dutch didn't sound pleased.

"Because it's a good chance for you to turn the house upside down looking for the diary again, but more importantly, Caity and I won't get arrested just for showing our faces around town. Sheridan still has a BOLO out on you."

"Point taken, but the *monster behind the monster* could strike at any time." Dutch put an arm around each of them. "So please, be careful out there."

Chapter Twenty-Five

Monday, October 21
10:00 A.M.
Dallas, Texas

SELF-CONSCIOUSLY, CAITLIN TUGGED the sleeves of her tailored cotton blouse lower over her wrists, making sure her wounds were well covered. Not that either of the women in the room noticed much about her. They seemed to only have eyes for Spense, and really, how could she blame them?

Spense looked beyond handsome in his best sports jacket and tie. Georgia Keiser and Sue Ellen Zachek (formerly Sue Ellen James) sat across from him, stiff-backed and well apart on a Queen Anne sofa in a conference room at the Fairview Hotel. At first, Caitlin had a hard time telling them apart even though she'd studied their photos in the society pages. Both women were of a particular type. Brunettes who'd bleached their graying locks to near platinum, then teased the top, pageant style, and added extensions. Their wealth showed in their appearance. They wore designer clothing, and much time and effort had obviously been extended making them up to look "natural."

They sported Botox, filled cheekbones, full lips—but again, not overdone—and figures that spoke of salad dinners, personal trainers, and, perhaps, diet pills. These women were fighting the battle against aging and winning. But there was one fight they'd lost or at least in Georgia's case come close to losing: the war to hang on to their wealthy husbands' affections.

By all accounts, Cindy had been only one of multiple women to come between them and their spouses. Which begged the question, why would either of them single Cindy out for revenge. She couldn't have been the easiest target, and certainly not at a public event. And though it might be unkind for Caitlin to think it, neither Sue Ellen nor Georgia seemed to have the initiative required to commit murder, then keep her mouth shut about it. That sort of thing took fortitude.

"Thank you both for agreeing to meet with us," Caitlin said, noticing that the women kept their gazes on Spense even when she spoke directly to them. "I realize it's unorthodox to interview you together. But I want to assure you that we're not singling you out as suspects. And time is of the essence. However, if either of you want a separate conversation, we can arrange that at any time. Just say the word."

Sue Ellen smiled sweetly. "Which of us would you take, Agent Spenser?"

"Dr. Cassidy and I would both do the honors. One of you can wait in the other room until the other is done."

"So we wouldn't be alone with you?"

"No. Nothing to worry about on that score."

"I wasn't worried." Sue Ellen batted her eyelashes.

Caitlin swallowed her irritation. Since they'd returned from the stockyards, things had been gradually returning to normal between Spense and her. He no longer pulled away if she touched his hand, and she'd caught him watching her more than once. But he hadn't said he'd forgiven her, they hadn't kissed, and certainly, he hadn't come to her bed. So while Sue Ellen was a single woman and perfectly within her rights to flirt with Spense, who was undoubtedly the finest male specimen she was ever likely to come across, it cut Caitlin straight to the heart to have to watch. And if Sue Ellen thought she could game them, she had another think coming. "I see you've got a good rapport going already, Spense, so why don't you go ahead with the questions."

He shrugged as if to say he couldn't help his charm. And honestly, she didn't think he could. He was just naturally sexy without even trying.

Georgia shot Sue Ellen a disbelieving look. "I get that you're single, and I get you don't have any love lost for Cindy. She fucked my husband, too—when I was pregnant if you'll recall. But she's *dead*, Sue Ellen. Don't you think you could turn off your inner slut long enough to help the police catch her killer?"

The words *inner slut* set off warning bells in Caitlin's head.

"You're the slut, Georgia. And you hated her every bit as much as I did, so don't put on the phony-baloney sympathy act just because she's dead. You don't fool me one bit."

"I'm not pretending to be sorry she's dead. I *am* sorry. Believe it or not, I pitied her."

"How's that?" Caitlin asked, genuinely interested. This was something she hadn't expected from Georgia.

"Cynthia Langhorne was one of the saddest women I've ever known. After she ended the affair with Kip, she came to me and apologized. She had no idea that I was expecting . . . not that that excused anything. But she said she didn't know, and I believed her. She also said Kip told her we were separated."

"Was that true?"

"Almost. Before I found out about the baby, we were talking divorce. Kip was in the process of looking for his own place when the affair started. He took his sweet time ending it, though, even after we found out I was pregnant and after he'd agreed to go to counseling. I believe Cindy's story that Kip lied to her, because, as I found out later, she wasn't really that into him. Kip told me he thought Cindy had used him to make Dutch jealous. Apparently, she talked about her husband constantly. Even called his name out during sex. It was quite a blow to Kip's ego." She turned to the woman beside her. "Don't you dare look down your nose at me, Sue Ellen. Peter's no prize, you know."

"I'm not looking down my nose. I just can't understand why you stayed with Kip. I certainly wouldn't have taken him back."

"I was trying to give my unborn child a happy home. And I have. Besides, everyone knows you begged Peter not to leave you."

"That's a lie."

"You're a laughingstock."

"Ladies." Spense grimaced. "If we could get back to the matter at hand . . . the reason we brought you in is that we're hoping you can tell us more about Cindy Langhorne. After all you're both—"

"Gossips?" Georgia's face flushed.

"*In the loop* as far as the Dallas social scene is concerned." Spense looked to Caitlin for help. Perverse of her to let him go it alone, but she stayed silent. "Was there anything you heard via the grapevine about a new affair? Any speculation about who that might've been with?"

"Hasn't anyone told you?" Sue Ellen asked.

"No. No one's offered up any names up at all," Spense said.

Of course, the only other person they'd had a chance to talk to was Heather Cambridge.

Sue Ellen and Georgia exchanged a glance, then Sue Ellen continued, "Matt Cambridge. We tried to warn Heather, but she brushed us off. She said Cindy would never do such a thing to her."

Georgia smoothed her hand back and forth over the silky fabric on the couch. "I remember thinking how strange it was that Heather said *Cindy* would never do such a thing to her. She didn't seem to find it hard to believe that her husband, Matt, would cheat on her."

"He's a politician," Sue Ellen jumped in. "Heather's known for years about his wandering eye. She even told him straight out she didn't care what he did, only he better not get caught at it and ruin his chance at the White House."

"That's just a rumor."

"It's a rumor straight from the horse's mouth. Heather told me herself she warned Matt he better start keeping it in his pants or he'd wind up like Gary somebody or other."

"Gary Hart?" Caitlin asked Sue Ellen.

"Yeah. I think. Maybe. That sounds familiar. I didn't know who she meant, and I guess I was embarrassed to say so."

"He was a front runner for the Democratic presidential nomination until he got caught partying in the Bahamas with his mistress and had to withdraw from the race."

"When?" Georgia asked.

"I think it was '87 or '88," Spense supplied, impressing Caitlin.

"No," Georgia gave Sue Ellen a *how-could-you* look. "I meant when did Heather tell you that shit, and why didn't you ever tell me?"

"I don't tell you everything. Why should I? Heather told me in the limo on the way home from Vegas after my niece's wedding shower. She'd had quite a few margaritas, and we'd smoked a little weed in the car."

"I don't believe it. You must've been drunk."

"We both were. But I wasn't too high to remember the conversation."

Caitlin tried to pull the women away from their personal issues and back on track. "Do either of you think Matt Cambridge would risk his shot at the presidency for Cindy Langhorne?"

"For Cindy?" Georgia nodded. "Hell yes. He tried to hook up with her when he first met her, but she wasn't interested and passed him on to Heather."

That fit with what Heather had told them.

"He never got over Cindy," Sue Ellen said.

That, on the other hand, was new information. And coupled with what Caitlin had learned from the statements the protective detail had given Sheridan, things were starting to take a turn in the prime-suspect department.

"Besides, it's Heather who's always had her eye on Washington. If you ask me, which, hey, you just did, Matt would still be trying to make partner at that shitty little law firm if Heather hadn't taken him in hand. Not that I don't give him some credit for making it to the governor's office. He's got the charm. He just never had the ambition. Not until he met Heather anyway."

Spense wasn't generally a percher, but at the moment, he teetered on the edge of his chair. "You two seem pretty convinced that Matt Cambridge and Cindy Langhorne were having an affair."

"Look," Georgia said. "I really meant it when I said I'm sorry she's gone. And I want to be as helpful as I can. I can't say that

Cindy was or was not having an affair, but if she was, the number one candidate would be Matt Cambridge."

"Let me ask you one more thing," Caitlin said. "Who does your hair and makeup?"

Georgia's face brightened at the implied compliment, and she seemed unfazed by the abrupt change of subject. "Karina Peyton. She's does everyone in our gang."

"I could use a little makeover. May I get her number?" Caitlin tried for a demure smile.

"Well, now that you mention it, I think she could do a lot for you." Georgia reached for her purse and began rummaging for a card, then finally found it. She pulled it out with a tiny bit of gum stuck to it. "Oh, I'm so sorry."

"No problem," Caitlin wiped the sticky mess from her fingers while Spense escorted the ladies to the door.

When he returned he had a plaintive look in his eyes. "Please tell me you're not about to turn yourself into a Dallas Cowboys' cheerleader."

"Don't be ridiculous. I'll tell you what's up in the car. But I'm going to need some help on this one, and you're definitely not the right agent for the job."

IT WAS A stroke of luck that Gretchen Herrera was in Dallas for a regional conference. Caitlin could've taken any female agent with her to Karina Peyton's day spa, but she knew Gretchen from the Man in the Maze case, and felt comfortable with her. And since Gretchen's home office was Phoenix, not Dallas, she had no reason to discuss the matter with Jim Edison. Not only that, but with her stunning looks, she was perfect for the task at hand.

At the moment, they were sipping cucumber water, waiting in

the members-only spa-reception area. By dropping Heather Cambridge's name and mentioning Gretchen's status as a federal agent, they'd scored a last-minute, private tour.

Eventually, a petite woman, about five-foot-two, turned five-foot-eight by her Louboutins, entered the room.

"I'm Karina Peyton." She smiled and pirouetted as if she were on a runway.

It made some sort of sense, Caitlin supposed, because if you're going to advertise yourself as a professional makeup artist and stylist, you're a living sample for your customers. Karina really fit the bill, with her enhanced breasts, tiny waist, and hair that looked as though it never met a curling iron it didn't like. In fact . . . she might be mistaken, but Caitlin was fairly certain the woman had calf implants.

"Wow," Gretchen said, admiringly. "I like your style."

Caitlin suppressed a smile. No one was more natural than Gretchen. She came by her figure the old-fashioned way—in the field and in the gym. Caitlin understood that Gretchen ran around thirty miles a week and lifted daily. Her hair was natural blond, which was quite stunning in comparison to her dark, creamy skin.

"You're beautiful. Do you mind if I ask you, what's your heritage?" Karina asked Gretchen. "If we're going to do you over—not that you need it—it will help me pick a skin palette."

"Hispanic." Gretchen's tone was friendly and suggested she'd been asked the question many times.

"But you're blond."

"It happens." Gretchen shrugged.

Karina flushed. "Well, come on back ladies, and let's get started." She swept her hand out. "This is the dressing area. You can be assured of absolute privacy here. There's a separate entrance, so you won't need to worry about the customers out front. I'm thinking that with the FBI, that might be important."

"Absolutely. And thanks for showing us around on such short notice." Gretchen smiled warmly.

Caitlin was glad she'd brought her along.

"It's my pleasure. Anything to help my country."

Caitlin wondered if Karina was about to break out the pledge of allegiance. This was going to be cake. The stylist seemed thrilled to have the chance to win the Bureau's business. And maybe something really would come of it. Gretchen might put in a good word for her if she offered a good deal.

"Well, we're not talking espionage." Gretchen said with a friendly wink. "It's just that some of the female agents have been talking about finding someone reliable to help us look our best. The FBI likes their agents to make a good public appearance, and we're often invited to high-level functions. We're hoping you might be able to provide a government discount."

"Discount?" Karina recoiled. "This is a luxury salon."

"Well, we are civil servants so . . ."

Karina's patriotism quickly kicked back in. "I normally don't do discounts . . . but, I must say, it's exciting to work with the FBI."

"Just think of the state secrets you'll hear," Caitlin nudged Gretchen.

Karina's mouth gaped.

"She's kidding," Gretchen said. "But in all seriousness, we know you're trustworthy. Heather Cambridge speaks so highly of you."

"I think the world of her. And I never spill her secrets." She cleared her throat, suddenly a bit off-balance. "I hope you're not here to pump me for them."

"Oh!" Caitlin covered her mouth.

"That is why you're here?"

"Yes." Caitlin said. "We were so hoping you could let us in on what shade of lipstick Heather wore to last week's fund-raiser. She looked stunning. You did her hair and makeup, right?"

"Right. Whenever she's in Dallas, she always comes by the shop. But I couldn't possibly reveal the name of her lipstick. That's top secret, like Diane Sawyer's."

Gretchen rounded her eyes. "You really *are* loyal."

"I have my standards. I wouldn't get repeat business otherwise."

"So, then . . . what can you tell us about hygiene?" Caitlin pulled out a notepad and pen for effect.

"Hygiene? Mine's perfect."

"No. I mean, do you use the same cosmetics on multiple clients?"

"Of course not." Karina paled. "Each client has her own separate stock. I would never share brushes or product. The idea is completely unacceptable."

"May we see? Just for verification purposes," Caitlin explained.

"Of course." Karina led them into another room and showed them a cabinet with multiple drawers. Each drawer was labeled with a client's name.

"I see Heather has her own drawer." Caitlin tilted her head toward Gretchen.

"Yes. In fact, if you like, I'll show you the lipstick she wore that night. But I can't tell you the name of the color or the brand." Karina lifted a lipstick from the corner and swirled it up to display the color. Then she quickly replaced the cap and placed it back in the drawer.

Scarlet.

Caitlin drew in a sharp breath. Up until this moment, she hadn't been sure. But her own personal certainty wouldn't be enough to keep Dutch off death row. There was still work to do. "Thanks, and I have one more question. If that's the lipstick you put on Heather for the fund-raising ball, how did she go about reapplying her color?"

"I gave her a complimentary tube in the same shade to take with her. She usually applies it several times during an evening since she has to look fresh for the press."

"Makes sense." Gretchen checked her watch. "Thanks so much for the tour, but we've got to run. I'll definitely be in touch. I think we should set something up for the rest of gals at the Bureau." Then she patted her pocket. "Where's my phone?"

"Maybe you left it in the reception area," Caitlin suggested helpfully.

"Would you mind showing me the way back, so I can look for it?" Gretchen asked Karina.

"Of course," Karina said.

As soon as the two women were out of sight, Caitlin quickly opened the cabinet and found Heather's drawer. She pulled out the red lipstick and dumped it into a plastic bag, marked *evidence*, in her purse. The stolen lipstick might not be admissible in a court of law, but for what she had in mind, it just might work.

Chapter Twenty-Six

BEING CONFINED IN a vehicle with Monroe Sheridan all the way from Dallas to Austin was hardly Spense's idea of a good time, so when they arrived at the Governor's Mansion, his chest loosened with relief. Still, he had to admit the detective had been far more open-minded than expected. Instead of taking matters over Sheridan's head and making him look like an ass to his superiors, Spense and Caity had gone directly to the detective with the gaping hole they'd found in his case.

Then, apparently appreciative, Sheridan had listened without interruption and agreed to go along with a plan that could end Spense's and Caity's careers if things went south.

As a housekeeper escorted them into the library of the governor's mansion, Spense tugged at his tie.

This had better work.

There would be no more deceiving Jim, now. They'd gone too far, and if the SAC didn't yet know they'd disobeyed his orders, he would by the time the governor of Texas lambasted the FBI in the press. But with his brother's freedom, and possibly his life, at stake, it was a risk they were going to have to take.

"That's Davy Crockett," Spense told the detective, whose leg jittered while he gawked at the colorful portrait.

"Cool." Sheridan clacked his teeth and paced to the door and back.

"Maybe you should sit down," Caity suggested. "You don't want to seem nervous."

"I look nervous?"

"A little." She extended a suggesting hand toward an armchair. "It might be best if you're not prowling the room when the governor and the first lady arrive."

Sheridan immediately plummeted into a chair, and it screamed in protest.

Good thing they weren't relying on him to set the trap. But fortunately, they'd all agreed Spense and Caity would take the lead. That way, if their plan failed, which it certainly might, Sheridan could escape much of the blame. And if all went well, they'd be happy to let the detective take the credit—just as long as they got their man.

Impatient, Spense tapped his fingers on his knees. He gazed around the library. Yep, still green. An expectant energy filled the room, until at last, the governor, Mrs. Cambridge, and Brian Foster, her personal guard, joined them.

They all shook hands and after brief introductions, Heather offered tea. They declined, and she dismissed her man.

At Spense's nod, Caity raised an innocent finger in the air. "Just a moment, Brian, if you don't mind." Her smile was all gracious apology to the first lady. "We have a few questions for your guard."

"I thought you said you were bringing *us* information—about Cindy." Matt Cambridge, older than his wife by a decade, had that distinguished look of a gentlemen politician. His hair had been tastefully colored close to its natural shade of brown, with a hint of gray still showing at the temples. "We weren't expecting an interrogation." He raised an obviously displeased eyebrow. "What's this about?"

"About Cindy," Spense said. "Take a seat. We'll get to you in a minute."

The governor's eyes darkened. He opened his mouth, about to speak, but then his wife, took him by the hand and led him to the love seat.

"It's all right, Matt. We don't want to appear uncooperative at a time like this." She matched her tone and conciliatory smile to the one Caity had used, but she didn't fool Spense. Her eyes had turned slick and hard as polished agate..

"I'm the sitting governor of Texas, Agent Spenser; you'd do well to keep that detail in mind." He made a growling noise in his throat.

"May I quote you on that?" Spense flipped open a notepad.

Sheridan wiped his gleaming brow with a hankie and shoved it back in his pocket. "Take it easy, Spenser. Let's show the governor the respect he deserves."

"I'm showing him exactly what he deserves," Spense answered.

Brian looked to Mrs. Cambridge, then to the governor in apparent alarm. "Should I stay or go?"

"That's up to you, Brian." Heather raised her chin.

Brian crossed his arms high on his chest and widened his stance. "I'll stay for questions."

"Thanks," Caity said. "Just one or two. Won't take long at all." She handed a paper to Sheridan, who handed it to Brian. "Is that the statement you gave the detective last week?"

"Looks like it, yes."

"Would you mind reading it aloud?" She looked at Heather. "Not to worry, it's short."

"'On Sunday, October 13, I accompanied Governor and Mrs. Cambridge to Dallas, Texas. Governor Cambridge asked me to stay with his wife during the fund-raiser at the Worthington Mansion, stating he would make use of local DPS officers for his own protection.'" Brian looked up, "He wanted someone he trusted with Mrs. Cambridge, that's the only reason. Nothing out of order about that."

"Is that part of your statement?" Sheridan asked.

"It is now," Brian said.

"Then I'll make a note. For now, maybe get back to what's written."

Brian wiped one palm on his slacks and continued reading. "'During the entire time I was with Mrs. Cambridge, she never left the first floor of the mansion.'" He glanced up again. "That's it."

"Thank you, Brian." Heather gave him a grateful nod. "That will be all."

"Hang on," Caity said sweetly.

She could be swinging an axe over your head and still seem angelic. She had a way about her—a way that Spense liked. In fact, he liked pretty much all her ways.

"I haven't asked my question." She put two fingers to her lips.

"You're aware this is all going to be reported back to your superiors at the Bureau," the governor said.

"If you need the number, it's right here." Spense reached in his pocket and tossed his card onto the coffee table.

"What's the question, Dr. Cassidy?" Brian asked.

"Your statement is that during the entire time you were with Mrs. Cambridge she never left the first floor."

"It is."

"So then, what times were you with the first lady?"

"I don't understand."

"I think you do." Much to Spense's amazement, Sheridan lifted his chin and bravely waded into high water. Perhaps he hadn't given the detective enough credit. "What times were you with the first lady?"

"The entire evening . . ." Brian looked at Heather. "The entire evening . . . except for my dinner break. It wasn't a high-risk situation, and there were other officers standing watch at the event."

"What time did you take your break? Seven? Eight?" Spense asked.

"Ten o'clock."

"And how long was your break?"

The governor flushed. "Good God, Brian, I told you to stay on my wife. Now look at the position you've put us in."

"She dismissed me, sir."

"How long was your dinner break?" Spense asked again.

"Forty-five minutes."

"Thanks, Brian." Caity smiled reassuringly. "You can go now."

He sulked from the room, and when the door closed behind him, Heather reached for her husband's hand. "I'm sorry, Matt.

I shouldn't have gone against your wishes. Now it appears I don't have an alibi." With an anemic laugh, she turned to Sheridan. "Are you going to arrest me for giving my guard a dinner break?"

No one laughed back.

Sheridan held a recorder in the air. "Governor and Mrs. Matthew Cambridge, you understand you are not under arrest and are free to go at any time."

"This is asinine." Matt Cambridge leapt to his feet.

"Do you want a lawyer?" Spense asked.

"I want you to get the fuck out of my house." The governor's face contorted, and a small drop of spittle appeared at the corner of his mouth.

"Matt! This is being recorded."

Shoulders shaking, he dropped onto the love seat next to Heather. "You three are despicable. However, my wife and I are devastated by the loss of our dear friend, Cindy, so naturally we'll answer any questions you have. No matter how absurd they may be."

Spense closed in on Cambridge. "Were you having an affair with Cynthia Langhorne?"

The governor sank lower into the cushions of the love seat.

"Don't answer that." Heather's eyes widened until Spense could see white ringing all the way around the irises.

Matt took Heather's hand. "No," he said. "I did not have sexual relations with Cindy Langhorne."

Heather heaved a sigh of relief. "You see? You've all made complete fools of yourselves. You'll be laughed off the force and drummed out of the FBI, and Matt and I will be kicking up our heels with glee all the way to Washington."

"You're on the record here, sir. Do you want to reconsider your answer?" Sheridan ignored the first lady. He was showing some spine. There might be hope for him after all.

"I'm not under oath," Matt sputtered.

"No, but you're on the record, and anything you say can be used against you," the detective reminded him. "You keep on lying, and you'll not only be finished in politics, you'll be guilty of obstructing a murder investigation." He scratched his head, as if puzzled. "Maybe you think you'll look good in stripes."

The governor's eyes filled with water, then something close to a sob rattled out of his chest. "Heather, I'm sorry. But I just can't do this anymore. I know what the White House means to you, but I just can't give it to you. It's simply not in the stars."

"Don't say another word, Matt. You need a lawyer." Heather Cambridge hunched her shoulders and arched her back. Her screeching voice sounded more pissed-off cat than first lady.

The governor dropped his head to his chest. "I don't need a lawyer because I haven't obstructed justice . . . yet, and because I'm going to tell the truth. I'm sick of lies. Yes. I had an affair with Cindy Langhorne. I'd been after that woman for years, but she never gave me the time of day until about a month ago. Up until that point, she turned away my advances, always maintaining she loved both her husband and Heather." He turned to his wife. "She said she could never betray you."

Heather's lips went white. "Then why did she?"

"I don't know. If you want me to get on my knees and beg forgiveness, I will. I'll go to counseling. I'll quit politics—"

"Quit politics?" She turned to Sheridan, ignoring Spense and Caity. "He's overwrought. He has no idea what he's saying. You can't leak this to the press. It will ruin his career for nothing. He didn't kill Cindy. He's not guilty of anything except behaving like a horny teenager."

Just what the country needs in a president. Spense scooted his chair in closer. Sheridan and Caity followed suit. The worm was about to turn. "We know you didn't kill her, Governor," he said in a reassuring tone. "Unlike your wife, *your* alibi is airtight. But I do have a question for you. Did you ask Cindy to meet you at the ball, then stand her up?"

His hair stood on end from the way he'd been tugging it. "No. I would never rendezvous with her at a fund-raiser, with the press there, and my wife. For God's sake."

"That's funny." Spense tilted his head. "Because Cindy was expecting you to meet her. Someone claiming to be you arranged a meeting." He pointed an accusing finger at Heather and took another shot in the dark. "How did you do it? Send an e-mail from your husband's account?"

"You don't know what the hell you're talking about," Matt Cambridge sounded genuinely confused.

Spense kept his gaze on Heather, whose rigid posture suddenly crumpled. "You heard the rumors," he pressed. "But you didn't want to believe them. You had to see it with your own eyes. So you sent Cindy an e-mail, pretending to be Matt. You only planned to confront her, to plead with her not to ruin your chances at the White House."

Heather's hand trembled as she brushed a lock of hair off her forehead. "That's preposterous."

"Is it?" It was Matt, this time. "Did you do this? If you did, I'll stand by you. I'm as much to blame as you."

"Of course I didn't do it!" She half rose from her chair, then collapsed back down. Her eyes darted around the room, as if looking for a way out.

Spense didn't let up—she was about to crack. "But when you opened the door to the presidential suite, you never expected to find Cindy lying there, naked—what a careless risk to take with your husband's reputation. Your best friend had betrayed you on every possible level. She was not only fucking your man, she was fucking your chance at the White House—something you'd been dreaming of since you were a young girl. You pulled a revolver—no one but you or your husband could've gotten a gun through security. Then you slashed her dress and posed her body, leaving her humiliated for all the world to see."

"You're making this whole thing up as you go along. You can't prove a damn bit of it. Have you got a witness?" Heather raised defiant brows.

"No," Caity said, rummaging in her purse before pulling out a plastic bag with a huge red *evidence* label plastered on it. "But we do have a lipstick." She uncapped the tube and rolled it up. "I believe this is your shade."

Heather fell back on the love seat, and, for a moment, Spense thought she'd fainted, but then she sat up straight, rallying. "That's not my lipstick. I don't know where you got it, but it's not the lipstick I had with me at the party. You're bluffing."

"No. We're not." Spense took a deep breath, preparing for the big lie. They hadn't sent any DNA off because they didn't have a warrant. But Heather wouldn't know that. "This may not be the lipstick you took to the party, but it is *yours*. It's from your personal collection at Karina Peyton's spa. We pulled a DNA sample from this very tube, and it's a match."

"A match for what?" Sweat beaded around the governor's hairline, ruining his distinguished air.

Heather gritted her teeth, apparently prepared to call Spense's bluff. "Well, Agent Spenser, my husband's waiting for his answer."

"The DNA taken off your cosmetics from the day spa, matches the DNA found on Cindy Langhorne's forehead. You freshened up your lipstick at least once before using it to defile your best friend with the word *SLUT*."

"We've got the goods, Mrs. Cambridge," Sheridan said. "If you sign a statement today, I think we can work something fair with the DA. After all, it wasn't like you planned it."

"I-I didn't," she said, mouth gaping. She put her face in her hands and started to wail though Spense couldn't locate a single tear, and her mascara remained perfectly intact. "It was temporary insanity. It was like I was outside my body slashing that dress, writing that ugly word on her forehead. And then . . . I wiped her lips and put my own lipstick on her. Just to make her look pretty." Heather's body trembled, but without tears, Spense didn't know how much of her emotion was real, and how much was a ploy for sympathy.

But that would be for a jury to decide.

As they exited the mansion's back entrance, Spense noticed a strange absence of satisfaction. He didn't have the exuberance in his step that he normally did when they closed a case. He glanced at Caity and noticed the downcast turn of her mouth. Was she *not* feeling it, too?

Sheridan certainly seemed pleased. All traces of the man's nerves had vanished, and he spoke excitedly into his phone, making big confident hand gestures. Periodically, a huge grin split his face. As well it should since he was about to make national headlines.

So why did Spense have that uncomfortable dryness in his mouth, that restless feeling in his legs? Heather Cambridge had confessed to the murder of Cindy Langhorne. Dutch could now come out of hiding, and surely Jim would forgive them for making an end run around him.

This morning they'd simply laid the groundwork, getting Heather's confession. Now it was up to the police and the prosecutor to flush out the whole story. And there was one big question that left the case feeling unfinished for him. After Heather shot Cindy, she had to have been desperate to get her hands on the diary. It likely chronicled her affair with the governor, and therefore could not only ruin his presidential hopes, it would prove Heather's motive for murder. But . . . "How the hell did a woman like Heather Cambridge get hooked up with the Thresher?" he spoke his mind aloud to Caity.

"Maybe one of her goons . . . maybe Brian . . . found him for her," Caity suggested dubiously.

But that didn't quite fit. "When we pressed him, Brian told the truth. He didn't cover for Mrs. Cambridge. If he'd been the one to put her in touch with a hit man, I would've expected him to lie and maintain he'd been with her all night."

"Sir." Speaking of Brian . . . the guard headed over with an outstretched hand.

Spense shook it. "Yeah?" He wasn't without empathy for him. After all, Brian's job had been to protect the first family—and he hadn't actually lied. But his fellow DPS officers might not see it like that. Depending on how his omission was viewed—

Brian might be looking at formal charges for obstructing an investigation.

"I just wanted to say I never intended to derail the investigation." Brian looked Spense squarely in the eyes, then nodded to Sheridan and Caity.

Sheridan snorted and, turning his back in a deliberate snub, headed back into the mansion, apparently intending to finish his conversation in private. He looked over his shoulder, and said, "I'll meet you at the car in ten."

"You believe me, don't you?" Brian asked.

He did. "I'm sure you never thought Mrs. Cambridge could be involved in her best friend's murder. But what you did was wrong. You had to know your statement would be misinterpreted."

"I'm prepared to take the consequences."

Caity finally broke her silence. "An innocent man was about to be charged with murder. Think about *that* consequence. I'm ready to get out of here, Spense." She raised her hand to shade her eyes from the sun and scanned the parking area. "Dammit. There's a van blocking us in."

"I'll take care of it," Brian said, "and then I'll bring your car around."

"Not necessary," Spense answered, but noted Caity shifting back and forth on her feet. He knew she wanted to get back to Dutch and give him the news in person.

"It's the least I can do." Brian turned to Caity. "Just give me a minute to track down the van's driver."

Spense handed him the keys. If it made the guard feel better to bring their car around, it was fine with him.

"Back in a flash." Brian was already on his radio, running

toward their car, which was parked in the back section of the lot. As he neared their vehicle, a uniformed man jumped into the van and pulled away. Brian waved to Spense and Caity, then motioned toward their car with the key fob.

A deafening roar accompanied the ball of flames that burst into the sky.

Car bomb.

Spense muscled Caity to the ground, covering her body with his own. The ground shook, and his ears rang. Hundreds of tiny missiles rained down on him. Desperate to protect Caity, he wrapped his arms tightly around her.

Chapter Twenty-Seven

Tuesday, October 22
10:00 P.M.
Dallas, Texas

Spense wasn't sure what to expect when Jim strode into the conference room of the Dallas field office. Things could've gone either way. But he was pleasantly surprised to note the relaxed expression on the SAC's face.

"First off, I just got the report on Brian Foster—his injuries are minor. Thank God he clicked that remote from a good distance, or the news wouldn't be so happy." A deep furrow appeared in his forehead as he looked from Caity to Spense. "And thank God the two of you came out unscathed."

As Spense's chest expanded with relief at the news about Heather's guard, he noted a slight twinge in his ribs. Tomorrow, he and Caity might have some bruises to show for their narrow escape, but Jim was right. This was very good news indeed.

"And second . . . don't ever do that to me again, guys." Jim made the rounds at the table, first shaking hands with Caity, then clapping Dutch, and finally, Spense on the back. He took a seat at the head of the conference table. "You're not only damn lucky to be alive, you're lucky you still have jobs." He directed his words pointedly to Spense. "Going behind my back like that." Next he speared Dutch with his gaze. "Evading arrest."

Dutch shrugged and made a lame attempt at humor. "Don't know what you're talking about, sir. I was just down at the stockyards taking a break from all the insanity. I even went dancing at Billy Bob's. Sheridan could've clapped me in irons anytime he wanted."

"Hiding in plain sight is what you were doing. I've sat in on some of your lectures, and I'm well aware that's one of your pet strategies." Jim raised his brows at Spense. "And that lipstick stunt . . ."

"That was Caity's idea, sir." Spense was so damn proud of her.

"You took a hell of a risk lying to the governor like that."

"We got our confession," Caity pointed out. "And the smoking gun."

Heather Cambridge had already turned over her revolver to Sheridan. And a DNA sample, properly collected and secured by a warrant, had been sent for comparison to the material extracted from Cindy's forehead.

"As far as the Thresher . . ." Jim put his hands behind his head. "I have to tell you Violent Crimes is happy to have that guy off the streets. He was one homegrown, crazy, son of a bitch."

There was a long silence, and the mood in the room took a turn.

"You get one homegrown crazy off the streets, and another springs up in his place." Dutch finally gave voice to what everyone was thinking. Some questions had been answered, but other, pressing ones remained.

Jim flattened his palms against his chest. "We're not going to rest until we find the man who set that car bomb—believe me. But piecing it all together, it seems probable Heather Cambridge had a backup ready to step in for the Thresher. Now that she's behind bars, we hope this thing is finished." He made eye contact with each of them in turn. "But we're keeping surveillance on Matt Cambridge—in case he's involved, and we want the three of you to lay low for a while. We're prepared to offer you protection—"

"No thanks," Spense interrupted. They all knew adding muscle wouldn't keep them safe. He and Dutch could handle a direct attack as well as anyone Jim might assign to watch over them. "We need intel, not a bodyguard."

"I figured you'd say that." Jim nodded. "And we're working to get a bead on the car bomber, but so far, Mrs. Cambridge has only admitted to killing Cindy. We don't have anything—yet—to connect her to the Thresher, or to the attempts on your lives. From what you've told me, she had to have been desperate to keep whatever's in that diary out of the papers. Why else would she have sent the Thresher after it? And even though she's confessed to Cindy's murder, I doubt she wants the public to know the sordid details contained in the diary. If we had it in hand, we might have more leverage with her." He paused, then looked intently at Dutch. "You never found your wife's journal?"

Dutch shook his head. "I'm assuming she destroyed it before she died."

"Probably right." After a few pensive moments, Jim stood up. "Need my beauty sleep, kids. I've got a meeting with the folks from Washington again, in the morning. But give my best to Yolanda. You're heading to Jefferson when?"

"First thing tomorrow," Dutch said.

"We're planning on staying several days," Spense added. "We'll stick together and lay low."

"I'll do my damnedest to have Heather's henchman behind bars before you get back." Jim shook hands with each of them. "I'll expect a progress report on Yolanda. And if you turn up anything new . . . like say, Cindy's diary . . ."

"You'll be the first to know. You have my word, sir," Spense squeezed his mentor's hand, wondering when they were going to get around to having a long-overdue conversation about Jack. Spense hadn't told Jim yet, that he'd learned the truth about his father, but sometime soon, he'd like to hear his explanation for keeping it from him all these years.

Tuesday, October 22
11:30 P.M.
Dallas, Texas

AFTER THEIR MEETING with Jim, Spense, Dutch, and Caitlin had returned to the Langhorne home for a good night's sleep. Tomorrow, they'd drive to Jefferson to see Yolanda. Like they'd promised Jim, they planned to stick together and lay low.

But then Dutch had called Spense and her to the library. He said he had something to show them. And now here Caitlin stood, center stage, turning over a small volume, with a pink cloth cover, in her trembling hands. Despite its wispy appearance, Cindy's diary felt heavy—as if the importance of the words within possessed physical weight.

"When did you find it? *Where* did you find it?" she finally managed, after taking a moment to recover from the shock.

"Hiding in plain sight," Dutch said. "I should've thought of it before. While you two were in Austin taking all the risks, I decided I needed to pull my weight. I swore I'd either find Cindy's diary, or demolish the house trying. Like I'd done before, I checked every possible hiding place—but this time, I even pulled up floorboards and checked for hollow places in the walls. I looked absolutely everywhere . . . except the bookshelf. After all, who would hide a diary with all the other books?"

"A woman who'd heard her husband pontificate that blending in was the best way to become invisible." Spense let out a low whistle. "You're right, we should've thought of that before. But why did you lie to Jim? You're not thinking of withholding the diary from the police because I made a promise—"

"Not withholding it exactly. I'm just saying we don't really know what's in here, so how do we even know it has any evidentiary value?" Dutch brushed his hand through his hair, his eyes glistening with emotion. "You accused me once of hiding the diary to protect my wife, well, maybe that's the right thing to do. I sure as hell didn't protect her like I should've while she was alive. I don't want to let her down, now."

Caitlin had only seen him like this once before—the night he'd told her that Spense was his brother. "I agree with Dutch. Since she was his wife, he should read her words before anyone else."

Dutch shook his head. "I-I can't. The day I found it under her mattress, I thought of breaking the damn thing open. Did she really believe that flimsy lock could keep *me* out?" His laugh came out as a harsh, choking sound.

Caitlin lifted the journal and inhaled the musty smell of it. She ran fingers over the worn, cloth binding, stopping at the tiny bit of cold metal that secured Cindy Langhorne's secrets.

The lock.

She frowned down at it. Such a fragile fortress—one that could be broken into with nothing more than . . . *a bobby pin.* This was literally a diary meant to hold a young girl's dreams. The kind you could buy at any five-and-dime. It touched Caitlin that Cindy had chosen this, rather than a more impressive journal.

Cynthia Langhorne could've easily afforded one with a silver cover from Tiffany's, but she'd chosen to store her secrets here, in this childlike book, instead. She'd grown up devastatingly poor. Her family had been homeless for a time, and even as an adult, her life had been tarnished with scandal and shame. She tapped the book against her heart, wondering if the choice of this girlish journal represented Cindy's longing for a more innocent life.

She looked from Dutch to Spense. "I know this is evidence. Or at least we assume it will become evidence. But now that Heather Cambridge has confessed, I'm not sure . . ."

"Heather Cambridge was apparently willing to kill for what was written inside, and Jim thinks he can still use it for leverage to get her to admit she hired the hit men. There's still a paid killer out there somewhere." Spense didn't seem the least bit moved by the sentiment Caitlin felt oozing from the diary's pores.

"What you're really saying is we *think* Heather was willing to kill for what we *assume* she *believed* was written inside. That's a lot of uncertainty. And to me, this book seems like a place a young girl would hide her secret thoughts. We don't know how far back it dates . . . what if Cindy's been keeping it since she was in her teens?"

"We can't withhold it from the police."

She sighed. "It's not like they have a warrant for it."

"Like you didn't have a warrant for the lipstick?"

"I'm only suggesting that since this is such a personal posses-sion, we owe it to Cindy to open it first before handing it over. If it contains any evidence not already documented, anything at all that could be used for leverage, we'll turn it in." She heard stub-bornness creeping into her voice, but she wasn't going to back down. "Otherwise . . . I don't see the need to violate her any fur-ther. She's been humiliated enough."

Spense looked from her to his brother, and she could see in his eyes that he was wavering. He knew the degradation Cindy had suffered, just as Caitlin did. "It's Dutch's decision," Spense said at last.

"You should open it," Caitlin said to Dutch. "Some part of her must've wanted you to find it eventually . . . and read it."

He turned away. "I can't. It's going to list her affairs, her dis-satisfaction with our marriage. All the ways I let her down. I don't want to read about the other men she's been with. The way they put their hands on her, and the way they made her feel—the way I *didn't* make her feel. You open it, Caitlin. Someone has to read it, but it isn't going to be me."

Caitlin came around to face him. "Remember what you said before, about how you wish you hadn't turned away from the issues in your marriage? Well, you can't keep running forever. Cindy was your wife. Because you loved her, this falls on you. You're the one who has to open it."

He nodded, and she placed the delicate volume in his hand. He dumped a container of paper clips onto his desk, and then held his palm high over the pile, as if there were an electrified field repel-ling his hand. Caitlin held her breath. Several beats passed. At last Dutch swooped down, selected a paper clip, inserted it into the lock and before another heartbeat passed, the diary sprang open.

Dutch sent Caitlin an expression that seemed to be begging for mercy. But there's no reprieve from the truth. She met his eyes, not bothering to hide her worry. Perhaps the diary contained details of many more affairs than he suspected. It was possible that what he read there would scar him for life. But she wouldn't allow pity for him to overrule her judgment. There could be important evidence in the journal, and it wasn't anyone's place but his to find out. "Go ahead, Dutch. We're right here if you need us."

His bottom lip quivered, but only for a moment. "Where to begin?" With his finger, he parted the diary in the middle and began to read aloud:

"*My dearest Alex.*"

He smiled wistfully, and Caitlin realized for the first time she'd never heard anyone call Dutch by his Christian name, other than his mother. Even this small thing seemed such an intimate detail between husband and wife. But Dutch clearly wanted them present.

"*Tonight, sitting beside you at the ambassador's dinner, I felt so lucky to belong to you. Your hair is cut far too short, as always. You know how I loathe that aspect of your government job, but even a shaved head could not take away from your natural good looks. When you spoke of your work with the orphans of Guatemala there was such a fire in your eyes. My heart was bursting with pride, and I wanted to shout from the rooftops, or at least from the dinner table, that I was married to the smartest, kindest man on earth. If only that stuffy, diplomatic crowd knew the real you . . . like I do.*"

He stopped abruptly. Looked up in disbelief. "This is an old entry," he said. As if to dismiss what he'd read. "She didn't mean it."

Caitlin arched a brow. "You think she's lying to her own diary?"

He cleared his throat. "Let's move forward in time. That entry followed the year I'd returned from a long stint in Central America. She must've been lonely and glad for my return."

"She didn't say you made her lonely. She said you made her proud."

He flipped through more pages, both forward and back, blinking rapidly. "It appears these are all . . ."

He was clearly overcome with emotion. Spense looked at her, the concern for his brother apparent on his face. Her mind flew back to the night she'd found Dutch holding a pistol to his head. What if the details of Cindy's affairs were too much for him? She reached out her hand, for the diary, suddenly thinking she'd been very wrong to insist he be the one to read it.

He brushed a hand across his eyes. "These are all love letters."

Caitlin caught her breath. Cindy had written to her lovers via her diary.

Tears began to stream down Dutch's face. "To *me*. These are meant for me. I don't see anything at all here about Matt Cambridge, or any of her affairs."

He flipped to another page:

"*My darling Alex,*

This morning, we breakfasted on the balcony and as you reached for the teapot, your hand brushed the back of mine, then you smiled at me before going back to your paper. Small moments like these make me recall the way you entwined your fingers with mine, the first time we made love. I cherish every moment we spend together. My heart is bursting with the need to tell you how dearly I love you. If only I had the courage."

Tears pricked Caitlin's eyes, and her throat closed. Her heart began to beat faster in her chest.

Dutch turned more pages, skimming, running his fingers

across the words on the pages. Abruptly, he closed the book. "There's nothing in here of any use to the police." Then his knees seemed to give way. Spense buoyed him up with an arm around his back.

Dutch shook his head. "Don't look at me that way, brother. Do. Not. Feel sorry for me. I loved my wife, and she loved me." Then his eyes darted back and forth between them. "I'm keeping this diary. It's mine." His voice rang with sorrow for his loss, but more than that, with joy. "God in heaven. She *loved* me."

Clutching the journal to his chest, he strode across the room and threw open the door. "I need to be alone, now." Then he looked pointedly at Spense. "And you . . . my dear brother, I think you have something you'd better say to Caitlin."

The door closed behind him.

Spense's shoulders dropped, and he lunged for the door. She could see a faint tremor sweep his body.

"Wait." She went to him and rested her hand on his shoulder.

"I should go to him." He kept his back turned. "I know he said he wanted to be alone, but I should be there for him. This is one time I'm going to be the brother he deserves."

Her heart was in her throat, and tears were in her eyes. "You are that brother. You always have been."

"No. No. No. I turned away from him when he needed me. I can't help thinking that maybe somewhere deep down I knew the truth, but I just didn't want to believe it. And if I didn't know, I should've figured it out."

"You're not *that* good a profiler, Spense. He pushed you away, for his own reasons, and you reacted as anyone would. You can't blame yourself. Both of you are responsible for how you treated each other, but you have the rest of your lives ahead to be brothers. To build a real relationship."

He whirled to face her. "What about us? What do we have ahead of us?"

She raised her chin, choosing her words carefully. Dutch's voice echoed in her head: *Dear, God. She loved me.*

If only Dutch had known the truth while Cindy lived . . .

She wet her lips. What she wanted to say to him had been on the tip of her tongue for so very long. Why hadn't she told him she loved him? "Spense, I—"

He grabbed her by the shoulders. "I love you, Caity Cassidy," his voice was harsh, almost angry. "And by God, I'm not going to wait until I'm dead and gone to tell you in a letter."

"Thank heavens for that." She tiptoed up and pressed her lips to the corner of his mouth, then kissed her way up to his ear, and whispered, "I love you, Atticus Spenser. And I'm not going to scribble it in my diary hoping you find it one day. I'm going to tell you right here and now. And then I'm going to tell you again tomorrow. And every day after that."

His hands came around her waist, pressing her body to his, so tightly she could barely breathe. "I was a fool to wait so long. First, I was trying to give you the space you needed."

"And then you were mad as hell . . . and you had every right to be. I should've come to your room that very night. I should've woken you up and told you everything Dutch told me about your father. But I was afraid to put you in harm's way, and . . . the truth is, I couldn't bear to see you hurt. But I know now, by keeping secrets from you, I only caused you more pain." She cradled his face in her hands. "Forgive me."

Then he kissed her.

A long, hard, demanding kiss.

There was heat in the way his tongue thrust into her mouth, an obvious need in the way he crushed his body into hers, but there was something more than passion. There was a promise in the way he touched her—a promise that took her breath away. She wanted nothing more than to stand right here and kiss this man until the very moment her heart stopped beating.

But he broke apart.

"There's nothing to forgive," he rasped. "You made a mistake, but, baby, I've made them, too. No matter how badly I was hurting, I should've given you a chance to explain. I should've tried to see things from your side instead of shutting you out. I'm so sorry I let this come between us. I realize now we can't expect perfection, from each other or from ourselves. When Dutch was reading those letters from Cindy, all I could think about was how I never want that to be us. I don't want to hide my feelings from you anymore. Even if those feelings seem dark or dangerous."

She took his hand and placed it over her pounding heart. "I promise never to keep secrets from you again. I promise to trust that we can figure things out together. Because I love you, and I'm tired of pretending that I don't."

His lips were on her eyelids, then wandered down to her cheek and finally, reached her mouth. "You taste so sweet, Caity. I want you so badly, right now, I don't think I can wait another second."

She opened her mouth and his tongue swept over hers with an urgency that set her entire body on fire. She gasped, and pulled his head down for more. They kissed until her head felt so light she thought she'd faint. And with every stroke of his tongue, with every feathered touch of his fingers along her jaw, she heard his words echoing in her heart. *I love you, Caity Cassidy.*

Dizzy, she pulled back to look him in the eyes. She was so grateful to be alive and to have the chance to tell him. "I love you. I *love* you."

"About time we cleared that up." Dutch appeared as if from nowhere, and she all but jumped out of her skin.

Heat rose to her face. She fanned herself with her hand, then stepped a respectable distance away from Spense. No telling how long Dutch had been standing there, watching them. "You might've let us know you were here."

"I did . . . eventually. Maybe I was enjoying seeing the two of you enjoying each other."

Spense idly picked up a magazine and shifted it in front of his waist.

"Don't bother." Dutch said. "We're all grown-ups here, and what I've got to say will lower your flag soon enough."

Spense shrugged and tossed the magazine on the couch, revealing an impressive fullness in his pants. "Your timing sucks."

"I consider it my brotherly duty to interrupt you at the most inconvenient moments from here on out. I need to make up for not having had the chance to spoil your fun when we were growing up." In spite of his tone, his face seemed serious. "Anyway, I just finished reading Cindy's diary, and here's the thing—I don't believe it."

Spense threw up his hands. "What do you mean you don't believe it? Is your sense of self-worth so low you're back to thinking she lied to herself—in her own diary?"

"I don't believe she had an affair with Matt Cambridge, or . . .

let me rephrase." He waved one hand in the air excitedly. "I'm not making myself clear. I think she did have an affair with Matt—after all he admitted it."

Caitlin heard a *but* at the end of that sentence and waited for it.

"But I don't believe she was *cheating* on me. Not really." He looked imploringly at Caitlin. "I've read most of those entries in her diary and skimmed the rest. And I am absolutely convinced that my wife loved me. I don't think she would've had an affair just for the fun of it. She had to have had some compelling reason."

Caitlin's hand went to her heart. She'd had that feeling for so long now, that if only Cindy could speak to them through her diary, the mystery would be solved. Then Dutch had showed them the journal was filled with nothing but love letters, and though happy for him, she'd been disappointed it hadn't provided the answers they desperately needed. But she was wrong. The diary laid it all out in front of them. They only had to open their eyes to the truth.

Cindy loved Dutch.

That was the key to everything!

She squeezed her eyes shut. They had the key; now they just had to find the right door, and open it.

Spense sat down and crossed his legs. "I'm sorry. I understand how you'd want to believe she didn't willingly have an affair with Cambridge. But to me, it's consistent with her past behavior. She had affairs early in the marriage, and the best predictor of future behavior is past behavior."

"You're talking like a profiler, Spense." Caitlin's voice shook with excitement.

He turned his palms up.

"Speaking as a woman . . . and a psychiatrist," she continued,

"I'm going to have to agree with Dutch. Those early affairs were an attempt to get Dutch's attention. They weren't affairs for the sake of affairs."

"Why wouldn't that same reason—a cry for attention—apply to her relationship with Matt Cambridge?" Spense asked.

"Because it doesn't. The marriage had moved past that stage. Cindy no longer believed Dutch cared if she slept around. She'd tried that tactic to make him jealous in the past, and she knew it would never work."

The look on Dutch's face was like a knife in her heart, but she forged ahead. "Dutch was there anything at all in that diary to suggest *why* Cindy would sleep with Cambridge?"

"No. It didn't mention him at all. It's all about how much she loves me. About how much joy she took from the few moments I gave her of my time." He let out a long breath. "But . . . the most recent entries, those made just before her death seemed strange. She kept talking about how she'd do anything to protect me. As I was reading them, I kept wondering why she would think I needed protection."

Spense bolted to his feet. His hands jittered at his sides. Many times, she'd watched his expression while he struggled to organize the chaos in his head, and she knew exactly what he needed to help him focus. She dipped into her purse and handed him a miniature Rubik's cube. He hadn't pulled one out of his pocket in days—not since he'd learned the truth about his dad. The cubes were a poignant reminder of his father—and now, perhaps . . . his father's betrayal. "I noticed you haven't been carrying your cubes, so I snuck one out of your suitcase. I was afraid you'd throw them all away, then later regret it."

He looked at her a long moment, grinned, and accepted it.

"Smart lady. Thank you. I did throw the rest out, and I haven't been able to think straight since." He scrambled it and unscrambled it—twice. "Blackmail!" He tossed his cube in the air and caught it. "Remember our early theory that Cindy was involved in a blackmail scheme? At the time I thought it seemed half-right. What if Cindy wasn't the one doing the blackmailing? What if Cindy was the victim?"

Dutch steepled his fingers and rested his chin on them. "You're saying someone blackmailed Cindy into having an affair with Matt Cambridge. That would definitely be a compelling reason . . . but what would they be holding over her head . . . and why?"

"Caity, make a list." The cube was back, and Spense was on a roll.

"Hang on, let me get the board." She quickly located the whiteboard and markers and set to work while Spense dictated:

"Cindy had an affair with Matt Cambridge. Matt Cambridge was the frontrunner for the Democratic nomination for the presidency, and the only candidate who was at all likely to beat a sitting Republican president. An illicit affair could—and will—force Cambridge to withdraw from the race."

"So following that line of reasoning, the plan would've been to get Cindy to have an affair with Cambridge, then reveal it at just the right moment to destroy his presidential hopes," Dutch said. "Who would do that, and how would they convince her to go along with a plan that would devastate her best friend, not to mention betray me?"

"Let's stick with who; and then we can work on the how later," Spense said. "Who would stand to benefit *most* if Matt Cambridge had to drop out of the race?"

"The president," they all said in unison.

Abruptly, they all dropped into chairs. As the wind let out of their sails, Caitlin felt the ship running aground. "Do we really think the president of the United States blackmailed Cindy to get rid of an opponent?"

"No." Dutch poured himself two fingers of whiskey from the decanter on his desk. "But then again, the president doesn't do much of anything on his own. That man is *handled*, maybe more than any president in recent history."

It was true; the general consensus was that the president's advisors were the ones who really ran the show in D.C.

"Maybe one of the president's men, knowing that Matt had a longtime thing for Cindy, approached her and coerced her into the affair in order to ruin Cambridge," Caitlin offered doubtfully.

"To my knowledge, Cindy knows very few people in Washington. And frankly, if someone had approached her, she still wouldn't have done it. She loved Heather too much, and she wanted to help her get to the White House," Dutch responded.

"Unless whoever approached her had some major leverage."

"She certainly didn't need money, and she didn't care about power." Dutch nixed that idea, too.

Caitlin closed her eyes. Cindy was talking to them through her diary. All they had to do was listen. "She may not have cared for money or power, but there was one thing she valued above all else." She held her hand out. "You, Dutch. And her last entries were about protecting you. From what?"

"Tesarak?" Dutch frowned. "That's the one blemish on my record. Someone could've threatened to dredge it all up and ruin my career."

"Or worse. The Bureau cleared you, so the case never went to court. If the blackmailer claimed to have evidence against you—

that it wasn't a good shoot, you could still be tried for murder. But who's that loyal to the president and has the balls and the credibility to pull it off? Who has enough access to the Tesarak files to claim they had evidence against you, and to make Cindy believe it?" Spense asked.

The room went quiet, and then as if lightning struck them simultaneously, they all looked up at once. Caitlin saw Spense's face go ghost white.

"I can only think of one person," Dutch said. "But how in God's name are we going to prove it?"

Spense's face turned a slightly brighter shade of pale. "Does anyone remember where we put the decoy diary?"

Chapter Twenty-Eight

Wednesday, October 23
4:30 P.M.
Preston Hollow, Texas

SPENSE WAS FAIRLY certain Monroe Sheridan thought Dutch, Caity, and he, had gone off their gourds. If the detective really believed their new theory, he wouldn't appear so at ease. The way his shoulders slanted toward the ground made his stance seem almost a shrug—of course, that was partly due to the low ceiling in the surveillance vehicle. But his slack expression and periodic yawns smacked of stakeout boredom. Spense, on the other hand, had all but worked the squares off the face of his Rubik's cube but still couldn't stop his mind from racing, and Sheridan's constant chatter over the radio wasn't helping.

"Perimeter still secure? Who took charge of chow? Jarkowski's stinking up the damn truck with a liverwurst sandwich. I thought we talked about this shit before. No tuna. No liverwurst. Those are the rules." Sheridan squeezed into the seat next to where Spense sat eyeing the panel of video monitors. "This is a total waste of my time."

"Stakeouts are below your pay grade, huh?"

"Something like that." Sheridan spat into an empty paper coffee cup, then crushed it and tossed it into a wastebasket. "Particularly when it involves some harebrained theory about a presidential conspiracy."

"So why'd you show up?" Spense hadn't been sure he could persuade Sheridan to go along and had been relieved when he'd agreed to go all out.

"Because I was wrong about your boy, Dutch. And I figure I owe him one." The detective checked the monitors, stood up, nearly bumping his head on the ceiling. "And because you pulled a rabbit out of your hat at the governor's mansion yesterday. So I figure, if you can do that again, my career is set for the duration. And if your crazy-ass theory turns out to be wrong, I'll be standing right here, ready to say I told you so. Got myself a win-win, see?"

"Sounds fair enough to me." Again, Spense could care less who took the credit as long as they got their man. Only this time, he was hoping with all his might that he was wrong. He'd give anything to hear the words *I told you so* from Sheridan.

Because that would mean Jim Edison, his dad's best friend, the man who'd watched over him after Jack's death and mentored both him and Dutch into the FBI was not a dirty rat bastard who'd paid an assassin to bring back Cindy Langhorne's diary—at any cost. But the way Spense's gut was pinging on this one, Jim was about to crack one more piece off his already fractured heart.

Once Sheridan came on board, setting the plan in motion had been simple. Dutch contacted Jim and reported that he'd found Cindy's diary and was calling to keep him in the loop. But his priority, he told Jim, was to travel to Jefferson, along with Spense and Caity to check on his mother, Yolanda. Meanwhile, he said, he'd locked the diary in the library safe of his Preston Hollow home.

Jim had pressed Dutch with questions. *Had he read the diary? No. Why the hell not? Who else knew the diary had been found? No one? Good. Maybe keep it that way for now.* Five separate times, Jim had asked Dutch if he'd read the diary yet.

After much reassurance, Dutch had told Jim a half-truth. That he was having a hard time turning Cindy's secrets over to the cops. And that he wasn't sure he could face reading the contents of that diary. That was why he couldn't bring himself to open the book.

Jim had been very understanding and promised that upon Dutch's return from Jefferson, the two of them would turn the diary over to Sheridan together. He'd promised to be there to support Dutch when Cindy's secrets were revealed.

Then, with Caity waiting safe and sound down at the Dallas PD, Dutch, Spense, and Sheridan went to work. They'd locked the decoy diary in Dutch's safe. Since Jim would smell a rat if they made things too easy, they'd set the burglar alarm in Dutch's home. Security cameras were placed throughout the premises, and plainclothes detectives swarmed the quiet Preston Hollow neighborhood: walking borrowed dogs, checking water meters, and raking leaves.

If they got Jim on tape, breaking and entering, if they could catch him red-handed with the decoy diary, they'd have enough to detain him and get a warrant for his computer and phone. There should be a mother lode of evidence on Jim's private electronics. And there was always a chance, since Jim likely believed the diary detailed his part in a conspiracy to force Cambridge out of the presidential race and subvert the democratic process, that they could bluff a confession out of him.

If, in fact, there was a conspiracy.

A small voice in Spense's head continued to whisper hopefully that he might have it all wrong.

All that was left to do was wait and see if Jim took the bait.

Across the street, Dutch stood watch in a second surveillance van. They'd been looking out since 9 A.M., and nearly eight hours later, there was still no sign of Jim.

"You told him you'd be gone until Friday, but just so we're clear, I'm not tying my men up for three full days. If he doesn't show by sundown, I'm calling it," Sheridan said.

Spense didn't like those terms, but he'd expected as much, given the circumstances.

"Let's face it, if Jim Edison was worried enough about that diary to send a hit man after it, he's going to act fast. If he really believes that diary could implicate him in a conspiracy that leads all the way to the White House, he won't let the grass grow under those fancy ostrich boots of his." Sheridan spoke into the radio again, then said, "They got nothing."

Spense checked the feed in the library. Still working, just like the last ten times he checked it. Feed from the driveway camera and the entry were online, too. Bracing his hands behind his head, he leaned back to wait, and wait some more. He was sick to his stomach, and it wasn't just the liverwurst.

By five o'clock, a wave of optimism lifted his spirits. Sheridan had made a good point: Jim wouldn't wait long to act—if he were guilty. So maybe Spense's gut was wrong, and Jim was exactly what Spense had always believed him to be—a good guy. The sun ducked behind a large bank of clouds, and Spense noticed the eastern wall of the sky darkening with thunderclouds. A lightning strike crackled in the air, and a light rain pelted the side of the truck. Not good, since they needed the plainclothes officers to look natural wandering the streets. On the other hand, an impending storm might keep the neighbors safely behind closed doors.

But it wasn't long until the drizzle let up, and the sun popped back out, shining a spotlight on the rain-slick street . . . and then bounced its rays off a tan Dodge Charger, creeping down the road.

"Look alive." Spense thumped Sheridan between the shoulder blades.

The detective yawned. "That ain't him. Last time I saw Jim, he pulled up to the station in a red Porsche."

"He's not stupid enough to drive himself to a break-in in his personal vehicle. That Charger's a Bucar if I've ever seen one. He must've yanked it from the fleet." The optimism that had lifted his spirits disappeared, and a lead weight in his gut replaced it.

The Charger pulled curbside, several doors south of Dutch's home. Its driver exited the car, tugging a waterproof poncho over his clothing. Not unusual on a rainy day, but a bit much for a light drizzle like this one. Even though the electric smell of a storm hung in the air, Spense didn't think most guys would worry about a few stray raindrops mussing their hair. The poncho's hood hid the man's face, and its bulky profile concealed the shape of his body. As he made his way up the street, he hunched over, making it difficult to determine his height. His gait, one of the main cues Spense might use to recognize Jim with his face concealed, was useless, too. The suspect limped up the road, which made the hairs on the back of Spense's neck prickle. Either they were looking at a guy who cared more about his hair than most, had both a spinal deformity and an ankle injury—or that was Jim Edison on his way to steal Cindy's diary, trying to make sure the neighbors, if questioned, would be unable to accurately describe him.

The closer he got to Dutch's place, the more prominent the limp became. Finally, the Hunchback of Notre Dame ascended Dutch's front steps and knocked forcefully at the door. "Census." The microphone on the porch transmitted the sound of his voice.

Jim.

Spense's heart paused, then started back up with a vengeance, hammering rage through his entire being, smashing a lifelong friendship to bits, until no trace of sympathy remained, nothing that might stop Spense from taking this guy—this asshole—down. His mentor called out a few more times, "Census!"

Then, apparently satisfied no one was home, Jim made his way around to the backyard, where cameras caught him at the fuse box, disabling the alarm.

You motherfucking son of a bitch.

Jim removed his poncho, wrapped it around his fist, and smashed a back window. The cameras caught him climbing inside, then lost him again until . . . he entered the library. His eyes darted everywhere and finally landed on the portrait of Cindy that concealed the wall safe.

Using a handheld electronic device, Jim unscrambled the lock code and opened the safe. After removing several packs of small bills, he reached in and retrieved the diary. He stuffed the bills under his sport coat, as if setting things up to look like an ordinary burglary.

With a grim smile on his face, he examined the diary. Apparently satisfied, after turning it over in his hands—Caity had come up with the last-minute idea of adding Cindy's initials in gold lettering on the back—Jim tucked the decoy diary beneath his coat and exited the library. A minute later, he walked straight out the front door and headed for his car.

"Got him!" Spense said.

Maybe not enough for a conviction, but enough for an arrest and a warrant to search his home and computer—which ought to offer up all the proof they'd need. Giving terse orders over the radio, Sheridan put his men in motion. The plan was to surround Jim and cuff him just before he got into his car.

Plainclothes officers materialized in strategic locations.

"Proceed with the utmost caution," Sheridan ordered.

The last thing anyone wanted was for one of the officers to have to discharge his weapon in a residential area. Luckily, the street appeared clear of civilians for now. As a precaution, Sheridan decided to order a temporary roadblock to prevent an influx of residents arriving home from work—just until Jim was safely in custody.

The muscles in Spense's back ached from the way he'd been tensing his shoulders. He wanted out of this van. He wanted to be on the street so he could be the one to personally cuff Jim, but that privilege belonged to Dutch. He could see his brother, already on the move, wearing a hoodie of his own, with a bevy of detectives at his side.

"Looks like you pulled another rabbit out of your hat." Sheridan shot him an animated smile, his stakeout ennui a thing of the past. "I bet I make commander in under a year."

"We have to get him in custody first." Spense rubbed the soreness out of his tight jaw.

"No worries. You Feebies make everything a big deal. We'll have him cuffed and in a black-and-white before you can say . . ."

Spense squinted at the monitor. "Tell your men to stand down."

"What? No. Jim's nearly at the car."

"He just lost his limp, and he's doubled his pace. I think he made one of your guys."

"All the more reason . . . oh, holy shit," Sheridan yelled into his radio. "Stand down! Stand down!"

Headed straight for Jim, a kid pedaled fast and furiously—on a beat-up yellow bike with flower decals.

Aaron.

Spense ripped the radio from Sheridan's hands. "Civilian in the field. Stand down. Do not approach. Wait for my go."

Too late, the men dropped back.

Jim had made them all right. He kicked a large rock into the bike's path. Aaron swerved, and the bike tipped over. Jim plucked Aaron off the sidewalk and pulled him against his chest.

Aaron screamed, crying out for help. His feet dangled, kicking in the air. Then Jim locked an arm around his throat, and the boy went still, and silent.

"Back off. Back way off," Spense ordered into the radio as he scrambled out of the van. He ran full tilt to where the detectives encircled Jim and the boy, weapons drawn.

Aaron had ridden up out of nowhere at the exact wrong moment. But Spense knew it was no coincidence. He'd egged the kid on with all his talk of profiling, telling him he'd make a good agent someday. Aaron had probably had Dutch's house under surveillance ever since the news reported him missing. This was on Spense. He knew it, but now wasn't the time to let guilt mess with his head.

Now was the time to act.

He put his hands in the air and stepped inside the circle, keeping a yard or so between him and Jim. "Drop your weapon. You got no reason to hurt an innocent kid."

From behind him, Sheridan called for Spense to drop back.

No fucking way.

Spense took another step toward Jim and Aaron.

"I'm ordering you to take cover, Agent Spenser," Sheridan had a bullhorn now.

Hands high over his head, Spense kept walking. Then another set of footsteps sounded beside him.

Damn it, Sheridan.

"Get back," Spense said through gritted teeth, and then, out of his peripheral vision, he caught sight, not of Sheridan, but of his brother. He nodded, and together they halted a few feet or so in front of Jim and the boy. His mouth pulled up at the corners, just a bit, because one the best hostage negotiators on the planet now stood by his side.

"Let me handle this," Dutch said. "It's what I do. Step back and take cover."

"I'm not leaving your side, brother. Not this time."

"Okay." Dutch shot him a side glance. "Don't fuck it up."

"Not another step." Jim raised his pistol and angled it just inches from Aaron's scalp. "I thought you said you didn't read the diary."

"I lied." Dutch jerked his head up.

"Yeah, I got that." Jim narrowed his eyes. "You forget, Dutch, I took your class on hostage negotiation; your tricks won't work on me."

"Then you must not have been paying attention, or you'd know I don't use tricks. I just tell the truth. You know what I want, so let's make this go quick."

"You want me to surrender my gun. Keep dreaming."

"You got no way out, Jim. You know as well as I do this boy is not real leverage. The only way you walk out of this alive is if you put down your weapon. You know it already. I shouldn't have to spell it out for you."

"You expect me to take you at your word after you lied? You read the diary, and then you set me up."

"You want to talk about our lying to you?" Spense broke in. "Well I sure as hell wanna talk about your lying to me. Put down your gun, and we'll have a family conference."

Spense saw a faint tremor in Jim's gun hand. A sign his emotions were overtaking his training. Aaron's eyes had gone saucer wide, and his chest heaved rapidly. The kid was terrified, but Spense couldn't put his attention on him. He had to focus on Jim. "Let's talk, buddy. We can work it out."

Jim shook his head. "You can't beat me. This diary doesn't prove a thing. It's just Cindy's word against mine—and probably inadmissible hearsay at that."

"You should've thought of that before you took a hostage. You wanna talk about your scheme to bring Cambridge down, show us how smart you are? Drop your weapon. Let the kid go, and like I said, we can talk all day long. Maybe even deal. But no deal until you lose your gun."

Jim had no idea they didn't even have Cindy's words to use against him, that the real diary contained only love letters to her husband. Up until this very moment, it had all been speculation on their part. And while they'd take whatever semblance of a confession Jim might make, that wasn't the goal any longer. Nothing mattered now but getting Aaron to safety. But talking Jim down was the only way to do that. Spense took a chance to break eye contact with Jim for a split second, to signal Aaron with his eyes. *Hold tight, buddy. We've got you.*

Aaron's trembling chin came up, and Spense thought he'd understood.

Jim tightened his arm around Aaron's neck, in a true choke hold, so the boy couldn't speak or scream. "*My* scheme to bring down Cambridge? I'm not taking the fall for this. It was Hamlin who approached me."

The White House chief of staff.

"Drop your weapon. We'll make sure you don't get a raw deal." Dutch moved closer. Almost near enough to tackle Jim to the ground.

"Hamlin promised me the directorship in exchange for getting Cambridge out of the race. I shouldn't have to do the president's dirty work for the honor of being handed an office I've already *earned.*"

All those meetings with the boys from D.C. The rumors of a presidential appointment for Jim were true. He was after the directorship of the FBI. And he'd been willing to do anything to get it. Even go against the principles that had led him to the Bureau in the first place.

"Put the gun down, and let's talk about it. You were coerced," Dutch said.

Spense nodded. His arms ached from holding them high in the air. "I'm going to lower my arms now, Jim. They hurt like hell."

When Jim didn't object, Spense knew they were making headway. Like Dutch had taught him, he'd appealed to Jim's human side and given him an easy request. It was a simple way to make inroads. Get the cooperation ball rolling.

"The directorship is rightfully yours," Dutch said. "No tricks, just truth, here. Put down the gun. Let Aaron go. That's his name, and I know you don't want to hurt him."

"It's too late." Jim choked out the words, but it made no difference to Spense. He could cry like a baby, and he wouldn't have an ounce of pity for the man.

"Not too late. Not if you put down the gun. You've done a great service for your country, Jim." Spense tried to remember what he'd learned from Dutch. Keep it personal. Call him by his name. "All the cases you've solved."

"The terrorist threats you've thwarted." Dutch lowered his arms, too. Still no objection from Jim. "You'll get yourself a great lawyer, and he'll get you a sweet deal. Think of what concessions they'll make to take down the president's inner circle. *You* can do that, Jim. What you know about the plot to get Matt Cambridge out of the race—*that's your leverage.*"

"Not the boy." Spense made eye contact with Aaron, then shifted his gaze toward a large tree that could provide some cover, hoping he'd understand the signal. "Let him go, Jim."

The pistol wobbled in Jim's hand.

"Aaron's dad is out of the picture. The boy wants to be a profiler." Spense tried to appeal to Jim's paternal instinct. In spite of everything, Spense knew he had one.

"That true?" Jim asked Aaron, loosening the choke hold but keeping his pistol aimed at his head.

Aaron looked at Spense, then nodded. "Y-yes. I wanna go home."

"I *know* you don't want to hurt this boy." Dutch moved in closer, with Spense in lockstep. "The way you looked after Spense and me when Jack died, I don't believe you ever meant any harm to come to us. And I know you don't mean Aaron any harm now. So do the right thing, Jim—it's what you do best."

Jim's legs trembled beneath him. "I never meant for anyone to get hurt. This whole thing is on Heather and Cindy. I told Cindy I could prove you killed Tesarak in cold blood. She told me she'd go through with the affair with Cambridge, but she had everything documented in her diary. She said her diary was safe and if anything ever happened to Dutch or to her, the truth would come out. She shouldn't have threatened me like that, Dutch." His voice carried an expectant plea, like he really believed that once he'd explained himself, Spense and Dutch would understand. "That's the *only* reason I went looking for a hit man who could get rid of Cindy and bring in the diary. But Heather caught wind of the affair. Heather killed Cindy *before* the Thresher could do it right. Because Heather ruined everything, I *had* to send the Thresher after you. When you ran, Dutch, I was sure you had the diary."

"Of course, it was my fault for running. Like you say, you had to send the Thresher. And the car bomb—you thought we all knew more than we should."

"*And* you all betrayed me. I warned Spense away, but he disobeyed my orders. I never wanted that guard, Brian, to get hurt, either. I waited until I saw Spense exit the building to set the timer. How was I supposed to know someone else would get there first?"

Jim set the bomb himself. Tried to murder the sons of the man who'd saved his life in combat. The Thresher was a sicko, but Jim was the real monster.

"Put down your gun. Let's get you a lawyer. Dutch and I forgive you," Spense said. "And a jury will understand, too." He threw out a Hail Mary. "Unless you fuck it all up by hurting this innocent kid. Drop your weapon. Let him go."

"A jury? You think I care about convincing a jury or making a deal? No matter what I do now, my life with the Bureau is finished . . . and the Bureau is my life."

The deadweight of Jim's words hung in the air. Spense could feel the tension vibrating off his brother. They both knew what those words meant. Now they were the ones who had no leverage because Jim did not plan to walk away from this alive. They had to get him to release Aaron *now*.

"Let Aaron go. Maybe you think your life is over, but this kid's got his still in front of him. Just like Dutch and me, he wants to be like *you*. He wants to serve in the FBI. How do you want to be remembered? As the man who betrayed his country, or as the man who followed his conscience and let a young boy go free? A goddamn hero! Be a hero, Jim. Let him go."

Tears streamed down Aaron's face. The wind died down, and a dreadful stillness replaced the rain.

"Don't let one mistake negate your entire life of service. Don't let it define you. If this is going to be the last thing you do," Spense paused, trying to get control of his voice, "make it the right thing."

Jim's arm wobbled down to his side. He shoved Aaron in the back. "Get the hell out of here."

Aaron ran toward Spense but stumbled and fell. Spense yanked him up. "Walk fast, but don't run. Other side of the street. Do *not* look back."

Aaron's breath came in spurts, and a hoarse grunt rushed out of his throat.

"Go!" Spense said.

One. Two . . . Aaron made it to the other side.

"Thank you." Spense released a shuddering breath.

"Now put your gun on the ground. Let's hammer this out," Dutch said.

Jim's arm jerked, and the sound of gunfire shattered the stillness in the afternoon air. His body thudded to the ground. Blood poured from the gaping hole in his head, mixed with water from the rain, and drained down into the sewers.

Chapter Twenty-Nine

Thursday, October 24
7:00 A.M.
Preston Hollow, Texas

THERE'S SOMETHING ABOUT death that makes you want to live. Really live. Caitlin pried herself away from Spense's magnificent, bare chest to enjoy her view of his face while he slept. Unlike some people, who look very different when sleep strips away their defenses, Spense looked the same. Granted, his mouth didn't usually gape, but his day face was generally as unguarded and devoid of pretense as it was at this very moment. He was a good man, and she was a lucky woman.

A *very* lucky woman.

"Spense," she whispered, though the way she shook his shoulder negated the purpose of her gentle, low voice. "Open your eyes."

Awakening next to a slumbering Spense was not unlike rising early on Christmas morning, only to have to wait until later to unwrap your presents. She shook his shoulder harder. "Wake up, please. I want some more."

He popped one eye open. "More coming right up. He checked beneath the sheets and grinned. Yep. Up and ready."

She swatted his arm. "I meant that I can't wait to get the day started, you know, as a couple."

"That's exactly what I'm talking about," he said, and pulled her down for a hard kiss.

Then something vibrated between them—his phone. She threw her hands up in surrender. But in truth, she didn't mind. He'd kissed her breathless, and she needed air before going back in.

"I cannot wait to get you to Tahiti." But as he looked at his cell, his grin turned to a groan. "I've got a secure message."

She brushed her hair from her eyes, and tried to wipe what she assumed to be a love-struck smile off her face. "Well, are you going to tell me what it says? Or is it above my security clearance?"

He shook his head, and the faintest lines appeared around his eyes. "It's actually for all of us."

She made a show of looking around, then peeked under the covers, as if wondering who else might be in the room, but she knew, of course, the message must be for Dutch, too.

Spense barked a laugh, like he currently had his hand on Ellen DeGeneres's naked ass instead of plain ole Caity's—she loved a man who got her humor. And she loved a man who grabbed her ass in the morning. "We've been cordially invited to appear at the field office at oh eight hundred sharp."

He yanked her back on top of him. "That gives me just enough time to take care of a little personal business first."

AT OH EIGHT hundred sharp, Anthony Logsdon lumbered into the Dallas field-office conference room. Spense scrambled to his feet to greet the director of the FBI.

"As you were." Director Logsdon motioned for them to take their seats around the glass-topped table. "I should be rising to my feet for you three."

Caity blushed prettily. Spense tried to assume a humble posture, but the director had a point. They'd done good work, and he was proud of it. The upward tilt of Dutch's chin told Spense he felt the same.

They all sat down, and a hush fell over the room. Spense hadn't exactly expected the director to fly down and meet with them in person, but he wasn't that surprised, either. After all, they'd busted open a can of conspiratorial worms that couldn't be buried. Not to mention the Dallas field office wasn't going to run itself. Until a new SAC could be installed, someone would need to oversee its operations. The director of the FBI was one logical choice.

"Dr. Cassidy, it's a pleasure to meet you in person. I can honestly say that after your contributions over the past months, the Bureau is going to be seeking your services for a long time to come. In fact, you and Agent Spenser are currently topping the FBI's most wanted list."

"Thank you, sir," Caity's cheeks pinked again. "I'm honored to serve in any way I can."

"Good. Because . . ."

"Sir, respectfully," Spense cleared his throat. Not that he planned to make a habit of interrupting the director, but he felt a case request coming on. That *FBI's most wanted* remark would undoubtedly come with a price tag. "We'll be requesting time off before our next case. We've worked three back to back—I know this one was off the books, but—"

The director held up his hand. "I agree. It's not wise to put you two right back out there. And around here, there's always going to be another case. You should set boundaries, but . . ." His eyes swept back and forth between Caity and Spense. "I'll let you make your own decision once you know the details. Meanwhile . . ." He turned to Dutch "This place can't run itself."

"I'd be honored to serve under you, sir. I'll help any way I can."

"Glad to hear it." The director flashed a wry smile. "Because I do need your help. While I'm well aware of your recent loss, I also know you love the Bureau. And frankly, if I'd lost my Nancy, I wouldn't want to be alone in the house, mourning. I'd want to be right here, doing good where I could, surrounded by my second family . . . the men and women of the FBI. I'd want to make Nancy proud."

Dutch nodded—vigorously. "Understood. And sir, if you're asking me if I want to come back to work, the answer—"

"Hear me out." He folded his arms across his chest. "Normally, I'd stay and run things for however long it took to find the next SAC. But my wife is ill. I don't want to be away from her any longer than necessary, so I'm announcing my retirement within the month. Jim was the frontrunner to take over my spot, but thank heavens we have a backup. My point is, I can't take over Dallas. Nancy comes first."

"You must have backups for Jim, too, though, since you were planning to move him into the director's spot." Dutch sounded confused. But Spense saw exactly where this was headed and grinned proudly.

"We do." Logsdon leveled his gaze at Dutch. "We've been set on your taking over Jim's spot since before the tragedy with your wife. And frankly, I still believe you're the right man for the job. You might not be the most popular guy in the office, but you're the most respected. You've earned it, son. So while I'll understand if you decline, the position of Special Agent in Charge of Dallas is yours—if you want it."

Dutch's shoulders drew back, and his eyes gleamed in the morning light. "I want it, sir. Thank you."

Spense's chest swelled with pride. Under the table, Caity touched his hand. Finally, something good for Dutch.

"Congratulations." Caity sent Spense's brother one of her big, sweet smiles. At first, Spense had been jealous of the attention she'd paid Dutch, but now he was glad they got on so well. He and Dutch had a ways to go to build a real relationship, but they were brothers, and Dutch was going to be a part of his life—of their life—from here on out.

A phone, sitting in the center of the table rang. They all jumped. The director stood to answer, as if he knew who'd be on the line. His face turned grave. "Yes, sir. They're right here."

He pulled his shoulders into a military stance. "I have the commander in chief on the line."

Even in life-and-death situations Spense had nerves of steel, but right now, knowing that the president of the United States was on the phone gave him a bit of a quiver in the old gut.

"You're on speaker, Mr. President. I'm here with Agents Spenser and Langhorne, and Dr. Cassidy's present, too."

"Pleasure to speak with you all." The president's Vermont accent, which had been imitated by every impersonator in the country, rang over the speakers.

"Likewise," Dutch said.

Spense couldn't help smiling at the dueling accents—Dutch's Texas drawl and the president's Yankee twang.

A round of "my pleasures," came and went. There was a brief, awkward pause—after all, the three of them had recently implicated the White House chief of staff in a conspiracy to interfere with a national election.

Then the president got down to it. "I want you to know, Agent Langhorne, how deeply sorry I am for the loss of your wife. And how truly grateful I am to you and to Agent Spenser and to Dr. Cassidy for exposing the snake in my lair." Another beat passed. "I'm not going to ask for your discretion—if that's what you're expecting."

In fact it had been. But Spense was relieved to learn he'd been wrong. He didn't want to believe the president had knowledge of the conspiracy.

"I'm going to ask you, instead, to make damn sure that every member of the FBI understands that as commander in chief, I will *never* ask you to engage in illegal activity. And if I were to do so, I would hope you'd expose the truth and chase me from the Oval Office with a broom. But the fact is I did not condone, nor did I have knowledge of this reprehensible scheme. I've already appointed a special prosecutor to look into the matter, and everyone involved, including my chief of staff, is going to be dealt the full measure of the law."

Silent nods of approval went around the table, then the president continued, "When this breaks, I may look guilty to the man on the street, and I might even lose my bid for reelection. But I will not cover up this scandal. The country deserves the truth, and the country shall have it."

"Thank you, Mr. President." Spense didn't really have another response, and maybe he was being naïve, but he believed the man.

"Now that I've gotten that out of the way, I do have a favor to ask."

If discretion wasn't it, Spense had no idea what it might be.

"Agent Spenser, and Dr. Cassidy, your reputation precedes you. And I'm afraid I've had some terrible news. My dear friend's, Senator Chaucer's, daughter has gone missing in Colorado. Local law enforcement, the Colorado Bureau of Investigation, and Denver area FBI are all involved, but . . ." Spense could hear the slightest vibration in the president's voice. "I want the best men possible on the case. I'd consider it a personal favor if Cassidy and Spenser would join the team. I hear you're due a vacation, but I'm not above using whatever influence I have to persuade you."

Spense caught Caity's eye. Ten minutes ago he couldn't have imagined a scenario that would make him accept another case.

He should've imagined harder.

"What do you think?" he mouthed at Caity.

"I'll pack my winter things," she mouthed back.

Leaning toward the speaker, Spense barely resisted the urge to salute. "That's a yes, from us, Mr. President. We'd be honored."

Acknowledgments

FIRST AND FOREMOST, thank you to my readers! I'm humbled and honored that you take precious hours out of your lives to spend time with my characters. I'd also like to extend my heartfelt thanks to my family, Shannon, Erik, Bill, and Sarah for your love and support. I'm so blessed to have a wonderful group of talented friends who are always there to cheer me on, brainstorm, and lift me up. Thank you to Lena Diaz, Leigh LaValle, Courtney Milan, Brenna Aubrey, and Tessa Dare for being my collective rock. Thanks to my talented and supportive Kiss and Thrill sisters—Lena Diaz, Rachel Grant, Diana Belchase, Krista Hall, Manda Collins, Gwen Hernandez, Sarah Andre, and Sharon Wray. Thanks to my incredible beta reader, Carmen Pacheco, who is always there when I need her. Thank you to my agent, Liza Dawson. I can't wait to start a new journey with you. And finally, a huge thank-you to my brilliant and kind editor, Chelsey Emmelhainz. How lucky am I?

Want more Cassidy & Spenser?
Don't miss Carey Baldwin's heart-pounding thriller

FALLEN

Available now wherever e-books are sold.

An Excerpt From
FALLEN

YOU. ARE. FINE.

Twenty-five hundred for a couple hours of work, Susan reminded herself. She waited, and she waited some more. The breeze in the alley was bringing her smells from the coffee shop and a pizza joint, and it made her stomach growl. The sting in her ankle was subsiding, though, so that was good. She checked her phone again and noticed it was after ten. Maybe this guy was full of shit. How was he going to get into Waxed after hours anyway? He might work there, but that didn't add up. It was mostly kids making minimum wage manning the desk and counting the tickets. Of course he might own the place. Or maybe . . . he was one of the artists who made the wax figures. She'd heard each statue cost over 150 grand to create, so the sculptors could definitely afford a girl like her. Her phone beeped again:

Are you in yet? Lucy asked.

No, she typed back. But just then, she heard creaking, and the back door to the museum swung open.

"Hang on a minute. I gotta check in with my boss." She raised one finger in the sticky night air, making a point that she was texting on her phone. Then she typed *I'm in* and hit SEND. Her phone made the reassuring blurp of a message sent. She dumped her cell in her bag and focused on the positive: They were sneaking into the wax museum. One of the perks of working for Madam Lucille was that the clientele were not only connected, they were often creative. This guy right here was wearing what looked like a custom silk suit . . . in addition to a Charlie Chaplin mask. Tonight could make for a good story, like that Oscar extravaganza.

The john was playacting at being someone he wasn't, and she was doing that, too. After all, she'd been pretending to be Gina since she went to work for Lucy. Her real name, Susan Smith, wasn't nearly as catchy as Gina Lola. She'd renamed herself after Gina Lollobrigida because if she was going to be someone else, she figured it might as well be someone she wished she could be—like an exotic Italian movie star with long legs. Life was so much easier when you pretended.

You got this.

Her shoulders relaxed.

Charlie Chaplin motioned her inside, and the door slammed shut behind her, sending a cool wind across the backs of her knees. Compared to outside, the air in the narrow stairwell felt heavy and oppressive in her lungs. It was creepy dark here, but she could see light seeping around the edges of a door on the landing. It was that light, and the draw of $2,500, that kept her from calling things off right there and then.

"I'm Gina," she said, blinking hard, waiting for her eyes to adjust to the low light. Until she walked up those stairs, she hadn't fully committed.

Wordlessly, Charlie turned his back to her and headed toward the landing, which was somewhat reassuring, as she thought this was his way of showing her that she could stay or leave as she pleased.

Damn straight.

But, apparently, he wasn't the talkie type—probably why he was wearing a silent film star's mask and wig—and this was not good news for her. The talkers were the ones who didn't require much out of a girl, and since Charlie didn't seem to want to bend her ear, her guess was he'd have plenty of other stuff he'd want her to do for him.

Likely things he wasn't proud of. But the mask would also keep his secrets . . . She'd never be able to identify him.

Thinking again of the fallen angels, she hesitated.

He was halfway up the stairs, and she could turn around and go if she wanted. Lucy had a no-repercussions policy. Anytime a girl felt like it, she was free to shut things down, no questions asked.

Twenty-five hundred dollars.

She followed Charlie upstairs, her high heels clicking on the industrial metal steps, her hand trailing reluctantly along the cold railing. When she reached the top, he flung open the door, and they stepped into the A-List party room at Waxed.

Her breath caught. She couldn't help it.

Wow.

This was probably as close to being invited to a Hollywood bash as she'd ever get. To her right, Fred Astaire, dressed in black tie and tails, was dancing cheek to cheek with a lovely, and very lifelike Ginger Rogers. Ginger was wearing a beaded brocade gown that was simply too beautiful to be true. Susan walked over, reached out her hand, and let her palm slide over the heavily textured fabric. She wondered if it was a real costume from one of Ginger's movies.

Throughout the museum, rope lights, like those used to guide your path in a dark theater, lined the perimeters of the walls. The overhead lights were off, but there was moonlight sifting in through breaks in the drapes, imparting an eerie glow to the hordes of wax figures. They looked so real, she got the feeling they might come to life and start following her with zombie arms any minute.

Her stomach flipped over.

She really wished he'd turn the lights on, but they were not supposed to be in here, so it made sense he'd keep them off. Anyway, there was plenty of ambient light for them to move around without bumping into furniture or statues or anything, so she decided to immerse herself in the experience and enjoy her private tour of Waxed. She really did want to please her customers. Especially one like Charlie, who'd be paying well for her time. "This is cool."

Moving forward, she all but tripped over George Clooney and Matt Damon, who were laughing and clinking champagne glasses. Closing her eyes, she sniffed. She thought she could smell their aftershave. She wasn't sure if it was her imagination, or the statues, or Charlie Chaplin over there, but she liked the scent. No, it couldn't have been aftershave. The smell seemed too sweet for a man's cologne. In her head, soft music played. Enchanted, she swung around, wishing she had on a full skirt that would fly out as she twirled, but then . . . she remembered why she was there. She clapped her arms down to her side.

With a tilt of his head, Charlie motioned to her, and she followed him into another statue-filled room, then another and another. At least ten minutes passed, and he still hadn't spoken. She was starting to feel like she needed to take charge, or they might be here forever. She noticed Charlie wasn't that tall for a man, and that gave her a mental advantage, made it easier for her, someone who bought her clothes in the Junior Petites department, to assume control of the situation. "Tell me what you want," she commanded in her sultriest voice.

He shook his head.

"Show me then."

Still, he said nothing.

Maybe he wanted her to guess. But the clock was ticking. She still might have time to squeeze in another client if this one didn't keep her tied up all night. "Charlie, baby," she whispered, then licked her lips and slowly unbuttoned her blouse, just enough to reveal the tops of her breasts and her lacey red push-up bra. Even if the john didn't specifically request it, it was a good idea to wear sexy lingerie. Lucy had a big walk-in closet, filled with specialty and designer items for the girls to borrow. Looking down at her small tits, she thought about the $2,500 that, along with Lucy's plastic-surgery discount, would all but pay for her implants. It wouldn't be long until she could broaden her customer base and start making real money, like Lucy said some of her other girls did. Smiling, Susan gave Charlie a come-hither finger.

At last, an obedient Charlie closed the distance between them. *Finally!*

"That's a good boy. Now, don't worry about a thing, baby. Just tell me what you like, and we can get started."

He stared at her, and above the silence she thought she heard the wax figures breathing. Charlie raised an arm and gently swept soft fingertips over her eyelids. She'd just bet he was one of those guys who got manicures.

"You want me to close my eyes," she guessed.

He nodded, and she did what he wanted. In the next few seconds, she heard a faint rustling of fabric followed by a tearing noise. A spasm of unease closed her throat. What was that? Did he open a condom? Whatever he was doing, he was taking his time, so she let her lids flutter slightly open and peeked out from beneath her lashes. First, her heart stopped beating entirely, then it began to jackhammer in her chest.

Charlie was wearing latex gloves.

Unable to fully process what was happening, she froze. He raised both gloved hands toward her neck as if to strangle her

Now you panic?

Adrenaline jetted through her blood, unlocking her paralyzed limbs. She thrust her knee into his groin. Grunting, he doubled over with pain. She didn't miss her chance. She barreled past him, racing for the door. Behind her, she heard him panting. She ran faster.

Faster.

She passed a statue and from instinct, threw out her arm and knocked Richard Gere to the floor. A loud thunk was followed by a muffled cry. Daring a look over her shoulder, she saw Charlie sprawled on the ground over the statue.

Where are those stairs?

She flew to another room and realized she was going the wrong way. The stairs were in the party room. Then she heard them. Slow, deliberate footfalls coming toward her. Trapped, she spun around, desperately searching for a weapon. Anything she could use to defend herself. A few feet to her right, moonlight bounced off a shiny object.

A sword!

She grabbed it from a statue's hand.

But when she touched the tip, her heart sank. It was square and dull. Still, the sword was heavy, and it was all she had, so she hung on to it anyway. Wait, she had her pepper spray!

Thank God!

She reached for her shoulder bag and hot tears filled her eyes. Somewhere, somehow she'd lost her purse. With each passing moment, the footfalls grew louder, more menacing. Slow, taunting steps told her he was in no rush—promised her there was no escape.

Hide.

Edging around the room, she mashed her back against the wall, trying to find the darkest corner. That's when she felt cold steel pressing against her spine. Too scared to breathe, she found and turned the knob, then eased through the doorway behind her before closing it softly. There were no windows inside this new room, therefore no light seeping through the drapes. Only the rope lights guided her now. It took time for her eyes to adjust, a few seconds, maybe more, then, too late to cover her scream, she clamped her hand over her mouth.

Before her, on a long table, stood an entire row of heads. Her heart jumped to her throat. She couldn't pull air into her lungs, and after a minute, her fingers begin to tingle. Dizzy, she fell to her knees.

Get up, Susan!

Using the sword as a fulcrum, she managed to pry herself off the floor. Suddenly, her common sense kicked into gear. She was in a wax museum. Those heads—they weren't real. Her chest loosened, and she resumed breathing. This had to be the art studio. Maybe there was another entrance. It made sense the artists would want to avoid walking through the public areas. Squinting against the darkness, she felt her way along the wall again until she was stopped by heat wafting toward her, warning her not to touch what was up ahead. In the dark, she saw shadows. No, not shadows. White vapor dissolving into black air like smoke into a night sky. That sweet scent she'd smelled earlier was so strong here—as if someone had set a thousand candles aflame. The vapors triggered a spasmodic, uncontrollable cough. When her fit finally subsided, her mouth opened in a gasp. Then, as if compelled by some unknown force, she reached out her hand, waving it over what she now could see to be a bubbling cauldron of molten wax.

Those footfalls again.

The door creaked open.

He was coming for her.

About the Author

CAREY BALDWIN is a mild-mannered doctor by day and an award-winning author of edgy suspense by night. She holds two doctoral degrees, one in medicine and one in psychology. She loves reading and writing stories that keep you off-balance and on the edge of your seat. Carey lives in the Southwestern United States with her amazing family. In her spare time she enjoys hiking and chasing wildflowers. Carey loves to hear from readers so please visit her at www.CareyBaldwin.com, on Facebook www.facebook.com/CareyBaldwinAuthor, or Twitter www.twitter.com/CareyBaldwin.

Discover great authors, exclusive offers, and more at hc.com.